Find Me Where *the* Water Ends

Find Me
Where
the Water
Ends

a SO CLOSE TO YOU *novel*

RACHEL CARTER

HARPER TEEN
An Imprint of HarperCollinsPublishers

HarperTeen is an imprint of HarperCollins Publishers.

Find Me Where the Water Ends
Copyright © 2014 by Full Fathom Five, LLC
All rights reserved. Printed in the United States of America.
No part of this book may be used or reproduced in any
manner whatsoever without written permission except in
the case of brief quotations embodied in critical articles and
reviews. For information address HarperCollins Children's
Books, a division of HarperCollins Publishers, 10 East 53rd
Street, New York, NY 10022.
www.epicreads.com

Library of Congress Cataloging-in-Publication Data
Carter, Rachel (Rachel Elizabeth), 1984–
Find me where the water ends : a So close to you novel /
Rachel Carter. — First edition.
    pages cm
Summary: "When Lydia has the chance to see a future in
which the Montauk Project never existed, she knows that she
will sacrifice everything to make that vision of the world a
reality"— Provided by publisher.
ISBN 978-0-06-208111-7 (hardcover)
[1. Time travel—Fiction. 2. Experiments—Fiction.
3. Grandfathers—Fiction. 4. Science fiction. 5. Montauk
(N.Y.)—History—20th century—Fiction.] I. Title.
PZ7.C24783Fin 2014   2013037290
[Fic]—dc23   CIP
                                                              AC

Typography by Alison Klapthor
14 15 16 17 18   CG/RRDH   10 9 8 7 6 5 4 3 2 1
❖
First Edition

To my sisters, Mary and Emma Carter, for always having my back

CHAPTER 1

The dress is laid out on the bed, so dark red it looks black in the muted light of the hotel room. I run my hand down the fabric and it parts like water, the silk gliding across my skin, the deep color swallowing the paleness of my fingertips.

I take off the robe I've been wearing and lay it over the back of an overstuffed chair. Though the room is empty, I cover my nakedness with my hands, keeping my body angled toward the door. I am waiting for the knock, waiting for it to open at any moment.

I pick up the dress and quickly pull it over my head. It molds itself to my body, sweeping against the low heels of my sandals. It is a simple column, with a cut that reminds me of old Hollywood movies, where the women had smoky voices and everyone talked too fast.

The knock still doesn't come. I turn on another light next to the bed and the thick fringe from the lampshade sweeps across my hand. This one has a tinted bulb, which turns the room a garish pink, making the shadows deeper and staining the white floral wallpaper with slashes of red.

There is a mirror across from the bed, framed in gold and silver, ornate twists and circles that make me dizzy when I catch them from the corner of my eye. I stare at my reflection, barely recognizing the face that looks back at me. My old bangs grew out months ago, and my red hair falls in heavy waves around my shoulders. My cheekbones were always high, but now they are even more pronounced, making hollow grooves above my jawline. I dab a light gloss over my lips, ignoring the flatness in my eyes and the new muscles that curve along my arms and shoulders.

I'm not supposed to wear a lot of makeup, they said. No one in this time period does, and blending in is the most important part of being in an era that's not your own. I take care to use only a small swipe of mascara, a touch of blush, and though I run an ivory comb through my hair, I leave it down, skimming where the edge of the silk hits my lower back.

I step away and examine my reflection, still detached, as though it is a stranger's face and body that I am somehow controlling. The color should look wrong against my skin, but the red brings out the lighter strands in my hair and the sheath hugs my frame, making me seem curvier than I am these days.

It has been nine months since I faced General Walker in that bare gray cell, hidden so many feet below the ground. He told me I could walk away from my old life, join the Montauk Project and start traveling through time as part of a secret government organization, or I could die. It wasn't much of a choice, and so here I am, standing in this lavish hotel room, waiting for my contact on my first mission.

I have not met the rest of the team yet. I don't even know who they are, and the anticipation is crawling over me, like an itch I can't quite reach in the middle of my back. I pick at the fabric of the dress, pinching the silk between my fingers and then smoothing the wrinkles out again. I'm surprised at how nervous I am; I thought they had stripped all my feelings from me, that those endless months of training—not speaking to anyone but my commanding officers, not seeing my family or friends—had made me numb in a way that was permanent, in a way that would make me unable to feel anything ever again.

But there it is inside of me, curled in a ball, tucked low in the pit of my stomach—fear. Tonight I have to kill a man, and I don't know if I can.

The knock on the door is so loud it makes me jerk, and the comb falls from my hand to bounce against the glossy tiled floor. I take a deep breath, pushing my shoulders back, lifting my chin. I am a skilled recruit for the Project, just like whoever is standing on the other side of that door. They don't have to know that this is my first mission. They don't have to know that I'm afraid.

I cross the room quickly, the silk whipping around my legs. The wooden door is cool to the touch, and I lay my cheek against it, listening. "Who is it?" I call out.

The voice that answers is muffled. It sounds deep, but I can't quite tell through the thickness of the door. "It's Michael. Let me in. The fund-raiser is starting soon and the champagne will get warm."

It's my contact. He's using the code, even mentioning his alias. I slide back the old-fashioned lock and swing the door open.

There is a phrase I am supposed to say back so that he'll know who I am. "Darling, the champagne is on ice, don't—"

But the final words die in my throat.

Standing in front of me, dressed in a slim black tuxedo, is the boy who left me crumbled on the cold floor of a cell after betraying me to General Walker and telling me he never loved me. Wes.

The boy who broke my heart.

CHAPTER 2

We both freeze, unable to look away from each other. I had forgotten how dark his eyes were, more black than brown. The dim light of the room falls harshly on his face, and the shadows make his cheekbones look almost as sharp as mine.

Wes. I mouth the word, careful not to say it out loud. I don't want anyone lingering in the hallway to hear, but I'm also not ready to remember what his name feels like on my lips.

He frowns slightly, and I imagine he's reacting to my thinner cheeks, my wary eyes. "Samantha." He says my alias, then clears his throat, breaking my gaze to look behind me into the hotel room.

His voice. The last time I heard it was during my training, weeks after I learned of his betrayal. I was in a hallway in the Center in New York City, hidden from sight, watching a future version of him hug a future version of me, their faces glowing as their lips met again and again. I knew then that I would forgive him, at least one day.

But that doesn't mean that I have yet, and I step back to avoid contact as he enters the room. He doesn't seem surprised to see me, but then Wes was always good at hiding what he felt.

He does a quick sweep, his head moving back and forth to examine the reddened walls, the shadowed corners, and his hair falls over his forehead in a black wave. It is longer than it was the last time, almost touching the collar of his jacket.

The hotel is secure—we both know that—but he takes his time turning back to face me. I watch the way his fingers tap against the sides of his pants, an awkward move that doesn't match his usual grace, and I wonder if he's as nervous as I am.

"You're alone?"

I nod and shut the door, looking out the window. Outside, the lights of the city are like oversize stars, and I remember being with him in my bedroom in Montauk, New York, so long ago, his body covered in blood, my chest pressed against his, the night sky beyond my window looking a little like this one, though without the buildings or the busy streets.

With the door closed tight we are hidden from the

hallway, but we still don't make eye contact. Wes examines the fringed lamp, the gilded furniture, the creamy wallpaper. It is a blend of old-fashioned styles, with no modern sleek lines, no black or chrome metal. I see him take a deep breath and I know that he is thinking the same thing I am—this room looks like it could belong in the 1920s, the time we once promised each other we would run away to. In another life, this would have been our space, far away from the reach of the Project.

But Wes broke his word, and the large, holographic TV against the far wall proves that what I thought was love was not as strong as the pull of the Project. Now we are in the year 2049, near Washington, DC, and in just under three hours we will attempt to kill the president.

Wes finally faces me, and when he speaks his voice is lower, softer. "How have you been, Lydia?"

It is hearing my name that brings my anger back, boiling and churning, and suddenly I am on that cold floor again, hearing him tell me I was just a mission, that he never loved me.

"Stop." I spit out the word, keeping my face turned toward the window. "Don't say it."

"It's your name." I hear the rustle of his tux as he moves closer. "You can't forget that."

"My name is Seventeen. I'm a number now, just like you."

His mouth tightens, his full lips thinning. Small lines fan

out from the sides of his eyes, even though he is only nineteen—nearly the same age I am. But the life of the Montauk Project recruits is a hard one, and he has been working for them since he was eleven years old.

"You know we're more than a number. Some of us remember our real names."

"You're the one who told me to think of you as Eleven. You told me to forget W—" But I can't bring myself to say his name, and I turn from the window, staring at the white bedspread, now a faint pink in this red-lit room. "When I die, another recruit will become Seventeen. Isn't that what you told me? We're just numbers; our lives don't mean anything. There were hundreds of Elevens before you and there will be more after you die."

I hear him suck in a breath and despite how angry I am, I instantly wish I could take back the words. When we were in 1989, Wes told me he was dying. That the prolonged effects of the time machine were slowly killing him. Since then I've wondered if he was telling me the truth, but if he was . . .

I lift my head. He's watching me, his jaw tight. "I'm sorry," I manage to say. "I shouldn't have put it like that. This is just too confusing. I didn't even know you'd be on this mission."

"I volunteered. I wanted to see you."

His voice is serious, measured and deep, but I shake my head. I couldn't have heard him right. Wes would never have come here just to see me. Not after what happened.

"Don't lie to me."

"It's true." There are several feet between us, but it's still too close. I inch away until I feel the cold glass of the windowpane against my back. Why would Wes say that? He was so convincing in the cell when he told me I was just a mission. But he looks just as convincing now, with his palms slightly open toward me and his black eyes steady on mine.

"Why now?" The question is too raw, and I lean back even farther, my head tapping the glass as he takes a step forward. "I haven't seen you in months. You knew where I was."

"Walker sent me out on a mission right after they took you. . . ." He trails off, staring down at the white and black tiles on the floor. "Then . . . I thought you probably wouldn't want to see me, after what happened."

I press my lips together, not wanting to remember what it felt like when he said he never loved me, that it was all a lie. Is this a lie now? I try and hold on to that moment I saw in the hallway between the future versions of us. There must have been a reason for his betrayal, otherwise why would future me forgive him? Or was she just so in love, so lost, that she was willing to forget how he made her feel? Was future him playing her, too?

Wes suddenly lifts his head, his eyes bright and seeking mine. "Lydia, we need to talk. I need to explain—"

There is a knock on the door that cuts into his words.

"It's the rest of the team," I say. My thoughts wrapped up in Wes, I had almost forgotten why we were here.

He runs his hands through his hair. "We never have enough time."

"I can't think about this right now. I need to focus on the mission." I start to cross the room.

"Lydia." He grabs my arm as I move past him, forcing me to stop. The skin of my wrist grows warm under his touch. "Before this mission is over, we'll talk. I'll explain everything."

I nod without looking at him and he peels his hand away from me, slowly, picking up his fingers one by one. As soon as I'm free I move toward the door again, ignoring the way my arm still tingles, ignoring the way he stares at my back as though he is trying to see through my flesh to what lies underneath.

The first recruit who enters is a petite, dark-haired girl. I take in her small, perfect nose, her olive skin, and I realize I've seen her before—in 1989, when I was posing as a recruit with Wes, in the Assimilation Center in the Project's main facility in Montauk, New York. She watched Wes then as she watches him now, like he is something she wants to consume.

Wes lifts his chin at her, no more than a slight jerk, and I remember him telling me that her name is Twenty-two. He said he'd never spoken to her before, but that doesn't mean anything when it comes to the recruits. They could have gone on countless missions together, traveled through time over and over without saying a word.

She enters the room with that deliberate prowl that all the long-term recruits have, brushing past me as though I'm another piece of furniture. She moves to stand next to Wes, and I turn to see a boy in the doorway. I immediately recognize his broad frame, his short brown hair. Thirty-one. He and I were sparring partners a few months ago, part of the same training group in the Center.

Now he enters the room, his black jacket hanging from one hand, as though he is going to his prom instead of attempting to kill the president. When he sees me, he stops. "You . . ."

I quickly shut the door, surprised that he would show his reaction so openly. Most recruits would act like Twenty-two, watching our exchange with a blank expression, her hands resting on her hips.

But then I see the way she leans in slightly toward Wes. Maybe she's not as impassive as she seems.

Thirty-one briefly glances at the other two before he turns back to me. "There are seventeen shells where the water ends."

I stare at him, blinking. It is a code phrase, one that all recruits use to identify themselves to each other in public. *But the rocks are too sharp*, I am supposed to say back.

"Oh wait." He shakes his head. "We're on a mission. I don't have to say that. I keep forgetting. I did it to her too." He gestures at Twenty-two. Her expression is still blank.

"That's okay," I say quietly.

His lips tilt up. It's not quite a smile, but his eyes are warm. "I didn't know you'd be here."

This time I don't answer.

Twenty-two looks directly at me. "You two know each other?"

"We were in training together," I say.

Thirty-one opens his mouth to respond, but Wes moves so suddenly that everyone freezes, even though he is just crossing his arms over his chest. He is taller than Thirty-one by several inches, but not as muscular—Wes's body is long and lean where Thirty-one's is sturdy. "This isn't a reunion." His voice has changed again, remote but authoritative. That intimate, soft tone he used to tell me he volunteered for the mission has disappeared completely.

"You can call me Eleven," he says to the room in general.

The rest of us go around and state our numbers, a collective lottery ticket instead of a group of people.

"The hallway and the room next door are secure too." Twenty-two's voice is low and husky, like she has a perpetual cold. "I cut the camera feed in both, so no one will see us enter or leave. And we have weapons if we need them, though we won't be able to smuggle any of the guns into the party. We'll all be screened by their security."

"You think we'll need guns?" I ask.

She shrugs and looks back up at Wes. She is so small she barely reaches his shoulder. "Who's running the play?"

"I am," he answers. "You have the I-units?"

She nods. "And this." She reaches into the bodice of her white, slinky gown and pulls out a small vial. It reminds me of the first time I traveled into the past, to 1944, and met my great-great-aunt Mary, who told me the best way to hide your lipstick was in your bra. I can still picture us wrestling with the lipstick tube on her bed, laughing as our skirts tangled, but I push down the pang that the memory brings. She is now just another name on the list of lost people. Like my parents, and Hannah, my childhood best friend, who I left behind in my own time. Like Dean, Mary's brother and my great-grandfather, who disappeared in the forties, and then had his brain stripped in the eighties.

Like my grandfather.

Twenty-two's voice pulls me from my thoughts, though she addresses Wes only. "The I-units are in the next room. We can get them and I'll show you the other supplies."

But Wes hesitates, glancing over at me. I keep my eyes on the floor, not letting on that we know each other.

"Why don't we let them get reacquainted?" Twenty-two still speaks in that flat monotone. It's unsettling to sense her sarcasm but not hear it. "I'm sure they have a lot to talk about."

Thirty-one just looks amused by her words, but Wes's gaze shifts to the other boy, staring at him in a way that seems to suck the air out of the room.

"We don't have much time. The fund-raiser starts soon," Twenty-two adds. Wes finally nods and follows her to the door, though the rigid line of his shoulders never softens.

Thirty-one moves to stand next to me, and I can't help but think we're already pairing off—the two experienced recruits united against the newer ones.

As soon as the door shuts behind them, Thirty-one sighs and rubs the back of his neck. "I'm exhausted. The TM never gets easier, does it?"

He moves toward the bed and slumps down onto the mattress. I stare at the relaxed, easy way he moves his body. Most recruits are like coiled springs, their muscles tight, their eyes watchful. But not Thirty-one.

He raises his brows and I realize he's waiting for me to answer. "No." I think of the time machine—Tesla's Machine, or the TM as the Project refers to it—the way it rips your body apart, shooting you through space and time in broken pieces. "It never gets easier."

We are silent for a minute. I stare at the heavy wooden door, wondering what Twenty-two and Wes are doing in the next room.

Thirty-one is watching me closely. "I'm surprised you remember me."

"We sparred together under Lieutenant Andrews," I say.

"There were only ten of us on our team. Why wouldn't I remember you?"

He shrugs. "You seemed pretty out of it. And it wasn't just the sparring. I would watch you, sometimes, in the Center. Eating in the cafeteria, or walking down the halls."

I try to think back to that time, but it is a blur of empty hallways, endless lessons, white lights, and cold, blank recruits. "You did?"

"You didn't even notice." He spreads his legs wide and rests his forearms on his knees. It is too comfortable of a position. Everything about this boy is too comfortable, too casual. "You had your head down, looked kind of blank. But there was one day, a few months ago, when I saw you crying and I knew you weren't like the rest of them."

I remember that day. It was after my commanding officers had forced me to write a letter to my parents, saying that I was running away. They would put it in my bedroom the same night I disappeared, and a few days later a body matching my description would be found in a nearby ditch. My parents would never know the truth of what happened to me.

I had written it carefully and silently, my fingers not even shaking. It wasn't until I was out in the hallway that the impact hit me. I fell back against the wall, one hand pressed to my stomach, the other to my chest, trying to hold in the sobs I could feel ripping through me. Only a few tears escaped, sliding down my face to fall onto the white tiles below. I had thought I was alone, that no one had seen me, but obviously I was wrong.

"I am like the rest of them," I protest, but Thirty-one shakes his head.

"No. They're zombies. You're different, I think."

"I don't know what you mean."

At my icy tone, he shifts his weight, pulling in his arms slightly. "I'm going too fast, aren't I? My mom always said I speed through shit. Sorry."

"You remember your mom?"

He nods, his hazel eyes locked on my green ones.

"How is that possible?"

He shrugs again, the movement deliberately casual. "I don't know. I just do."

"Were you . . . were you brainwashed?"

He nods, keeping his body forward, his hands swinging in the space between his knees. I don't even know why I bothered to ask. Brainwashing is the first stage of training. It means the recruits won't run away when they're out on missions, because they have nothing left to care about. No family, no friends, just the constant fear that the Project is all knowing, that they will find you no matter what. It was why Wes wouldn't run away with me, in the end.

"Were you?" he asks, and my muscles go tight, my back stiff above the silk of my gown. He is digging too deep, and I cannot trust this person. I can't trust anyone anymore.

"I'm the same as any other recruit." I keep my voice even.

"I haven't met another recruit who would cry in a hallway."

"And I haven't met one who remembers their family."

"That's why I think we might be able to help each other," he says softly.

There is a silence. I keep my arms wrapped around my middle. I've been trying so hard to be numb, to forget those endless days of training. When they first took me I was in the Center, hidden below Central Park. That is where I learned how to be a recruit—how to fight, how to survive in the wilderness with no supplies, how to load a gun in seconds. Then there was the intelligence training: languages, codes, minute historical facts. It is the recruit's job to change small moments, to gather information, to act as a liaison between different time periods. If we are not careful, we could change the entire course of history.

All that information, crammed into six months, crammed into my head, crammed in a room with hundreds of other recruits, all children, all vacant eyed. In the beginning, I had so many questions. Who was the mysterious Resistor, who visited me at my father's hardware store in my time, who helped me realize I was destined to become a recruit? How did my grandfather have a disk with a list of future recruits that included my name? But no matter how much I churned through possible answers, I could never find clarity, and after a while, remembering was harder than forgetting. By the time I got to the facility in Montauk to practice on the TM, I had built a shell around myself, had learned to block out everything but the information they kept pumping into me. For months I've lived like this. Trying to let go of Wes, my family, my old life. General Walker didn't make me go through the brainwashing, but he might as well have.

"Do you remember your family?" Thirty-one asks.

I open my mouth but I do not answer. An image of my grandfather flashes through my head, standing next to the stove, stirring a pot of spaghetti and asking me about my latest article for the school paper. But then the memory shifts and he's curled in a tight ball on the floor of a cell, rocking back and forth, moaning in pain and fear.

My grandfather was the one who told me about the Montauk Project in the first place—and now they're using him as leverage so I'll work for them, knowing that the threat to his life is enough to keep me in line.

"I don't know why I remember mine," Thirty-one says when I don't respond. "I just do. I can . . . There are flashes of my mom. I had a sister. She was ten. We were close."

I stare down at the floor, at the way the black tiles meet the white ones in never-ending diamonds. "When were you taken?"

"A year ago, I think. Time gets muddled down there. You know."

I do know, only guessing at the nine months that have passed since I was taken. "Still," I say. "That's not long. Most recruits are kidnapped earlier, put through training for longer."

"General Walker said they couldn't have brought me in any earlier or time would have been messed up. I'm needed for this mission, I guess."

I look down at him. "Me too. He said it was my destiny."

"Do you believe him?"

"I don't know."

"They said they needed to speed up my training," Thirty-one says. "Maybe that's why the brainwashing didn't totally stick."

His words are light but his eyes are drawn at the corners and white lines appear around his mouth. It is a mask, his casual behavior, in the same way Wes's coldness is a mask, hiding the part of himself that the Project tried to strip away.

"This is why we can help each other. Even if it's just to have someone we trust."

Help each other? I think of what the Resistor told me, about how he was starting a movement against the Project. Since I've become a recruit, I haven't heard or seen any evidence that he has succeeded, but a small resistance could exist. For one brief moment, I consider asking Thirty-one, consider opening up to someone in a way I haven't in months.

There's a muffled sound from the hallway and I automatically take a step backward, away from the bed and Thirty-one. Wes and Twenty-two will be back soon. They can't find us questioning the Project. Wes might understand . . . at least, the old Wes would have. But Twenty-two is too much like the other recruits: unfeeling, hidden, more robot than human. I don't know if I can trust Thirty-one, or even Wes, but I *know* I can't trust her.

"We were chosen for a reason. If we're too distracted, we will fail." I mimic Lieutenant Andrews with his clipped, military tone.

Thirty-one stares at me, but I do not waver, keeping my expression empty, my mouth a thin line. Finally he sighs and stands up from the bed. "Right."

He sounds disappointed, but I can't be what he wants. I can't be his lifeline. The only person who matters now is my grandfather. I'll do whatever I have to in order to save him.

When Thirty-one steps closer to me I freeze, my new muscles flexing under my skin. Those hours and hours of training take over, and I have to fight the urge to twist his arm up over his back, to show him that even though he's strong, I'm quicker. But he stops just before he can touch me and looks down into my face. He's not much taller than I am, and even this close I do not have to tilt my head back to look at him.

He leans forward slightly, moving until his mouth is

hovering right above my ear. "Tim," he whispers.

I stop breathing.

"My name is Tim."

He pulls back, watching my face, waiting for my reaction. I do not give anything away, but when he turns his back to me, I finally allow myself to smile. It is just a small one, a tilt of my lips, the slight pressure on my cheeks. But for the first time in nine months, it's there.

Despite what I said to Wes earlier, I remember my name, my identity. *Lydia Bentley.* And so does Thirty-one . . . *Tim.* I had thought that all the recruits were like Wes and Twenty-two, broken and lost and cold. But maybe Tim really is who he says he is: different from the others, capable of memory, of feelings, not a mindless slave of the Montauk Project.

And maybe that means I'm not as alone as I thought.

CHAPTER 3

"*The* fund-raiser starts in less than an hour," Wes says to the three of us as we stand in a half circle in the center of the room. The red-tinted light is gone. Right after Wes and Twenty-two returned, Tim walked over to the lamp and switched it off.

"It's like a whorehouse in here."

"Leave it," Wes said. "Ly—Seventeen put it on."

"It's fine. The red was too overwhelming anyway," I put in quickly, afraid someone may have noticed his almost-slip. I do not want Tim and Twenty-two to know that we have any sort of history. Things are already too complicated as it is.

At my words, Wes gave me the same hard look he just gave Tim. I refused to flinch, refused to change my expression. He turned away first, but I saw how he closed his eyes for half a second, the deep breath he took.

Now he stands across from the bed, addressing all of us. "Alan Sardosky has been the president of the United States for the past five years, and is currently in his second term. Right now he is fairly well liked by the American public, but over the course of the next year, he becomes more and more of a recluse, and his paranoia increases to the point where he no longer leaves Hill House, this decade's version of the White House. This campaign fund-raiser is his last public appearance before that starts happening. Which is why General Walker chose it for our first assassination attempt."

Tim and I stand side by side, listening to Wes. It is information I already know: we've all been prepared for the events of tonight, and normally we would complete our task without discussion. But because it is my first time in the field—and most likely Tim's—Lieutenant Andrews explained that we would be briefed again before the mission. I still find myself hanging on Wes's words, knowing that the minute he is finished talking we will be sent down into the ballroom to kill the president.

"In a year and a half, Sardosky proposes, lobbies for, and signs an international nuclear arms act. Twenty other countries sign too, including Russia and China, all agreeing to disassemble their nuclear weapons and, ideally, end the threat of nuclear war for good. The two most problematic holdouts are North Korea and Iran. When the U.S. puts pressure on North Korea, threatening to invade if they don't cooperate, the North Koreans retaliate by launching a series of nuclear attacks. Within a week, North Korea bombs Los Angeles, New York City, Boston, Chicago, and Washington, DC."

"Sardosky and most of his staff live through the attack, and in response, the administration levels half of Asia. Millions die, and the radiation sparks a worldwide famine when crops fail," Twenty-two adds. She sounds almost bored. "We need to prevent it from happening by bringing down the man who put all this in motion in the first place."

"Even though he was trying to do something good," I say without thinking.

All three of them turn to stare at me, and I press my palms into my sides, feeling the silk of my gown slide between my fingers. "I just . . . he didn't mean to destroy the world. He was trying to help people. To end the threat of nuclear war."

"It doesn't matter." Twenty-two's expression is cold. "This isn't our first mission to stop the aftermath of this treaty. The Project has already tried to get Sardosky out of office before his second term. We've tried to stop him from proposing the treaty, to stop him from signing the treaty— to stop North Korea from reacting to the United States' pressure. Nothing has worked; every mission has ended in the same way: nuclear war. This is the next logical attempt to stop it from happening. Sardosky has to die."

I do not respond. The Project makes calculated choices, weighs the odds and experiments until they create changes that have the smallest impact on the time line. Killing someone as important as the president has a large impact, and they wouldn't do it unless they'd considered every option, unless this was the final choice.

But could this really be my destiny, as General Walker told me it was? Killing a man who's trying to make the world a better place, even if he doesn't succeed?

I don't know if I believe in destiny anymore, but if I don't go along with what the Project wants, then my grandfather will be the one who gets hurt. Either way, someone dies. It may sound heartless, but I will always save my grandfather over Alan Sardosky.

"If we fail to kill Sardosky on this mission, we'll be sent back again and again, won't we?" Tim asks. He is standing straighter than he was before, looking more like a recruit than he did when we were alone together. "And what if killing Sardosky doesn't even work? What if we still end up with a nuclear war?"

Wes gives Tim a grim look. "We don't know yet if killing him will stop the war, but it's the only viable option left. The Project believes this is the solution, so we need to do our best to succeed tonight. If we can't kill the president, then we'll come back again until we do. It's our job."

Tim doesn't answer.

"Remember that as soon as we leave this room, I am thirty-year-old Michael Gallo, a financial analyst at an international shipping company. I've been invited because one of the president's friends, a Mr. Tierney, is trying to set up an export business in Washington and he wants to do business with the company Michael Gallo works for." Wes glances at me, but when our eyes meet he looks away. "Seventeen is Samantha Greenwood, my fiancée. Twenty-two is Bea Carlisle, Samantha's cousin, and Thirty-one is posing as a waiter. Everyone is clear on this?"

We nod.

"Twenty-two is a dead ringer for Sardosky's mistress, who's been away from the capital for weeks. She'll seduce the president, and try to convince him to meet her in a private room." He gestures at the other girl's small, dark features, her petite frame. She doesn't smile at Wes—she probably hasn't smiled in years—but her mouth parts slightly, her head tilts down and to the side, and suddenly I believe she's capable of seducing anyone. It makes me inch toward Wes, though I refuse to let myself think about why.

"Thirty-one can't hold on to the poison; the guards physically search the waitstaff. Seventeen and I will pass it off to him after we go through security. He'll doctor a drink and deliver it to the president. I'll infiltrate the control room of the hotel and disable the security cameras in the room where Twenty-two leads the president. It will take one solid minute for the drug to take effect, at which point the president will have what appears to be a completely typical heart attack. If Sardosky gets help too quickly, then he could recover, which is why we need the attack to happen in private. By the time Twenty-two runs out of the room looking for help, the president will be dead. In the confusion, we disappear. Seventeen." He turns to me, but keeps his eyes on the wall behind my head. I wonder if it is hard for him, seeing and treating me as another recruit. But why would it be? He's the one who put me in this position. "Do you understand your job while this is going on?"

"I'll create a distraction in the main room that will occupy security long enough for them not to notice that the feed of an adjoining room has been cut. It has to last at least five minutes," I answer. "Thirty-one will act as my backup in case something goes wrong."

"What will you do?" Tim asks me.

"Huh?"

"How will you distract them?"

"There's a congressman from Michigan who's having an affair with his aide. Both his wife and the other woman will be there tonight. The wife likes champagne and apparently has a temper. A few whispers, and she'll make the scene for us."

"Really?" Tim makes a huffing noise. It is not quite laughter, but it's close. Twenty-two looks at him sharply.

"According to her history, she likes to throw things,"

I say, a little defensively. "It's the best way to keep a large number of people distracted."

"Fine," Wes says. "I'm running point for the mission. Once we put in our I-units, we won't be able to communicate as ourselves. From that point on, you will all become your aliases. Here." He hands us each a small contact-lens case. Inside is an I-unit, the future's version of a cell phone and personal computer, all in one, made to become a part of its wearer.

"You both know what an I-unit is, right?" Twenty-two asks us, unable to keep the condescension from her voice.

"Of course." Tim is impervious to her tone, and I realize how seriously he is taking this; even though he looks like a bumbling Captain America, he knows that this mission is life or death. If we fail, the Secret Service will descend, and as soon as we run they'll start shooting. We have no real identities in 2049 beyond the ones that have been created on our I-units. If the Secret Service doesn't shoot us on sight, then we'll be faced with treason charges and locked up, or possibly executed. We're relying on success or on the Project coming to rescue us—and I don't trust that they will.

The lights around us dim, then brighten, then dim again, and the room is almost dark now, with the streetlights outside the window glowing yellow against the glass. "Solar power." Twenty-two opens the contact case and squints down at the see-through lenses. "You'd think they'd have perfected it before they made the whole country switch over."

"It only flickers at night sometimes," Tim says. "Besides, oil couldn't last forever. Especially not after the waters rose."

Climate change had started in my time, with a growing number of floods and hurricanes and tornadoes, until there was one major natural disaster a year, then five, then ten. By the 2020s it was bordering on apocalyptic, with whole towns washed away by floods, and thousands dying in the storms and the aftermath. In the beginning people were rebuilding the cities and towns, but when the waters rose permanently it became impossible. It took almost twenty years for the weather to stabilize, but by then the damage was done—the oceans had risen by several inches, and cities built near the coasts or on swamps, like Washington, DC, were underwater. The government banned carbon dioxide emissions and shifted to solar energy. And now we are standing in New Washington, DC, the reconstructed capital of the country, several miles inland.

I had seen the new city, gleaming with glass and metal, when I was brought here from Montauk and delivered to the hotel, but it still feels unreal to me, like a hologram projected out into the sky.

Twenty-two shrugs, dismissing Tim, dismissing the whole idea of global warming, and I wonder how many times she has seen it happen, how many ways the world has crumbled for her, before being pieced back together as she jumps through time again and again.

"You two should leave," Wes says to them. "Twenty-two, you're in the room next door; we'll meet in the hall in ten minutes. Thirty-one, you need to report for duty in the kitchens."

"Got it." Tim looks over at me and smiles slightly. "Good luck."

"You too," I whisper, aware of Wes watching us both.

Twenty-two doesn't say a word, but her brown eyes linger on Wes until the moment she closes the door behind her.

When they are gone I turn around and place the contact case on the bed.

"Lydia." I can feel Wes standing right behind me, though I never heard him cross the room. I know that if I move at all we will be touching, and I stay rigid, my back slightly bent toward the bed.

"Don't put them in yet," he says.

"We don't have time for this."

"I need to explain."

"I . . ."

As I hesitate, his hand reaches out and curls around my wrist. The front of his arm is pressed to the back of mine, and I feel the soft material of his black jacket against my bare skin. I stay perfectly still. For months I obsessed over that moment I'd seen between the future versions of us, wondering what it meant, why I would forgive him for pretending to love me in order to fulfill his mission. I waited for him to find me, to explain. But time kept passing, a slow trickle, until I began to lose hope. And Wes still didn't come. I thought I felt him sometimes, watching me train, standing in the back of the room during my history lessons. But when I turned to look for him, he was never there. I learned to stop looking. I learned to rely only on myself, realizing it was the only way I would survive as a recruit.

But that was easy enough to feel when I was lying by myself on a hard mattress, staring up at the underside of a white bunk, the facility's fluorescent lights bright even in the dead of night. Now, with Wes so close, his large fingers curved around the delicate bones of my wrist, I feel that resolve start to waver. I want to know what he has to say. I want to know why the future me forgave him, and how he made her smile like she forgot, if only for a moment, that she had become a slave to the Project.

"I missed you," he whispers, his deep voice so low, so soft, and I close my eyes. But then his fingers trace the scar that covers the pale skin on the underside of my wrist, and I pull away.

"Don't."

He steps back. I feel the heat of him leave, and I am only cold in its place. "I'm sorry. I didn't mean—"

"Twenty-two will be waiting. I have to remember why I'm here." I look down at my arm, my back still to Wes. In the shadowed light of the room you almost can't see the slim, raised white ridge. But I know it's there. I always know it's there. Somewhere under my skin, tucked against the muscle and the white, ropey tendons, is their tracking chip. The way the Project follows my every move through their facility, through the outside world. It is the thing that marks me as theirs.

Wes doesn't say anything, and I ignore his presence as I carefully open the case, pull out a thin lens, and place it over my eye, repeating with the second one. I blink, and it takes a minute for my eyes to adjust, for the tears to settle, for my vision to clear. It is my first time wearing an I-unit, though I have been practicing with ordinary contacts for weeks. It is against Montauk Project policy for inventions to be shared across eras, so although I know how an I-unit works in theory, I have never worn one in practice.

Menu, I think, and a scrolling list appears before my eyes with words like *Contacts, Calendar, Messages, Internet.* I can see through the black lettering, though the world behind it is slightly fuzzier.

Off, I think, and the menu disappears.

I swing around the room, imagining that it will look different somehow, with this thing creating a veil over my eyes. But no, there is the wooden dresser, the gold picture frame against the wall, the TV, dark and quiet.

My eyes settle on Wes. He is staring back at me, and I know he's wearing his I-unit too. As soon as I focus on his face, faint red lines shoot out in front of my eyes, mapping the angles of his features, his head. It is not just scanning his image, but linking to a database that stores his online presence, including his social media sites, his work history, and pictures of him that have been posted on the web.

A small profile appears. Because our aliases have a relationship, I have access to his entire I-unit profile, full of milestones, dates, and pictures of events we've both attended. Michael Gallo, it says, with a photo of Wes and a brief résumé. *Engaged to Samantha Greenwood.* I see the words on the bottom. And there is the history of us, or the fake us. *Met in 2042, senior year in college. Traveled to England, France, Russia, and South Africa from 2043 to 2048. Engaged in Johannesburg June 15, 2048.*

Wes's eyes are unfocused, and I wonder if he's reading the same words I am. Not that it matters. This is a fake life, for a fake couple. Once I thought we would have that kind of future together, and I believed it enough that I left behind my family and friends to follow him into the past. But I was wrong, and even the memory of the future us embracing in that hallway is not enough to make me believe that we can ever start over again.

CHAPTER 4

Wes offers me his arm. I rest my hand on his jacket as we walk down the long hallway. To our right are framed portraits of men and women long dead; to our left is a balcony that looks out over a ballroom. In between the tall columns of the banister I see a flicker of light from the chandeliers, the swirl of a couple spinning on the dance floor.

My heels clink against the marble, loud even above the swelling of the violins that seeps up from below. Wes is as quiet as he usually is. We haven't spoken a word since we left the hotel room, not even when we went through security—metal detectors that scanned for everything from weapons to foreign chemicals. Luckily the poison, hidden in the bottom of a lipstick tube in my clutch, was undetectable. But not one of us is armed, and I cannot help feeling nervous as we reach the top of a large, gold staircase.

The hallway was dark and narrow, but now the party is spread out in front of us: light and noise and people in a room the size of a football field. There are floor-to-ceiling windows, dozens of round tables at the far end, and a small orchestra set up next to the dance floor. Like the hotel room upstairs, it is decorated in an old-fashioned style, from gilded chandeliers to simple 1930s fashions.

"Are you ready?" Wes asks me softly.

My body is stiff next to his and I force myself to relax. "Of course, darling."

He smiles at me, though it never reaches his eyes, and we start to descend the stairs. The guests are a collage of tuxedos and gowns, broken up only by the waiters who dart in and out, carrying silver trays heavy with champagne. The band ends one song, but it blends into the next, the classical notes rising and falling over the buzzing noise of hundreds of murmuring voices.

There's a rustling among the guests closest to the staircase, and a few people turn to watch us. A woman points at me, then whispers something to the man next to her.

I glance up at the sharp line of Wes's jaw. His expression is neutral, though his eyes are warm. It's an act, I can't forget that. Right now he is not Wes, he's Michael. I try to put the same level of warmth into my own eyes. I am not a natural actor, not like Wes has proven himself to be, but I have no choice but to become Samantha Greenwood tonight. A bored socialite, perhaps tired of following her fiancé from country to country, with no real friends left in the United States.

"Why are people staring?" I ask him quietly. "Do I have something on my dress?"

"They're staring because you're beautiful," he answers. "Don't be nervous, Love."

Love. Wes has never called me that before. I dig my fingernails into the silk of the clutch I'm carrying in my opposite hand. I know he is being Michael right now, but it is *his* voice, *his* lips saying the words. I look away before the confusion can show on my face, before I fall into his arms because I know, at least as Samantha, that he'll catch me.

I hear the tap of another pair of heels on marble and turn to see Twenty-two coming down the stairs behind us. She is transformed, flashing white teeth as she smiles, her eyes wide and bright. "Bea seems like she's having fun."

"Your cousin is a lovely girl." Wes sounds as though he is holding in laughter, delighted by her every move. This time Twenty-two's smile is for him, even though he has his back to her, and I wonder where the act stops and the real person starts.

We finally reach the bottom of the stairs. Wes lets go of my arm and puts his hand on my exposed back, moving me into the heart of the crowd. There are people on all sides, and I am jostled closer to him. He puts one arm out in front of us, angling our bodies in to each other so that we are like a tiny ship moving through rough waves. I brush against men in black suits, women in simple silk gowns like mine, but all I feel is the pressure of Wes's fingers on my skin.

"Do you want champagne?"

He has to lean down to whisper the words, and his breath stirs the hair near my neck. I nod. He stops a passing waiter and picks up a flute, the carved crystal catching the light that spills from the chandeliers overhead.

"Mr. Gallo!"

A short, dark-haired man pushes through the crowd to stand in front of us. Who, I think, and my I-unit flickers in front of my eyes, scanning the man's face and pulling up his profile. *Lee Mal-Chin,* it reads at the top. It is a limited profile, as we are not friends on any social media sites, but I see a link to a site describing his job and his business associates, and a public folder of pictures from events he has attended.

I do not bother following the link to his job; I have already studied this man's face in my pre-mission training. He's a business associate of Michael's from South Korea, though they've never met before tonight. I turn and see hundreds of familiar faces in the crowd—senators and socialites, businessmen and -women who make up New Washington's elite. I have seen file after file on them, not needing to rely on my I-unit the way most people do in this time period.

I-units are issued by the government in 2049, available for

all citizens and not monopolized by one company. They're encouraged and free, but as a result, the government has access to almost all your personal information—where you go, who you see. Some groups complain about the lack of privacy, but no one can deny that with the countless witnesses and eyes on the streets it has cut down on a large amount of crime. Even if you choose not to use an I-unit, other wearers can still scan your movements. Unless you have resources like the Project does, it makes hiding your identity almost impossible—especially at an event like tonight's, where they won't let you in without an I-unit so that security can monitor every movement and every conversation in order to keep the president safe.

Luckily, Michael Gallo is as real as anyone in this room, representing a France-based international shipping company where he's "worked" for almost a year. The company is fake, but the Project has spent months establishing its identity overseas, setting up business accounts, and using simulation technology to mimic Wes's voice on conference calls. In order to create our I-units, the Project hacked into the American I-unit database and planted our fake identities, including birth certificates, an internet presence, and forged family connections. Only Tim's alias, Paul Sherman, was a real person who the Project disposed of, and changed his photos to match Tim. Another casualty for the greater good.

"I heard a rumor you would be here tonight. My wife

and I flew all the way from Seoul just to see if it was true." Mr. Lee's voice is heavily accented, but his English is flawless. He holds out his arm to a brunette woman who appears to be in her mid-thirties. The loose, casual way she wears her hair reminds me of Hannah, who always dressed like a flower child. She would have fit in here, in 2049, with the simple silhouettes and the emphasis on sustainability. And though I'm glad that she never got caught up with the Project, a small part of me wishes I had her here now.

I blink away the memory and Mr. Lee's wife blinks, too. She is still, her eyes scanning me, then Wes, as she uses her I-unit to read the situation.

"It's a pleasure," she finally says, holding out her hand to Wes. "Mal-Chin speaks of you often."

Her voice is soft, with a slight English accent, and though I've already memorized her file, I scan her with my own I-unit while Wes takes her hand. *Sophia Lee, maiden name Jones. Born in London, England, February 1, 1995.*

1995. The year I was born. In another lifetime she and I would have been contemporaries, experiencing the last thirty years at the same time. But here we are in 2049, and I am just barely eighteen, while she is fifty-four.

Not that she looks it. Stem cell technology has advanced significantly, and even ordinary people have access to what it can do. People take it like a vitamin in order to stretch their life spans, and boost their metabolism, with the added benefit of making them appear younger by decades. It is why Sardosky is not considered too old to be president, though he's pushing eighty-five.

"I trust your flight wasn't too long." Wes is smiling at Mr. Lee in a wide, pleasant way I've never seen before, and I sip my champagne to cover my reaction. The bubbles fizz all the way down my throat.

"Ahh, these new airplanes." Mr. Lee waves his hand in the air dismissively. His other arm curls around his wife, a mirror of the way Wes is holding me, and I know it is deliberate. The world may have changed significantly by 2049, but in this moment, Sophia Lee and I are only arm candy to these men. "Even run with solar power, they're so fast. It only took a few hours to get here. What will they think of next?"

"I hear they're working on teleportation," I say, and his eyes shift to me, taking in my dress and working his way up. When he gets to my hair he jerks his head back as though surprised.

Wes catches his reaction and his arm tightens around my waist. "We really should be going." He is already stepping away from the couple, smiling and nodding. "We'll talk later."

"I want to hear what you think about that report I sent last Thursday," Mr. Lee yells after us and Wes lifts a hand up over his shoulder before we are swallowed by the crowd again.

I want to ask if he knows what Mr. Lee's reaction was about, but I know I can't. Wes must sense it though; his hand moves up my back and into my hair, the dark-red strands tangling around his fingers.

He suddenly stops, his hand twisting now, and I have no choice but to look up at him. With my head tilted back, the chandeliers above seem overly bright, like staring straight into the sun. But it is only an illusion; the room is as dim as candlelight, and Wes's face is framed in shadows.

"Mr. Lee seemed nice." I cannot think of anything else to say.

Wes smiles, and it is more like him this time, half of a lip tilt, his expression soft. "He's an ass. But he runs a good business."

I feel my lips crack too, the unused muscles straining upward, and Wes's eyes drop to my mouth. I take a deep breath, my chest expanding under the low bodice of my gown. We are so close I know he feels it too, and then he pulls me in toward his body, his head dips, and his lashes lower to half-mast. He is leaning in, leaning down, and I do not pull away. Why shouldn't I let him kiss me? We are not Seventeen and Eleven right now, not even Lydia and Wes, but Samantha and Michael, two people who think nothing of holding each other in a crowded room. But then someone bumps into me from behind and I fall forward against Wes, one hand coming up and landing on his chest. I feel his muscles flex beneath the crisp white shirt of his tux and I push back, looking down and tucking my hair behind my ear.

Wes clears his throat and carefully pulls his arm away,

until we are standing close, but not touching.

"Where did Bea go?" His voice is even but forced. He is trying too hard to sound normal, unaffected.

"I don't know." I turn around, grateful for the chance to avoid looking at him. The space is so filled with people that I have trouble seeing past those closest to us. Most of the guests are standing in the center of the room, waiting for the dinner and the speeches to start, but I spot the president seated at a table in the corner. Secret Service agents in black suits stand against the wall next to him, their arms crossed over their chests and their heads turning back and forth as they survey the crowd.

"Bea!" I call out when I see her standing not far from us.

She is already talking to someone, an older gentleman in a tuxedo similar to Wes's. When she hears her name she waves at me through the crowd. "Coming, Sam!"

She beams up at the man, says something to make him laugh, and then shimmies over to us. Several people turn to watch her walk past, and I wonder where she learned how to be so open and free. It can't have just been the Project's training. Maybe this is how Twenty-two would have been without the brainwashing and the time traveling. Maybe she's just slipping into a role she was always meant to play.

"This room is amazing," she says when she reaches us. She throws out her arm, narrowly missing an older woman, and I follow where she's looking, to the cream-colored walls, the deep-red curtains pulled back from the windows with heavy gold rope. "I'm so happy you brought me along."

"Why wouldn't we?" Wes smiles down at her.

"You're such a charmer. Oh, champagne? I want some."

Wes spots a waiter near the dance floor. "Hold on, I'll be right back." He steps into the crowd and is quickly lost among the other guests.

Twenty-two and I are alone. I stare at her warily, but she just smiles and touches me lightly on the arm. "I'm so glad to be here with you, Sam. It's been forever since we last saw each other."

"Years, right?" I struggle to keep my voice as affectionate as hers.

"I was at your old house just last week, and your parents were asking about you."

I can't help but picture my own parents on the night I left, lying in their bed under their summer blanket, no idea that their only child was slipping out into the darkness.

"Don't you miss your mother? Your father? They're missing you terribly, you know."

"It seems . . . like a really long time since I last saw them."

Twenty-two steps closer. "It'll be okay. Family is so important, but I'm here now; don't worry. You're not alone."

She's acting. This is an act. I repeat the phrase in my head, but it's difficult to remember when she squeezes my arm, when she says the words I've so desperately needed to hear these past few months.

"Here you go." Wes is back, and Twenty-two steps away, taking the glass from his outstretched hand. "What were you two talking about?"

He looks directly at me and his eyes narrow slightly. I take a shaky breath as Bea sips from her glass. "Oh, nothing," she says. "Just about our family and how hard it is for Samantha to live so far away."

Wes frowns, but I wave my hand in the air. "It's fine!" My voice is overly high and I clear my throat. "I'm fine. Having Bea here reminds me of what I'm missing, that's all."

"Oh, cuz." Bea smiles and reaches out to touch my arm again. "I'm happy to see you, too."

Wes looks from her fingers against my skin to the confused expression on my face. His frown deepens, and he carefully steps between us, forcing Twenty-two to drop her arm. "Bea," he says, his voice low. "I wanted to introduce you both to one of my business colleagues. He's at that table over in the corner."

She has to stand on her toes to see around the other guests, and when she spots the table holding the president her back straightens the smallest amount. She turns to smile at Wes. "I'd love to meet him."

It is even harder to get through the crowd with three people, and we end up forming a straight line, with Wes in the front and me at the back. We pass a congresswoman, a governor from Texas, a current movie star I recognize from her file on my I-unit. I spot Tim a few feet away, holding a silver plate of hors d'oeuvres and smiling as he offers it to a simpering woman in purple silk. Her hair is up in an elaborate white twist, a large feather wrapped around her bun. It is an ostentatious hairstyle for a decade that stresses natural simplicity, and I watch Tim trying to dodge the feather as the older woman leans toward him.

There is a gap in the crowd in front of the president's table, and we realize why when a member of the Secret Service steps forward and puts his hand on Wes's arm. "State your name."

"Michael Gallo. I have business with Lawrence Tierney."

The agent looks over his shoulder. There are only men sitting at the large circular table—the first lady couldn't attend tonight, which is part of the reason we picked this event. The president is in profile to us, laughing at a joke someone just made. He's an attractive older man, and looks more like he's in his early sixties than his eighties. Next to him is a small, thin man with dark hair. He glances over at us and when he sees Wes his smile widens. "Michael!"

Seeing his reaction, the agent steps back and lets us pass. Wes and I go first, with Twenty-two following closely behind.

"Tierney." Wes puts his hand out. "It's great to finally meet you."

Mr. Tierney gets up from the table. He can't be much taller than my five feet six.

"I was starting to think you were a myth." He has a surprisingly booming voice for such a small man. "You and I are meeting tomorrow to discuss that proposal. No getting out of it this time."

"Of course. I'll be by your office first thing in the morning."

"I look forward to it. I can't believe I couldn't even get you on video chat. It's unheard of."

"Who knew my I-unit wouldn't work in Tanzania." Wes shrugs. "We've been traveling so much these days, we haven't had a chance to catch up with anyone yet. Samantha and I are exhausted."

Tierney looks at me and his smile wavers. I tilt my head at the odd look on his face. It quickly disappears and he says politely, "Ah, right. You must be Michael's fiancée, Samantha."

First Mr. Lee, now Tierney. Have I done something wrong? Am I not blending in?

Tierney looks behind us and his eyes glaze over for a second. We all wait until he has finished scanning Twenty-two.

I know that our I-units are foolproof, but I still have a small moment when I tense, waiting to see if Tierney will know that Twenty-two is a fraud. It is almost impossible to fake an I-unit, and the ones you can find on the black market are mostly useless. But the Project has resources we can only imagine, and I trust that our new identities are enough to get us through this evening. Still, if we are caught, blood tests and deep background checks will show the truth—that there is no real record of Michael, Bea, and Samantha.

Though the Montauk Project emerged from a U.S. government program, it works independently in this time period. Only a very small number in the government know of its existence at all, and an even smaller number know what they do. If something goes wrong, we will be four fugitives with no identities, completely at the mercy of an organization that has proven again and again that its recruits do not matter.

But of course Tierney just smiles, and I let out a slow breath. "You brought a guest."

Twenty-two steps forward. "Bea Carlisle." She says her name as though Tierney doesn't know it yet, and he smiles at her and nods. It is strange how the I-unit has worked itself into social custom, how much you can know about someone you've never really met before.

"Bea is staying with us while we visit New Washington," I say.

"It's a pleasure to meet you." Twenty-two cocks her head to the side. "I don't want to sound forward, but is that really the president?"

The breathy way she says it makes Tierney move toward her. "It is. He's a close friend of mine."

"This is all so exciting." She clasps her hands together, and Tierney's eyes fall to the bodice of her dress.

"You'll have to forgive Bea," Wes cuts in. "She's not used to events like this."

The shorter man inches closer to Twenty-two. "We'll take good care of you, don't worry."

"I'm from a small town. Peaksville, New York." Twenty-two laughs. It is a throaty sound that makes one of the Secret Service agents glance over at her. "I haven't seen Samantha in years, and now here we are in a ballroom with the president."

"Did you say Peaksville?"

The four of us turn. President Sardosky is standing now, watching our conversation. "I have family in Peaksville."

"Really?" Twenty-two's smile widens. "I didn't know that."

"I used to visit my grandparents there every summer." He pushes away from the china-laden table and moves to join us.

"Don't you miss it, stuck in this big city?" Twenty-two drops her voice, forcing the president to lean in close to hear her.

"Every day."

"I'm Bea Carlisle." She holds out her hand.

President Sardosky takes it in his, though he doesn't let go right away. "A pleasure. I'm sure you know who I am." He smiles, and thick creases spread out around his eyes.

She does. We all do. And not just that he's the president. We know about his childhood on the streets of Brooklyn, about his rise to politics. His daily routine, down to what type of coffee he drinks in the morning—Brazilian, imported, rare in this time period.

We also know that in some ways he is a contradiction: a president who will do anything to create peace across the world, while his own household is in upheaval. He is notorious for his indiscretions; he keeps a mistress, and there have been more than a few rumors of what happens with the young, dark-haired interns at Hill House. The first lady staunchly ignores the rumors in public, but the tabloids are constantly writing about the screaming fights overheard by their staff.

Twenty-two keeps her voice light as she says, "Oh, of course, Mr. President." She sounds in awe of him, and he stands a bit straighter, expanding his barrel-shaped chest. He is a broad man, just a little shorter than Wes, with thick graying hair and a mustache that hangs down over his top lip.

"This is my cousin and her fiancé."

The president uses his I-unit to scan us all, but when he gets to me, he blinks several times. I feel Wes's hand settle on my back again and I automatically move in to his touch.

Twenty-two starts to speak, but Sardosky cuts her off. "I'm sorry. But . . . your hair."

"Is something wrong?" I touch a strand that has fallen over

my shoulder. Sardosky follows the movement with his eyes.

"The color. This might be rude, but do you dye it?"

He is insulting me by asking this, since no one in 2049 dyes their hair. It is considered taboo to try and alter your appearance in such a drastic way, perhaps as a response to the plastic-surgery boom of the early twenty-first century. Even though stem cells make everyone appear more youthful, they're considered medicinal, not cosmetic.

I remember a passing comment from Lieutenant Andrews, who told me that my red hair might stand out in this era. I was so nervous tonight that I had forgotten all about it, assuming I was making some mistake that was drawing people's eyes to me. But now when I scan the room, I see that most people have black or brown hair. There are only a few blonds, and no other redheads.

I had asked Andrews if I should dye it or wear a wig, but he'd said it was better to look natural, that if people even suspected I altered it, I'd be ostracized. I hadn't realized that people would assume mine was fake.

"Of course I don't."

Sardosky raises one bushy eyebrow.

"She doesn't." Wes's voice is firm. "It's natural, I assure you. The color runs in her family." And it does—Mary and her mother, Harriet Bentley, had red hair too.

Tierney turns to the president. "Michael Gallo is an honest man. If he says so, then it must be true."

The president is still staring at me. "I haven't seen red like that in years, and certainly not on such a young woman."

"I thought it was extinct," Tierney adds. "You're a lucky girl."

Wes raises his arm and drapes it over my shoulder, twisting a section of my hair around his hand. It is a deliberately possessive move, and when Tierney sees it he looks down, fighting a smile. Sardosky is too focused on that spiraling length of hair to react to Wes.

"Thank you," I say to both men, as though I'm used to hearing comments like this all the time. "People often think it's fake. Sometimes I consider dying it just so the speculation will stop."

Tierney and Twenty-two both laugh, but President Sardosky shakes his head. "You shouldn't. It reminds me of . . ." His voice trails off and the corners of his lips drop. He reaches back toward the table. One of the men there shoves a glass of dark liquid into his hand, and he quickly swings it up to his mouth.

No one says a word while he drinks, slowly chugging the entire glass, his Adam's apple bobbing up and down against the weathered skin of his neck. When the cup is empty he pulls it away with a gasp, and his eyes find mine again.

Wes's arm presses into my shoulders and I smile tightly. This is not good. Sardosky is supposed to be noticing Bea by now, not paying so much attention to me.

"Mr. President," Twenty-two cuts in smoothly. She

takes a small step forward, subtly angling her body in front of mine. "I'd love to hear more about your memories of Peaksville. Perhaps we have acquaintances in common?"

"Perhaps." The president seems flustered, his eyes slightly glassy, but he turns toward Twenty-two. "I haven't been back there in years."

Wes looks at Tierney. "Would you please excuse us? My fiancée wanted to dance before they serve dinner."

"Of course."

"You'll sit at our table," Sardosky says before we can leave. "I'd love to have you as my guests." He is addressing Wes, but he glances at me as he speaks.

Wes nods and turns us both. It's not until we're a few feet away from the table that I feel him relax.

"I can't dance holding this." I shake the purse in my hand, trying to distract him. We need to pass the vial off to Tim before Bea can get the president alone.

Wes nods and I watch his eyes come back into focus. I hand him the clutch and he holds it up a little. Suddenly Tim is there, pushing through the crowd. "Excuse me!" I hear a woman gasp as he nudges past her.

"Can I help you with something, sir?"

"We seem to have forgotten about this when we were at the coat check. Would you mind taking care of it for us?"

"Certainly." Tim bows slightly and takes the bag. He is gone as quickly as he came, and finally this mission feels real. We are not just playing dress up—Twenty-two is with the president, Tim is getting ready to poison his drink, and soon I will need to do my part in killing a man who just admired my hair.

Not many people are dancing yet, and Wes smoothly slides his arm around my waist as we join the slowly moving couples. Everyone waltzes as though it has been choreographed, twisting in a wide, orderly circle on the floor in front of the orchestra. The music is staccato and the strings get louder, then soft again, the uneven tones making it hard for me to find the beat. It feels like we are in some eighteenth-century novel, but for 2049 this is the latest fashion. Children learn how to waltz at a young age, and even public high schools have formal dances now.

Wes moves me through the box step, one hand at my waist, the other kept stiffly in the air. There's a foot of space between us, but he is holding me in the circle of his arms and I can smell him—pine needles, the forest, a heavy rain. We have been on a dance floor in every era we've been to and each time has been different. I remember him holding me close in 1944, kissing me in the club in 1989. I turn my head so that I don't meet his gaze. This is too confusing, and now I'm the one who doesn't know where the acting starts and ends.

"I wonder what they're serving for dinner," he says after a moment of silence.

I stare at the pale curve of his ear, partially hidden by his black hair. "I'm sure it will be delicious."

"Maybe chicken. It's been so long since I had American food."

"Then you'll probably want it to be hamburgers."

He laughs, though I hear how fake it sounds, how forced. Now that we've been seen talking to the president, security will be monitoring our I-units even more closely. We'll need to be careful. We cannot say what we're really thinking—that the president's interest in me could present a problem.

And so, as usual, we do not speak as Wes leads me in a stiff arc across the floor.

CHAPTER 5

Twenty-two is sitting next to the president when we return, both elbows resting on the white tablecloth as she cradles her chin in her hands. Sardosky bends down closer to her and some of the tension leaves my body at how attentively he is listening to whatever she has to say. But then she catches my eye and runs her index finger down the edge of her cheek. Wes goes solid, and my breath leaves my body in a long, low rush.

It is a nonverbal code—one of many we have for this mission—indicating that the plan has changed. Twenty-two is telling me that she doesn't believe she can successfully distract the president, and now she and I have to switch roles.

"We've been waiting for you!" Twenty-two's voice is

still bright, cheerful. "I've been telling the president all about you, Sam. He's very curious."

Sardosky looks up at me. "Sam? Is that your nickname?"

I take a small step away from Wes. "Only for my closest friends."

He smiles. "Something to strive for."

Wes keeps his arms tight against his sides, not reaching for me even though I can tell he wants to. But what I don't know is why. Is he just acting as my doting fiancé, bothered by the interest of another man? Or is there another reason, one that's tied to that moment in the hallway where he pulled the future me flush against his body and she never seemed to doubt his love?

I do not have the time to find out now, and all I feel is relief when Tierney says, "Take a seat, Michael. We need to discuss that venture in Japan."

"Of course," Wes responds, and Twenty-two narrows her eyes at him, hearing the same strangled quality in his voice that I do. But he folds himself into the chair next to Tierney and doesn't try to stop me from walking over to a smiling Sardosky.

When I get closer, the president stands. "Samantha, why don't you sit by me? They're about to start the speeches."

I take his outstretched hand, lowering myself into the seat next to his. Beside me, Wes whips out his napkin with more force than is necessary, but then Tierney says something on his left, capturing his attention.

The president turns to me. "Bea tells me you grew up in Boston."

I nod. "Yes, I miss it."

"It's a beautiful city."

We continue to make light conversation, and Twenty-two excuses herself, turning to flirt with the older man on her right. The president pours me a glass of champagne himself, even though there are several waiters hovering behind us.

He asks me about my family, where I went to college, even how I met Michael, which I'm surprised by. I give him the answers I've memorized, and for a minute I pretend that Samantha is real, and that her life is mine, and I almost enjoy talking with him. I've spent the last nine months alone, with the Project hurling instructions at me. Classes and combat and orders. No friends. No Wes. Sardosky is attentive and focused, and there's something about him that reminds me of my grandfather. It might be his bushy hair, laced with strands of gray and white, or the wire-rimmed glasses he puts on to read the menu that one of the waiters places in front of him, or maybe it's just that he's paying me attention, in a way that makes it seem like he doesn't want anything back in return.

That can't be right. I must be reading the situation wrong, lulled by the friendly way he offers me some of the organic freshwater trout on his plate. I was told that, based on his reputation with women, the only interest he would show in Twenty-two or me would be sexual. But his attention doesn't feel like how I thought it would. It's politely friendly, not sleazy. Which might present a problem. Now that I've switched roles with Twenty-two, I am the one who is supposed to get him alone.

I lean in to him, making sure my side brushes against his arm. "Why don't you tell me more about yourself, Mr. President?"

He pulls away, reaching for his glass of whiskey. "Oh, there's not much to tell."

We are no longer touching, and I sit back again, defeated. Behind Sardosky's back, Twenty-two is watching me. When our eyes meet she raises one of her small shoulders. I give a tiny shake of my head, and I see her look down at the table as she sighs.

Sardosky turns to me and I smile, but we both jump when Twenty-two abruptly stands, pushing back her chair with a long scrape against the marble floor. "Michael, dance with me."

Her voice is loud enough to carry halfway across the table, and most of the conversations around us trail off. I feel a rush of gratitude for her, that she would try to help me complete my part, that she would recognize how Wes's presence might be a distraction for Sardosky.

Wes shifts in his seat, his body finally angled toward mine. He has spent the entire dinner physically turned away from me, as if he is trying to block out what is happening at his back. Now he takes in the way I'm twisting my fingers together in my lap, the way Sardosky is staring into his whiskey and turning it around and around until the liquor is a mini-tornado trapped in the glass.

I watch as Wes's eyes close for a second, as he realizes that he needs to leave in order for me to get Sardosky to make a move.

"Go dance. I'll be fine here," I say.

He hesitates, both of his hands coming up to rest on the table in front of him. That's when I see that his fingers are shaking. It's just a minor tremble, but I look up at him in alarm. This was one of the symptoms that suggested his body had started to fall apart because of the damaging trips through the TM and that he didn't have much time left. Once the Project noticed, they would experiment on his body while he was still alive to try to learn more about the long-term effects of time traveling on a recruit. He would eventually die, but it would be slow and agonizing. It was why I wanted us to run away together—to get him away from the Project and to save his life.

Who knows how many times Wes has traveled through the TM since the last time we were together, feeling the way it tears through your skin, separating molecules and shoving them back together again? It is why the Project uses only young people—our bodies are able to hold up longer, to take the abuse more easily. But even then we need a special serum in our blood, called *polypenamaether*.

If the TM is hard on a new recruit, leaving us white and shaking, what is it doing to Wes, who's been through it hundreds of time?

I put my arm out, but before I can touch him he clenches his teeth together, his hands slowly steady, and he gets up from the table in that careful, measured way of his. "Let's go, Bea." He offers Twenty-two his arm and bows slightly toward Sardosky. "Mr. President, please excuse us." His voice sounds strained, and he won't look either of us in the eye.

Sardosky inclines his head. Twenty-two pulls Wes away, and they disappear into the crowd. I stare at their backs, not paying attention to the waiters clearing the plates around us or to Sardosky, who has turned to study me.

"He's a good man?"

Startled, I shift in my seat to face the president. "I'm sorry?"

"Your fiancé. He's a good man?"

I open my mouth but no words come out. It is not what I expected him to say. "I . . . yes. I guess he is."

He puts his tumbler down roughly and the whiskey swings back and forth in the glass. When he turns to me, his hand falls out to the side to brace himself against the table. He is drunk. I hadn't realized it before, even though he was steadily drinking throughout dinner, but now his eyes are unfocused, and his body matches his whiskey, swaying a little from side to side.

"You're not sure?" he asks.

I stare at the condensation that beads on the edge of his glass. The table is littered with the remnants of our dinner: dirty forks and water-stains on the once white cloth. "I don't know. I think there was a time I would have said yes without reservation. But now I'm wondering if I ever knew him at all."

"Relationships change." The bitterness in his voice makes me look up.

"Mr. President, are you okay?"

He takes a heavy breath that flutters through his mustache. "I think I might need to rest for a minute. I'm usually more careful at events like this."

This is my opportunity. I lean into him and lower my voice. "Why don't we go somewhere quieter? No one would have to know."

He nods his head, his eyes half closed. I cannot tell how drunk he is, but his body is steady as he pulls himself up from the table.

"If you'll excuse me for a minute, gentlemen."

The other men murmur their good-byes, and I ignore the way they look at me with knowing eyes.

The president walks on his own, his back straight, his large chest pushed out in front of him like a sail that has just caught the wind. At first we are side by side, but I slowly move in front of him until I'm leading the way, angling us toward the small library where I know Twenty-two had been planning on taking him.

We pass by Tim, who's carrying a tray heavy with dishes. I put my hand out to stop him. "Bring two glasses of water to the reading room, please."

He nods.

Sardosky and I continue through the crowd. It is different walking with him. Instead of fighting my way through the guests, everyone parts before us, a Red Sea disguised as silk gowns and dark suits. A Secret Service agent follows behind, and even when the crowd is dense I can feel him at our backs.

When we are near the orchestra, almost to the edge of the room, I turn my head and see Wes and Twenty-two on the dance floor. Their arms are wrapped around each other, his hand on the bare skin of her back, and he appears to be holding her more closely than he held me. For one second I think our eyes meet, but then he whips her around in a fast circle, and the moment is gone.

I lead Sardosky out of the ballroom, down a short hallway, and into the small library. When I open the door, he looks over his shoulder at the agent who followed us. "Wait outside."

The younger man's face is like granite as he nods.

The room is empty, the walls lined with bookshelves from ceiling to floor. A pale green love seat sits in the center, and there are no windows, just the overwhelming smell of musty books.

Sardosky steps inside while I shut the door behind us.

"How are you feeling?" I ask.

Now that we are away from the staring crowds, he is like a marionette with his strings cut, staggering forward until he reaches the couch. He slumps down onto the silk cushion and lifts his hand to his forehead. "Unsteady." He narrows his eyes at me from under his hand. "Will you get in trouble for being in here alone with me?"

"Michael didn't see us leave."

"I suppose it would look bad, if he did."

Before I can respond there's a knock at the door. When I open it, Tim is there, holding a tray with two tall glasses of water. I step back to let him enter.

He sets the tray on a side table next to the couch. Sardosky does not acknowledge him; he still has one hand pressed to his forehead, but now his eyes are tightly closed. Tim glances at me, then nudges the glass closest to the lamp. I tilt my chin down and he bows low.

"Please let me know if you need anything else," he says before he leaves the room.

When I shut the door behind him the click it makes sounds ominously loud, and I stare at the wood for a second, at the wavy lines of the grain running parallel, up and up. I imagine them as part of a tree, alive and stretching toward the sun. When I turn back around, Sardosky is in the same spot, his head against the back of the couch.

"I hate these things," he mumbles.

"The fund-raiser?"

"Just a bunch of blowhards standing around bragging about who has more money, with politicians kissing their asses."

I don't say anything.

"I know, I know." He laughs without opening his eyes. "I'm one of those ass-kissing politicians. It's the game you have to play, if you want to make any sort of change."

I lean back until I'm pressed against the door. I know the type of change he wants to make, but I can't tell him the consequences of it. It makes it worse, that his intentions are good.

"You should have some water," I say.

He sits up fully. It takes a minute for his eyes to focus on me. "Not yet." He runs a hand down his face, stroking his mustache, his chin. "I don't usually drink this much. But seeing you . . ."

I tilt my head, my hair sliding across the smooth wood. "What about me?"

"You remind me of someone. That's all."

"Who?"

He suddenly lurches to his feet and stumbles over to the bookcase on the far wall. He was holding it together for the partygoers outside, hiding how drunk he really was, but here, with me, he is letting down his guard.

So that is why he has been so focused on me: because I remind him of someone. It would explain why he drank so much, if it was a person he lost long ago.

I walk to the side table, reaching for the glass of water with the poison in it. It is cold in my hand, the ice cubes clinking together when I pick it up, and I'm amazed by how normal it seems, this thing that will soon kill a man.

"How old are you?" He still has his back to me, and I watch as he runs his finger down the spine of a book. It looks old, but that could mean anything here. Maybe it was written when I was a girl.

"Twenty-nine," I lie.

"You look younger. But then, everyone does these days. I remember when twenty-nine looked like twenty-nine. And eighty-five looked like eighty-five. Did you know that's how old I am?"

"Yes." I step forward, skirting the side of the couch. The condensation from the glass slides down my fingertips. "But you don't look a day over fifty, Mr. President."

"Call me Alan."

"Okay, Alan." The word feels unnatural on my lips. In training we never referred to him as anything other than Sardosky or the president. It's hard enough looking at his face, knowing I have to kill him. I don't want him to have a name, too.

He finally turns around, propped up against the bookcase, unable to stand on his own. I clutch the water glass in my hand.

"I had a daughter, once."

"You did?" I act surprised, but of course I knew. She died when she was sixteen, not much younger than I am now. He and his wife never had any more children.

"I did. But not anymore." He drops his eyes to the hardwood floor at our feet. "She had leukemia. It was slow. Back then they couldn't fix it like they can now."

"I'm sorry."

"Me too."

I'm not sure why he's telling me this, but I want to rush forward and cover his mouth with my hand. I do not have a choice about what happens tonight. Even now, Wes is in the control room, knocking out the guards and cutting the video feed to this room. Twenty-two is in the ballroom whispering, scheming, orchestrating a scene that will distract security while Tim hovers near the hallway, watching and waiting. I have to play out my part too.

Sometimes the Montauk Project is monstrous, kidnapping and torturing children like Wes. Stealing my future from me. Changing the course of time in what it thinks is its favor, regardless of the consequences. But this time they could be right; if we do not alter the time line now, the world as we know it could end.

So when Sardosky holds his arm out, I only hesitate a second before I push the glass toward him. He takes it in his large, clumsy hands and lifts it to his mouth. I close my eyes so I don't have to watch him swallow.

According to General Walker, this is my destiny. These

few moments are the reason I was trained to become a recruit, the reason my grandfather is trapped in a cell right now. But how is that possible? I refuse to believe that my destiny is to be a killer, even if this man's death is necessary for the greater good.

In the end, does it even matter? I am not here because of my destiny; I'm here to keep my grandfather safe. The only way to do that is to obey the Project. If killing Sardosky will keep my grandfather alive, then I have no other choice.

The glass is empty when Sardosky holds it out to me again, and I take it from him gently. It is warm now, from his hands. He leans back against the bookshelf again, closing his eyes as he breathes deeply.

One full minute until it takes effect. I start counting the seconds as I place the glass carefully on the side table.

"Penny. That was what I called her, my daughter."

Twenty, twenty-one, twenty-two.

"She had red hair, just like yours. It was why it was such a shock, when I saw you earlier. At first I thought you were her."

This is who I remind him of. Not a lover, but a lost daughter. The Project must have known this was a possibility. That is why they didn't want me to change my hair color, because they were hoping it would be another avenue to get to Sardosky. Perhaps they didn't warn me because they wanted a natural reaction—surprise when he noticed my hair, confusion at his attention. They were worried that the new recruit wouldn't be able to handle the pressure, or maybe they were just testing me, trying to see how I'd react if the mission shifted in the moment.

"I'm sorry," I repeat. I cannot think what else to say.

"We were never the same afterward. My wife and I."

Thirty-five, thirty-six.

He straightens, pushing away from the bookcase until he's standing right in front of me. He seems less drunk now, more alert, his eyes wide and focused on mine. "I know . . . I know this is inappropriate. But would you mind if I hugged you? Just once?"

I lean back automatically, my hands clutching the fabric of my skirt. He sees my reaction and frowns. "It's just that you look so much like her. I just want to pretend for a minute that she's still here."

Oh God. What have I done? I want to refuse, to run from the room, but I can't save him now. I have to see this through.

"Okay," I whisper.

Forty-nine, fifty.

I stay perfectly still as he moves forward, as his arms close around mine until my face is pressed to the hard surface of his chest. He smells like whiskey and stale cigars, and it reminds me of my grandfather so much that I close my eyes and pretend it is his chest I am leaning on. That instead of killing this man, I am saving him.

Sardosky pulls back to look at me, but it is in that

moment the drug courses through his system, filling his arteries like cement, the blood trickling in drops, his heart slowing, slowing, faltering, stopping. His eyes roll back into his head and he crumbles, his arm knocking against the side table and sending the glasses to the floor where they shatter around us.

I drop down next to him, cradling his head in my hands. His mouth is open, gaping, like a bloated fish struggling to reach the water again. "Shh," I murmur. "It's okay."

His eyes dart frantically from side to side and his hands claw at his chest. He understands what is happening to him, understands that I'm not trying to help, and the accusation in his gaze is unbearable. I rest his head on the ground and turn away. The glasses have splintered into hundreds of pieces, some large enough to cut, others light as dust. I stare at the broken shards, covering my ears with my hands so that I won't have to hear his desperate gurgling anymore.

A sound at the door distracts me. It swings opens, and I shoot to my feet. *Please be Wes,* I pray. But no, it is a member of Sardosky's Secret Service.

CHAPTER 6

The agent takes in the scene: the fallen glasses, the puddle of spilled water, Sardosky's feet sticking out from behind the love seat, twitching and shaking. I freeze, unable to say or do anything to explain.

"I need an ambulance and backup," he calmly states. It sounds like he is saying it to me, but I know the noise is carried like lightning through the airwaves, arriving at the I-units of his fellow Secret Service in less than a second.

"What happened here?"

I jump, realizing he's speaking to me.

"I . . . I . . . he fell, he just started shaking. I don't know what's happening." I am scared enough for my voice to tremble naturally. What do I do now? Backup is already on its way. I could disable the agent and barricade the door until Sardosky is dead, but then they'd know I had a hand in this. I would never make it out of here alive. And who knows what would happen to Wes, Tim, and Twenty-two?

The Secret Service agent skirts the couch and falls to his knees next to Sardosky. The president's lips have turned blue, his eyes still open but glazed over, unseeing and empty. "Why didn't you get help?"

"It just happened. I haven't had time."

He presses two fingers to Sardosky's neck. "He's still breathing. The ambulance will be here in seconds. Move to the side; I'll deal with you later."

Time to abort.

"Please . . . my fiancé doesn't know I'm here. Can I leave?"

The agent looks up at me quickly, taking in my wrinkled gown, my shaking hands. "Just go. You'll only get in the way."

"Thank—"

I can't finish the word before the door swings open again. It is Tim, wide-eyed and frantic. "It's mayhem out there. We need to go."

I wave my arm through the air in a stopping motion, but it is too late. The agent heard every word. He springs to his feet, and I see Tim jerk back, not realizing that someone else was behind the couch. The agent takes in Tim's waiter uniform and my formal dress, and his hand falls to the gun at his side.

"You two know each other?"

"*Go.*" I spit the word at Tim, then run for the door. I hear a shot fired, and the bullet hurtles past my cheek, close enough for me to feel the heat of it. Another shot, but it misses too and I grab Tim's arm as I pass, pulling him behind me. We run out into the hallway, then quickly enter the ballroom. People are running in every direction and the screaming is so loud I'm surprised I didn't hear it in the library.

"Samantha!" Wes is halfway across the room, fighting the crowd to reach me. Twenty-two is right behind him. Tim and I run toward them, shouldering and pushing people out of our way.

"We heard the president had a heart attack," Twenty-two says, still in character.

"They know." I let go of Tim and clutch the lapel of Wes's jacket. "They're coming. We need to leave."

Wes looks over my head. I follow his gaze to see a cluster of Secret Service agents pointing in our direction.

"Come on, before they seal the exits." Twenty-two turns and we follow her as she pushes through the crowd, using her small body as a battering ram. A loud noise comes from somewhere above our heads—a siren, an announcement. *Please remain calm. Due to an investigation we ask that you remain in this room so that we can question those involved. You are in no danger.*

People around us murmur, then still, gathering into

tight groups as they speculate about what happened. It is the mentality of those witnessing a fire or a car accident—the need for companionship, for information, to see the disaster firsthand.

Twenty-two reaches up and pinches her eyeballs, pulling out her I-units and throwing them to the ground. She grinds her heel into each one. Wes, Tim, and I copy her actions. Other people can still scan us, but at least now the Secret Service won't be able to track our movements.

"What do we do?" Tim whispers. He is hunched over slightly, trying to hide his unmistakably large frame.

"The windows." Wes's voice is impassive, blank, despite the men in suits who are pushing through the crowd to find us. "There's no point in being subtle now. If we try for the doors, then they'll either lock us up or shoot us."

"Would locking us up be so bad?" Tim asks. "Then maybe the Project can get us out later."

Wes turns to him. "Is that a risk you want to take?"

Tim doesn't answer, and I shake my head. "We'll run. It's our only option."

"Get to the windows," Twenty-two says.

The four of us keep our shoulders bent, our faces away from the I-units of the other guests as we make our way past the table where the president was sitting only minutes ago. The Secret Service agents push through the crowd, searching for us, but without our I-units we have become harder to find in this teeming mass of people. It doesn't take long to reach the edge of the room. The ballroom is on the ground floor, overlooking the front of the hotel. The window is tightly locked and stretches up at least twenty feet. Wes is right—this won't be subtle, but there's no choice now.

He picks up a chair and throws it through the window in front of us. We all duck and cover our heads as glass pours down like beating hail, small slivers bouncing off our hair and shoulders. I feel a piece slice into my upper arm and the rush of blood that follows. Someone screams, and the mood of the crowd shifts again, louder, on the verge of frenzied. I see a woman run past, her silk dress slapping against her legs. The Secret Service seem to disappear, lost in the panic and noise.

Twenty-two uses her hand to push some of the remaining glass out of the frame. Blood from her palms smears across the window ledge as she launches herself through the open space. Tim is slower, trying not to touch the jagged pieces. "Go, go, go," Wes yells. I follow, leaping through the frame. My long gown gets caught on a protruding shard, and it tears through the thin fabric. I land half on a bush, half on the sidewalk and I quickly scramble to my feet, turning to watch Wes jump through after me. For a second he appears frozen in midair, silhouetted in the dim light, splinters of glass reflecting all around him.

He falls hard beside me, landing on his back against the pavement. Twenty-two and Tim are already in the street, running for a parked car. I help Wes get up, and we keep our fingers linked together as we chase after them. In the distance I hear more sirens. They are getting closer.

Twenty-two kicks through the back window of the car. There's no way to get the doors open without an electronic key, so she dives inside despite the glass. She crawls into the front seat. Tim follows her, clumsy, like he has forgotten how to move his body.

Wes lets go of my hand and climbs in first, reaching back to help me up over the rounded hood. My knees, now bare where my gown was ripped, sink into the broken pieces of glass, but I don't have time to check and see if they're cut. I slide through the window and join Tim in the back as Wes moves to the passenger's seat.

"Can you start it without the key?" he asks.

She shakes her head. "It wouldn't matter anyway. They've frozen the grid."

I look out the window. Drivers don't exist in 2049; vehicles run on a system of automated tracks that are built into every road, eliminating accidents and traffic jams. But now they are at a standstill, motionless in the middle of the street. The Secret Service must have shut down transportation as soon as they realized there was an assassination attempt.

"We need to get it off the grid," Wes says. "I'll disconnect it from the mainframe. You hot-wire the engine."

"Okay." Both of their voices are calm, maddeningly so, as though they are discussing what to eat for dinner. I feel

Tim dig his fingers into the seat next to me, the tension coming off his body in waves.

"Here." I take off my shoe and toss it to the front of the car. "Use this."

Wes jams the pointed heel into the plastic box under the steering wheel, prying it open to reveal a tangle of wires. Thank God this is an older model of car, and it still has a steering wheel, still has the capacity to be driven off the grid. It means we have a chance.

Twenty-two bends down, ripping through the hardware with her hands while Wes uses my heel to force open the dashboard. He starts fiddling with the wires there too, a mess of red and blue and green and white lines. Twenty-two is successful first and the engine sparks, catches, and rolls over, humming underneath us. But we're not moving. Wes is taking longer to override the system, and I see his hands start to shake, the vibrations traveling all the way up his arms until it seems that his whole body is trembling.

"Shit," Tim breathes, and I turn to see a dark-suited member of the Secret Service standing just inside the broken window of the hotel. She raises her gun and points it at the car.

"Hurry, Wes." I try, but cannot keep the panic out of my voice. "You can do this. Just breathe."

Sweat falls from his forehead, sliding down into his hair, and finally the shaking subsides. I hold my breath as he connects two wires. "Do it now." His voice is strained.

Twenty-two steps on the pedal and the car surges forward, just as the gunshots start. I hear the bullets crack against the pavement behind us.

"Go, go, go," I whisper. Twenty-two yanks us into the road, swerving around the frozen, stalled cars. I turn to look out the shattered back window. Three Secret Service agents have emerged from the front doors of the hotel and are now climbing into their own black car. In less than two seconds they are following us, easily breaking out of the grid.

"They're right behind us," Tim says. Shots ring out again, ricocheting off the back of the car in a torrent of metal on metal. Tim and I both duck down, folding our bodies in an effort to stay out of range.

"Faster!" I shout at Twenty-two.

She swerves us to the right, left, right again. There are parked cars everywhere and it's like we're in a post-apocalyptic world, trying to navigate a suddenly abandoned civilization. But these cars aren't empty, and the people inside stare at us as we pass. I wonder if the I-units of these strangers are being monitored even now, telling the Secret Service exactly where we are. A human tracking system.

We leave the new city and pick up speed on the highway. In the distance I see where the ocean has risen, where the old city is crumbling into the sea. A few buildings remain, their windows broken and empty, half buried in the water at their base. In the distance, the Washington Monument rises out of the waves, a single beacon left standing in the ruins.

I slump down farther. With the back window gone, the air whips through the car like a funnel, ringing in my ears and sending my hair flying around my head. The black car isn't far behind us, and now another has joined it. They're both gaining speed.

Wes glances back at me. His hands are clenched in front of him, and I know it is killing him that Twenty-two is the one driving, that he is not in control. "Keep down. Your hair is like a bull's-eye." Every word he says is shouted over the wind.

"I'm trying." I hear more gunshots, loud even over the whipping air, the roaring engine. One flies through the car, cracking the windshield, and now it is a spiderweb of glass with a neat hole where the bullet has flown back into the night. Twenty-two shifts her body, trying to see through the side that's still clear. Tim, hunched over, his muscled frame pressed against his knees, turns his head toward me. His eyes are too hidden to see in the darkness of the car, especially now that we have left the city and the streetlights are gone, but I know he is scared. He puts his hand out on the seat between us. Like mine, it is spotted with blood. I stare at it for a second, at how broad his palm is, open and exposed, his fingers slightly curled. When the gunshots start again I reach out and clutch his hand to mine, assuring us both that the bullets have not found us yet, that we are still alive.

We are getting farther from the city, and the new-growth forest emerges, lining the side of the road. This highway is emptier than the dense city streets were, but there are still cars dotted in our path. Twenty-two weaves us in and out, back and forth, making my body slide across the seat—first into Tim, then pressed against the window. I try to brace myself, though the turns are too quick, we are going too fast.

But not fast enough, and the cars behind us are creeping closer. Up ahead a semitruck is lengthwise across the road, halfway through a turn when the grid shut down. Twenty-two cuts the wheel to the right and we skid along the asphalt, narrowly missing a minivan with two little kids inside, their pale faces pressed to the darkened windows. "Hold on," I hear her say, and I know it is serious because her voice has finally changed, finally lost that detached, unshakable quality. Now she sounds shrill. Panicked.

She jerks the wheel to the left and the car angles so quickly that it seems we will flip over. My stomach drops as if we are on a roller coaster, the very moment of descent. Tim grips my hand in his as I squeeze my other one into the battered leather seat, trying to hold on.

"On the left!" I hear Wes shout, and then something slams into the side of the car in a blast of noise and sparks and screeching tires. I am thrown forward and feel Tim's fingers slip away from mine. My body is in the air. My head collides with something hard. I fall back against the seat as the window explodes, as the metal erupts, and my body, just skin and blood and bones, is no match for the force of it.

CHAPTER 7

"*Lydia.*" Someone is shaking me. "Open your eyes."

I feel pain, a fire burning up my leg. I blindly reach out with my hands. Something touches my fingers, forces them down.

"Open your eyes," the voice repeats, and it is so urgent, so desperate that I do. All I see is black.

"You need to try and move. We only have a few minutes." It is Wes, and I turn my head toward his voice. He looks fuzzy at first, but then his shape forms, standing in the doorway of the car—though there's no door now, just a twisted clump of metal pushed to the side.

"I'm pinned." I choke out the words. "I can't move."

"You're not pinned." He puts his hand on my forehead, slides it down the side of my cheek. He is so warm that I lean in to him, trying not to close my eyes again. "I pulled the metal away. You have a cut on your leg, but it's not too deep. It already stopped bleeding."

I look down. He has ripped the hem off my dress and used it to bandage my lower thigh. The silk is sticky, but the blood doesn't look like it's spreading.

I sit up, wincing when the movement reaches my left leg. Wes's hand falls away from my face. I see Twenty-two standing near the headlights, her gown torn off at the knees, blood trickling from a cut under her eye. Tim is propped against the open driver's-side door, one hand clutching the opposite elbow, his face chalky, his lips cracked. Only Wes is unscathed, though his dress shirt is ripped across the collar and I see a bruise forming on the sharp line of his chin.

"Hurry up," Twenty-two snaps. "They're coming."

The crash. The Secret Service chasing us. We need to keep moving. I push up from the seat and take the hand that Wes offers me. Both of my shoes are on again; he must have slipped the other one back on my foot while I was unconscious. He pulls me out of the car. My leg is not as bad as I first thought; it only throbs a little when I put my weight on it.

"The woods," Wes says. "We can lose them there."

There's a car flipped over across from us, dark and silent, and from somewhere behind the semitruck, orange flames throw black, tar-like smoke up in the air. I can't find any agents, but a small group of civilians stands near the side of the road. Their hands are pressed to their mouths, their bodies turned toward each other. They have seen everything with their I-units, which means the rest of the Secret Service won't be far behind.

"We need to move quickly." Twenty-two walks away, her strides long for her small body, her ragged dress hanging from her shoulders. The three of us follow. Wes easily matches her quick steps, and soon they are almost running, their heads tucked low as they cross the dirt-packed breakdown lane—a remnant of the old highway—and enter a short patch of grass that separates the road from the forest up ahead.

Tim and I run too, but we are slower, and I limp stiffly while he never lets go of his elbow. The pale skin of his arm has turned dark with blood and I wonder how badly he's injured, if maybe we should stop. But behind us I can still hear the crackling of the fire. It is only a matter of minutes before backup arrives.

The grass around us is high, brushing against the shreds of my gown. It smells like turned-over earth and new leaves, almost erasing the heavy metallic smoke that coats my nose, my throat.

"There's another car coming," Tim whispers, panting around the words. My ears ache from the crash, the gunshots, the screaming wind, and I barely hear him. "It's getting closer. Can't you hear the engine?"

"Not yet." I jog a little faster. "They won't stop looking

for us. Wes is right; the only way we'll have a shot is if we can disappear into the woods."

"The Project will find us first." Tim moves until he's running next to me, until we're pushing through the long grass side by side. "They'll track us using our chips. We won't be out here for long."

I bite my lip, not answering, not wanting him to hear the doubt in my voice. Walker may have gone on and on about my destiny, but if Sardosky is dead, that means I've already fulfilled it. I don't trust the Project not to leave us out here, four more casualties of the mission.

In front of us, Wes and Twenty-two are two hunched figures, their heads tucked low. Despite the moonlight over-head, the fire at our backs, I cannot make out the details of their bodies, and when the forest claims their shadows, I force myself to move faster, to fight my way to the hollow safety of the woods.

The trees around us are top-heavy pines that stretch six feet before their branches start. I walk the way the Project taught me: on the balls of my feet, bringing my weight forward and putting almost no pressure on the ground. It is easy to be silent here, with this carpet of pine needles beneath us and almost no underbrush to crush or snap.

We walk and walk, not talking, not slowing. We are pacing ourselves, moving quickly but not running, always aware of who is hunting us. Sometimes we can hear them—the faraway bark of a dog, a shout carried on the wind.

The thick boughs of green create a canopy overhead, blocking any moonlight that might slip down through the leaves. Wes leads our way, ducking under low-hanging branches, moving us north and east, toward the ocean. Twenty-two follows directly behind, her back straight, her shorter legs quickly scrambling over a fallen branch, around a large boulder. They never seem to tire, never seem to fade. Tim and I keep up, but barely. I hear him stumble behind me, know that he is still clutching his arm to his chest, face white as the blood continues to seep. I push myself forward, refusing to think about water or food or rest. The fire in my leg has turned to lava, hot and boiling under my skin.

When the light is starting to streak gray and watery through the pines, Wes finally slows. It has been hours since we heard any noise from behind us, and there are only the sounds of the forest—birds singing to each other from across the treetops, the rustling of the needles in the wind. A while back we found a small stream and crossed it several times, my sandaled feet sinking into the cold water. The fragile satin of my shoes is still not dry, but it was enough to fool the dogs, to put a few miles between us and them.

"Up ahead," Wes says. "Through the trees."

I look where he's pointing and see a barn, one side caved partway in, the roof slanted down, the red color faded and worn. A house once stood nearby, but there is only the foundation left, a slab of concrete already crumbling at the corners.

"We can rest," I whisper.

"No." Twenty-two sounds almost angry, so different from her usual blankness. "We'll be too exposed. We need to keep moving."

"We can't keep going on like this. You and I are in gowns. Someone needs to bandage Ti—Thirty-one's wound. And we need food."

"Someone owns this." She puts her hands on her hips. Her skin is flecked with dried blood, and I see tiny cuts where the glass bit into her. "What if they come back?"

"Anyone who used to live here is long gone." Tim is still pale, but his voice is clear and strong. "The house was probably lost in a flood years ago. This area is all floodplains now. But it's summer, and the waters are low. The barn should be dry."

These woods stretch all the way to the dunes, and the newly formed beaches where the waters rose. After the string of natural disasters, people learned from past mistakes and stopped trying to rebuild near the oceans or on old floodplains. Now the waters rise naturally in the spring, spilling over from the rivers and the oceans and onto land like the woods we've been hiking through all night.

The nearest town or city isn't for miles, the old ones swept away years ago, the highways and roads rebuilt farther inland. We are in the middle of nowhere out here, lost in a wilderness where there used to be none.

"We'll stay long enough to get cleaned up," Wes says. "We could all use new clothes, if we can find them."

Twenty-two opens her mouth, but shuts it when Wes gives her a look. She scowls and keeps her hands firmly on her hips, though she follows us through the last few feet of the pine forest. At the edge of the old lawn there is a tangle of weeds and brambles to cross, and they pull at the ruined silk of my dress, scratch the swollen skin of my ankles. After the protection of the woods, it feels overly exposed in this small clearing, and we sprint as we push through the long, untamed grass of the forgotten yard. The barn door is at an angle, and we slip through just as dawn breaks against the edge of the trees.

Inside it smells like sweet hay and dry wood and the musky, warm scent of horses, though the barn is long empty. The caved-in wall is on the right side, resting on the wooden beams of the old animal stalls and letting in light through the splintered boards. It's a large space, with a hayloft above our heads and a tack room in the back. I can see a strip of darker wood that runs near the floor— the flood line, where the water rose, and still rises in the rainy months. The way the color fades as it gets to the top reminds me of the rings on a tree, a slow marking of time.

"If there are clothes, they'll be in the back," Wes says.

"I'll look." I walk forward, the heels of my sandals sinking into the soft dirt floor. Wes moves to follow me, but

Twenty-two holds him back with a hand on his arm. It is the first time she has touched him not in character as Bea, and I stop, frozen, unable to look away from where she curves her fingers into his mud-spattered black jacket.

"Come on." Tim stands beside me. "I want to see if they have any medicine."

"Fine. Let's look." It is such a small thing, her hand on him, so why does it make my chest hurt so much? I touch the exposed skin near my collar, remembering a time when Wes's pocket watch would have swung there. It was the only thing that he had from his old life, from his family, who died or abandoned him so long ago. When he first gave it to me, I knew that he loved me. But then he took it back in 1989, and I was no longer sure of anything.

I turn, knowing Wes is watching, but then Twenty-two whispers something and he whispers back. Tim and I are already too far away to hear.

The tack room is on the left side of the barn, spared from the fallen roof. We push open the door to see a small workbench, a cot, a set of drawers. The walls are lined with old tools—a rusted scythe, a saw with rotting wooden handles. Propped against the wall is an old shotgun.

Tim picks up a box of shells on the desk. "At least we'll have a weapon we can use."

I find clothes in the drawers: old workpants, T-shirts, moth-eaten sweaters. This room must have housed a field hand at some point. Judging by the size of his clothes he was around the same build as Wes. There are also two pairs of scuffed boots tucked up underneath the cot, and a boxy TV sits on a milk crate in the corner. It is not a plasma, not a hologram, not even solar powered, and I wonder if maybe this place was abandoned long before the flooding.

I find a bottle of rubbing alcohol in a chipped enamel cabinet on the wall. It will have to be enough; there are none of the modern 2049 bandages that automatically clean the wound and knit the skin back together, eliminating any risk of infection. Tim stands next to the high bench, finally letting go of his elbow and laying his left arm flat on the rough wood. The gash there is deep, running the length of his forearm. The bleeding has stopped, but it has not scabbed over yet, and the wound is still a deep red, the color of ripe cherries. I rip up an old T-shirt and soak a strip in the alcohol. It stings the small cuts that line my wrist. When I start to clean his arm, Tim grits his teeth, his hand clenching into a fist then opening over and over.

There is dirt caked in the open wound and I carefully pick out the larger chunks with my fingers. "Was this from the crash?"

"I think from when the door was pushed in, but I don't really remember. It was hazy."

"You didn't black out?"

I glance up to see him shake his head, his thick neck barely moving. "You were the only one who did. The impact was right on your side."

"It felt like I was being crushed."

"You were." He is silent for a beat. "Eleven was worried."

"Was he?" My voice is carefully even.

"He was out of the car before we'd even stopped moving. I don't know how he was strong enough to rip that door away from you."

"I'm a member of the team. Of course he'd try to help me." I keep my head bent, my eyes on his cut. It starts to bleed again, a slow, steady trickle, and I press the cloth into it.

"I don't think that's all it is."

I stay quiet.

"You two have a history?"

He says it like a statement instead of a question, and again, I do not answer. His wound is clean now, and I wrap a new piece of cloth around it, tying the ends together tightly.

"How is it possible? We were in the same training group. When could you have met him?"

"I don't know what you're talking about." I gather the bloody, alcohol-soaked rags and move to turn away, but Tim reaches out, his hand circling my wrist.

"You can trust me, you know." His eyes look almost as green as mine, soft in the morning light that creeps in through the cracks in the walls. "You don't have to hide from me."

"I'm not hiding."

"Then answer one question."

The dust from the barn dances in the air between us. I don't respond, but I don't pull away from him either.

"Were you brainwashed?"

I shake my head, so slightly I barely move, but I know he sees it when his eyes crinkle at the corners.

"You remember your family, don't you? I'm not the only one?"

"I . . . was close to my grandfather. He helped raise me." Now I do pull away, holding the dirty rags close to my chest.

"Where is he now? Back in your own time?"

I shrug, trying not to think about the floor of that cell, my grandfather rocking back and forth, lost and alone.

"I'm sorry, Seven—" He makes a scoffing noise. "I feel ridiculous calling you by a number. Will you tell me your name?"

I open my mouth, but then slowly shut it again. In the hotel room when he first said his name, I felt a rush of belonging, of understanding. But now our situation is even more hopeless, and knowing his name seems pointless. I am Lydia, but whether I like it or not, I'm also Seventeen. If we make it through these woods, if we can evade the Secret Service and not get killed or captured, I still have years and years of working for the Montauk Project ahead of me. I cannot even try to escape, because they'll kill my grandfather if I do. Will telling Tim my name only hurt me in the long run? Do I even want to remember that I'm still Lydia, when my future as Seventeen is laid bare in front of me, bleak and endless?

I turn my face from his. "We should get back to the others. Can you carry these clothes?"

Tim sighs but doesn't protest as he helps me grab what supplies we can find. In silence, we walk back out into the main part of the barn. Twenty-two is speaking to Wes urgently, but when she sees us she stops abruptly. Wes has his arms crossed and he looks up as we approach. I cannot read the expression on his face.

I dump the clothes at their feet. "I don't know if it will fit, but at least it's better than what we have on now."

Wes kneels, sifting through the pile. He hands me a bundle, then Twenty-two. She sets it on one of the wooden posts and reaches for the hem of her dress. Wes turns his back but Tim stares directly at her as she yanks the torn fabric up over her head. She is wearing underwear, a scrap of silk, but no bra, and I widen my eyes at Tim until he looks away, coughing, his face burning red.

Her casual nudity is typical of the recruits—as though their bodies have no meaning beyond a tool for the Project. I am still more modest, and while Tim and Wes are turned away I quickly pull on a black T-shirt and jeans several sizes too big.

The pants are too small for Tim, but he yanks on one of the T-shirts, the old cotton stretching across his biceps, tight on his abs. I do not look away when he changes, and I'm surprised at how muscular he is, like a bodybuilder with his tapered waist and thick chest. There are freckles on his shoulder that seem out of place on his stocky frame. Wes catches me looking, his eyes narrowed, and I glance away.

When Wes changes into the rough work gear I whip around until I'm facing the wall. But Twenty-two just stares at him, taking in his long, lean form, so different from Tim's. I clench my hands together to keep myself from grabbing her shoulder, from forcing her eyes away. I shouldn't care, I tell myself. Wes and I are nothing now.

"There's some food," I say when everyone is dressed. "Not much, but a few old cans of beans."

"We can eat one now, save the rest for later," Tim adds.

Twenty-two looks at Wes and he shakes his head. She moves two fingers in a slight waving motion, and before I can process what is happening, she lunges forward. My body rocks backward as she locks her arm around my neck, a knife—she must have found it somewhere in the barn—pressed to my throat. I gasp, twisting and trying to find leverage, but she just tightens her hold. The blade pushes forward and I know that she's going to kill me, but then she sees that Wes has not moved and her arm stills.

"What the hell?" Tim jerks forward. Twenty-two digs in the knife and I flinch.

"Let her go." Wes moves one leg in front of the other as though he is getting ready to spring.

"What are you doing?" Twenty-two demands. "You're supposed to grab him."

Tim sinks into a crouch, his arms rising, but Wes barely glances at him. "I said we weren't doing this."

"They'll slow us down. If we kill them, it'll distract the Secret Service. We'll be able to get away."

I feel the blood drain from my face as I think back to the fund-raiser, to the way she touched my arm and talked about my parents so lovingly. I *knew* she was acting, but I was still taken in by her, lulled into thinking we were on the same side. She tricked me, with her soft voice and her words, and without meaning to I had started to equate her with Bea. I had started to trust her.

All along she must have been planning on killing me and Tim so they'd have a better shot at survival. But Wes wouldn't agree to that. Would he?

I close my eyes. I once thought I would love this boy forever, and now I'm wondering if he's capable of plotting my murder.

When I look up Wes is staring right at me. He tips his head forward as though he is trying to tell me something, but I just hold his gaze, letting him see my anger, my confusion.

"Let her go," he repeats. His black eyes flicker from the knife to my face to the tense set of Twenty-two's shoulders.

Tim plants his feet and lifts up the shotgun. Maybe Twenty-two didn't see it before, or maybe she cannot even fathom the idea that Tim or I would be a threat. "Drop the knife or I'll shoot you."

"Take care of this," Twenty-two snaps at Wes.

"The only way we'll get out of here is if we work together." He sounds different now, more soothing, less cold, though he does not shift his weight from his forward stance.

"It's their fault we're here in the first place." I feel moisture hit my cheek as she spits out the words. It is a shock to hear her so angry, so emotional. "They screwed up the mission. They blew our cover. They're too slow. Too inexperienced. We have to get rid of them before they get us killed too."

Wes puts his hand up. "Remember what Walker said."

"Oh right, destiny." Her voice is thick with sarcasm. "She's the special one. She has to make it out alive."

I picture General Walker sitting across from me in that cell, his hair speckled with gray, his large frame imposing as he leaned forward so urgently. I figured it was something he told all the recruits, that our destiny was to go on certain missions. But what does *the special one* mean? Am I different from the rest of them somehow?

Twenty-two's hand tightens, the point of the knife biting into my skin. Her other arm is wrapped tight around my chest. "It's not true. She's just the same as us. Worse, even. They're dead weight, Eleven. If they don't die now, then we will later."

I breathe slowly in and out. She may be a skilled recruit, but I am no longer a scared girl, waiting for someone to save me. I lock my muscles. All I need is one second, one chance.

"Do you think we want to be here?" Tim actually laughs, though the sound is empty. "We're not like you. We know there are people out there who miss us. We're not mindless drones of the Project."

Wes's face is like stone, his mouth a pressed line. I think of Tag, his best friend from his time on the streets, who took us in when we were in 1989 and treated Wes like a long lost brother. I want to tell Tim he's wrong about Wes, maybe even about Twenty-two, but I don't dare move. She is angrier now, and bound to make a mistake.

The sunlight coming in through the boards is getting brighter by the minute, picking up the lighter brown high-lights in Tim's hair, making Wes's skin seem golden. I wait, my muscles aching, for the moment Twenty-two lessens her grip.

"When did they take you in?" She demands from Tim. "A year ago? I've been here for six years. You have no idea . . ." She swallows hard, dropping the knife by barely a centimeter, but I am ready. I grab her wrist and spin until I have her bent over, her arm twisted behind her back, the knife fallen in the dirt.

"We have no idea what?" I grind the words out.

"What they're capable of," Wes answers softly. He reaches

down to sweep the knife up off the floor.

I let go of Twenty-two and she straightens, stepping away from me. Her olive skin is slick with sweat, her brown eyes wild. Like Wes, she doesn't know how to handle her emotions, and her anger is a simmering pot that doesn't boil but explodes.

Now I know why she is so mad. It's not just that Tim and I are inexperienced, or that General Walker wants me protected for some reason. It's that we are not like her or Wes and she knows it. Even though Tim was tortured and brainwashed, even though I watched them kidnap my grandfather, we have not been broken by the Project and therefore we have not lost ourselves completely.

"We have no choice in this either." I push up the sleeve of my T-shirt, revealing a small raised mark on my upper arm. It is the mark of the traveler, the place where I was injected with the time-traveling serum. "I've had this scar since I was a baby. They've been planning to bring me in my entire life. I wasn't taken off the street. I have a family. But I was destined to end up here, just like you. I never had a chance."

Wes—the one tasked with bringing me in, the one who lied about loving me in order to complete a mission—turns his face away.

Twenty-two doesn't soften. "You don't know. You don't know what it's like to forget everything and everyone you loved. To know that the Project is all consuming, that they will hunt you down no matter what happens. You learned your combat and your history lessons and you think you know what they're capable of. But you have no idea."

"Can we please stop playing this game of 'Who suffered more?'" Tim drops the end of the shotgun and it falls into the dirt. "Can't we just agree that all of our lives suck?"

"If you kill us, General Walker will kill you," I say to her. "And you know it."

She juts her chin out, her dark hair in soft waves around her face. It's not fair that it still looks so pretty after hours and hours of hiking.

Suddenly Wes lifts his head, his ear cocked toward the door of the barn. "Do you hear that?"

Twenty-two listens, and I watch as the emotion drains from her face until she is carefully blank again. "It's a helicopter."

Tim takes a step forward. "It must be the Project, coming to find us. We should go out there."

Wes grabs Tim's arm to stop him. "Do you think the Project would be that obvious? It has to be the Secret Service. At this point maybe even the FBI and the CIA."

"It's an all-out manhunt," I whisper. "Just to find us."

"We tried to kill the president; what do you expect?" Unlike her expression, Twenty-two's voice is still cutting, a new blade against my skin.

"They'll have infrared," Wes says. "If they scan the barn, they'll know we're here."

"They might think we're just animals." Tim gestures up at the roof. "Infrared never works the way it should."

"It doesn't matter. We need a plan," I say. "We can't keep wandering through the woods."

Twenty-two drops to her knees, gathering all the dirty clothes into a heap. "We have a plan. We go north until we hit Montauk. The safest place for us right now is with the Project."

"The only way to reach the Facility these days is through an underwater tunnel, but I know the codes to access it. Going to Montauk is the best choice," Wes puts in.

When the waters rose, Montauk was one of the first towns on the coast wiped away in the flooding. There is only a tiny island left where the firehouse used to be. But the Facility is encased in stone and it never flooded, perfectly preserved inside the rocky cliffs of Long Island. The Project decided not to move, and now the Facility is even more hidden, with secret tunnels leading down through the ocean.

Tim shakes his head. "The safest thing to do is wait. The Project will find us eventually." He holds up his arm, revealing the thin scar on his wrist. "They're probably tracking us now."

"We can't wait." I turn to glance at the half-open door of the barn. "We don't even know if the Project will come for us, and soon these woods will be swarming with soldiers."

"They probably think we're headed north to try to get

to Canada." Tim lowers his hand, clenching it around the shotgun, his eyes locked on Twenty-two's curved back. He tenses every time she moves, though she seems oblivious to us as she straightens, the clothes in a neat pile at her feet.

"Which is why we should go south," I say. "We can stay in the woods but follow the coastline until we're past New Washington. It should throw them off; the last thing they'll expect is for us to go back in that direction. We can head down into Virginia and then move north again from there. Maybe the Project will find us on the way."

"By that point we might even be able to steal a car," Wes adds. "They won't be able to lock the grid forever. It's a good plan." He tilts his lips up at me, an almost-smile, but I turn away, still able to feel the point of the knife against my neck.

"Fine." Twenty-two jerks her chin toward the ground. "But we can't leave all this here."

Wes finds a box of matches in the tack room and we start a small fire on the floor, burning our torn dress clothes, the bloody cloth I used to clean Tim's wound. When they are ashes, we bury them in the dirt, smoothing it over until the floor is even again. Twenty-two and I shove our feet into the work boots I found, stuffing the toes with cotton to make them fit. I keep one eye on her at all times, but she is back in recruit mode, ignoring Tim and me, her emotions stripped away again. They are too unpredictable—her moods, her anger, and I am afraid that as soon as we're in the forest she will try to kill me again.

And what do I make of Wes, who told her to let me go, who seemed ready to leap forward and rip her arm away? But he didn't actually do it, and Tim was the one who lifted his gun to her, who fought for me.

We leave the barn and sprint across the exposed, sun-filled lawn. I can hear the helicopter in the distance, a metal hummingbird beating its wings. When we finally reach the woods, still dark from the heavy pines overhead, I should feel relief. But I stare at the harsh line of Wes's back, the tense set of Twenty-two's shoulders, and I know that I am far from safe.

CHAPTER 8

I step over a fallen branch, and the heel of my boot hits something hard. Concrete, dusty and eroded, covered in grass and moss. It is almost impossible to see, but it is still there, proof that once there was a road here, that once this was a place filled with people and homes.

We have been hiking for two days, using the stars to navigate our way south and keeping the ocean to our left. We are far enough inland that we don't see the waves, but sometimes I can smell the brine, the salty air, and it reminds me of Montauk and home.

It is hot and humid for June, but climate change has raised the temperatures everywhere. By noon, it is well over 90 degrees, the sun beating down on us even through the trees. We do not stop, except for short breaks, resting against boulders, sitting on the hard ground. We eat as we walk; the few cans of food we could find in the barn are gone by the end of day one, and so far all we've had today are the berries we scavenged from a cluster of tangled raspberry bushes—the remnants of someone's garden turned wild in the woods.

After that first night of running, I thought that I had nothing left. But I underestimated my new stamina, or maybe it is just the fear of knowing they are never far behind us, that the Secret Service will shoot on sight—either way, I have kept going. My leg barely hurts anymore, though I don't know if it's because it is healing or because I am numb. But I feel like I could keep walking forever, that constant repetition of foot over foot, leg forward, leg back.

By now the government has run our images through their databases, and they know that Michael, Bea, and Samantha don't exist. The mystery of who we are will just make them more anxious to find us. We haven't heard or seen any sign of the Secret Service yet, but I know it won't last long. We may have tricked them into thinking that we're headed north, but as soon as the trail runs dry they will start looking for us all over the eastern coast. We need to make it to Montauk, or hope that the Project will use our tracking devices to rescue us. But it has been days, and there's no sign of them.

When I close my eyes I see Sardosky twitching on the floor, the rows of books towering over us, his lips turning blue. The Secret Service agent said he was still breathing, but who knows for how long? If he's dead, then my supposed destiny is fulfilled, and the Project has no reason to come looking for me. Or any of us.

What happens to my grandfather if they abandon us out here? If he's no longer collateral, then what value does he have to them?

I push the fear away. Tim is probably right. The Project will come for us eventually; we just need to stay alive until they do.

The woods are filled with remnants of the past—a heap of scrap metal covered in vines, the rusted-out frame of a car, saplings sprouting from the broken windshield. And in front of me is a different reminder of my past—Wes. I try not to, but I can't help staring at the muscles in his back, at the way his black hair reflects the sunlight. He is usually in the lead position, though if he is too slow, Twenty-two is quick to speed in front. He will wait a beat, half a mile maybe, before he moves ahead of her again. They dance this way, back and forth, a silent battle for control. And though Twenty-two keeps her expression vacant, I can feel the tension coming off her. She is still angry—at me and Tim for not suffering like she did, at Wes for not helping her kill us.

Tim is sometimes next to me, sometimes lumbering behind. He is the loudest of us, snapping branches under his feet and heavily panting. When I turn to make sure he is still standing, he will give me a strained smile, his broad face wet with sweat, his teeth clenched. I do not know how much longer he can keep this up.

Wes does not speak to me, he doesn't turn around, but sometimes he will hold back a branch, pausing until I reach up with my own hand to keep it at bay. I feel him watching me on those short rests we take, leaning against a tree with his arms crossed, his eyes narrowed. There has already been so much unspoken between us, with his betrayal, with what I saw in the hallway, and now it seems like he and Twenty-two are pairing off against Tim and me.

I take a step, my boot falling on another jutting piece of concrete, when I hear a dull thud. I turn and Tim is on his knees, his right hand pressed into the dirt.

I crouch down beside him. "Tim," I whisper, too soft for the others to hear. "Are you okay?"

He hangs his head and shakes it slowly back and forth. "I can't keep going. I can't. I'm going to die."

"No, you're not. You're just hungry."

"And tired, and about to pass out." He takes in a gulping breath, his large shoulders rising and falling heavily. The short hair at his neck is dark brown with sweat and his shirt is stuck to his back. "At this point, I don't even care if that girl wants to kill us. I need to stop."

I hear footsteps. "What's going on?" Twenty-two asks.

"We need to camp for the night," I say. "It's almost sunset. We haven't truly rested in days. We need food and sleep if we're going to keep this up."

She scowls. Her lips are small but shaped like a perfect bow, and the sour expression sits oddly on her face. "You two have no stamina. If we stop now we might as well turn ourselves in."

Wes moves to stand next to her, staring down at Tim's bent shoulders.

"They're miles away." I gesture at the trees around us. "They think we're headed north. We have a little bit of time."

Tim lifts his head. There are black smudges under his eyes and the lines around his mouth seem to have grown deeper overnight.

I stand up, my own muscles aching. It is twilight and around us the woods are gray and shadowed. We left the pine forest half a day ago and now the trees are shorter, newer, with green leaves and crowded branches. "I'm not having this argument again. Thirty-one and I are camping for the night." I pause, careful not to look at Wes. "You can both keep going if you want."

Twenty-two glances over at him, but Wes is too busy glaring at me to notice. "I would never leave you here. We're staying together."

"We can't stop now. They have trackers," Twenty-two argues. "And infrared. It's too dangerous."

Tim keeps his head bent, wincing as I touch his shoulder.

"The trackers won't work in the woods—there's no

reception." Wes crosses his arms, his expression still dark. "And infrared only works if they can find us. They're tracking us with manpower and dogs. We can avoid them, at least for one night."

The trackers were invented a few years ago—small robotic scanning devices that look like remote-controlled airplanes. They follow movements, smells, and sounds, but like cell phones, they run on wireless technology. Out here in the miles and miles of wilderness, they have no way of transmitting information.

"We'll stay," Wes says. "We all need to rest."

"Who put you in charge?" Twenty-two asks.

"No one." Wes's voice is calm, though he does not take his eyes off my hand, still hovering over Tim's shoulder. "You're welcome to leave if you want. But I don't think you should. We have a better chance if we stay together."

They are hardly words of love, but Twenty-two's scowl melts away. Without her usual pinched expression she is even prettier, and I turn away from them both, reaching out to help Tim get back to his feet.

The four of us sit in a tense circle on a large patch of deep-green moss. We have no tent to set up and we cannot build a fire—without a roof the smoke would give our position away. The few supplies we took from the barn are spread out in the middle: an empty container for water, a solar-powered flashlight, and a rusted compass.

"We need food," I say into the silence.

"We have the shotgun." Tim lifts it up slightly. "We could hunt, though it's probably too loud." Ever since Twenty-two pulled the knife on me he has kept a firm grip on it, the bulky weight perched awkwardly in his arms.

"We can try and catch fish." I point through the trees. "The stream isn't that far from here."

"I can fish." Tim looks over at me and smiles. "I used to do it with my dad."

Twenty-two straightens, her head snapping up. "You remember your father?"

Wes frowns, glancing between Tim and me as though he's seeing us both for the first time.

"I'll go with you," I say quickly. "I'm not very good with fishing, but I can carry stuff."

"Great." Tim doesn't acknowledge Twenty-two's shocked expression. "You can be my helper."

"No," Wes cuts in. "Twenty-two can go with Thirty-one."

Twenty-two blinks as though she just stepped out into the sun. "I'm not going to the water."

"Why not?" I ask.

"I'm just not going." She keeps her tone even, but I think of three days ago when we first crossed the stream. Twenty-two would not put her feet in the water; she simply jumped from bank to bank. I suggested following it for a while, but she refused, steering us back into the woods.

"Is it the water?" Tim raises his eyebrows. "Are you scared?"

She doesn't answer.

Wes's mouth falls open just a bit, his eyes on the mossy ground. When he looks up he says, "Twenty-two will stay here. I'll go with Thirty-one."

I do not want to be left alone with her, and I feel the corners of my mouth turn down. Wes sees my expression and stands up, holding out a hand to Twenty-two. She stares at him for a minute before she folds her small fingers into his. They walk away until they're out of hearing range.

Tim leans back on his arms, his legs stretched out in front of him. "What do you think they're talking about?"

"Probably plotting our murders."

"Eleven wouldn't murder you." He looks better now that we have rested for a while—his rounded cheeks are pink again and he no longer has sweat trickling down the edge of his hairline.

I pick at the moss in front of me. "I'm not so sure anymore."

"I am. You don't stare at a girl like that if you're thinking of killing her."

"Maybe it was a killing stare."

He rolls his eyes.

Wes and Twenty-two bend their heads together, and I see how good they look standing side by side. Her coloring is more olive toned, but they have the same black hair and dark eyes. She is so petite it seems he will fold her into his arms at any moment.

They look comfortable, like they've known each other for years. I think of when I first saw her in 1989. Wes acted like they'd never met before, but now I wonder if he was telling the truth.

I keep picking at the moss, squeezing the spongy green between my fingers, pulling it up from the ground and exposing a small bare patch of the rock it grows on.

"It's the color of your eyes."

"What?"

"The moss. It's the color of your eyes." With another guy I might think he was hitting on me, but Tim says it in that easy way of his, like he's commenting on the weather.

"Bentley green. It runs in the family." As soon as the words leave my mouth I realize what I have just said.

Tim sits up again and rests his hands on his bent knees. "Bentley? That's your last name?"

"I—"

He grins. "I'm wearing you down. You know it's only a matter of time before you tell me all of it."

I stare at the bald spot I've made in the gray rock, refusing to meet his eyes.

"Bentley. Like a luxury car. I like it."

"I picked it out myself."

He laughs, and I lift my head, startled not just by the

sound but by myself—that I would make a joke again, however lame it is.

"Let's go." Wes's voice cuts across the small clearing, and Tim's laughter dies away. "If it gets too dark the fish won't bite."

"I know, I know." Tim gets to his feet, but then pauses and looks down at me, pointing to the shotgun. "Keep it. In case she tries anything."

"Thanks."

He nods and makes his way to the tree line. Wes gives me one last look before he follows him, and then Twenty-two and I are alone.

I expect her to say something, but she just sinks back down to the ground, cross-legged with her hands folded in her lap.

We are silent for a minute, then two, then ten, and she seems content to sit there, staring at nothing. But I am getting bored, and the old me, the Lydia who'd wanted to be a journalist, who'd wandered down into that open bunker at Camp Hero just because I needed answers, has never been very comfortable with silence.

"So you're not going to try and kill me again?"

She shakes her head, facing the trees. "Eleven said I couldn't."

"He did?"

"He said that you were too important to the mission,

and if I killed you then he'd leave me here alone."

"It seems like you'd rather be alone."

She turns her head, and although we are several feet away from each other, I see the animosity in her gaze. "I'd rather *you* be gone. And the other one. But Eleven and I will complete this mission together, just as we have all the others."

I scoot closer to her, ignoring the glare she gives me. "Exactly how many missions could you have been on together? W—Eleven introduced himself to you in the hotel room like you'd never met."

She lifts one tiny shoulder. It is deceptively small; I have felt the strength in it when she held me pinned with the knife. "Five. Maybe seven. He was introducing himself to the two of you, not me."

I feel my neck and face start to burn. "You've spoken before this."

"Of course we have."

Wes was lying to me. I squeeze my hands into fists, picturing the two of them in different eras, relying on each other to stay alive. I don't know why I feel so betrayed. It's not the first lie he's told, or even the worst.

"Not that we needed to speak much." With each word, her voice grows more and more bitter. "Recruits complete their missions. We don't need to discuss every tiny thing that happens. It's you and Thirty-one who are so insistent on opening your mouths."

"Just because we're not like you doesn't mean we're not capable of seeing this through."

"You have no idea." Her eyes flash. "What do you think happens if we get caught out here? We're not regular criminals. We have no identities. The law wasn't made to protect people like us. We're ghosts. If the Secret Service doesn't shoot us immediately, then they'll torture us to try to find out who we're working for. How long do you think you'll last? How long before you spill about the Project and your sad little life? I give it an hour. Maybe two, if you're feeling really strong. Do you think the Project will rescue you then? I don't care if you're the special one. It won't matter. At that point you'll just be a liability. They'll go back to the hospital on the day you're supposed to be born and shoot your mother in the head."

She is on her knees, leaning toward me. I press shaking fingers into the moss as I inch backward.

"Thirty-one remembers his dad. You weren't even surprised by that. There is no way you both could have gone through what we did and still remember. You don't know what it's like to feel electricity shooting through you, burning you alive. You don't know how it feels to have water poured in your face, to think you're drowning for hours and hours." She looks nothing like a recruit now, her eyes bulging, her upper lip curled.

"You're right," I whisper. "I don't."

She sits back, running a hand over her face.

I stand up slowly. Her words run through me like ice water, making my joints feel stiff and frozen. I know we are in danger out here; I have been briefed on what could happen if we're caught. I even took a training course on tactics for withstanding torture. But I'm not ready to hear the truth of our situation out loud.

Twenty-two stares down at the ground, one open palm pressed to her forehead as she tries to regain control. I suddenly need to be out of this clearing, away from her. I pick the plastic container up out of the supplies from the barn. "I'll just go get water," I say. She ignores me.

Before I leave the clearing, I grab the shotgun, tucking it underneath my arm.

Tim is standing knee-deep in the stream when I push through the trees and onto the tall bank. He has found a natural pool, where the water is still and glass-like this time of night. Wes is standing on rocks near the shore and when he sees me he puts his finger to his lips.

Tim lowers his hands into the water, so gradually that it's hard to see if he's moving at all. His fingertips break the surface, not even making a ripple, then slowly, slowly, sink down until he's submerged to his wrists. I see a large catfish nearby, spinning in lazy circles. Tim moves his fingers in small waves and the catfish comes closer. He waits until it is right on top of his hand, and suddenly there is an eruption of water as he hurls it toward the bank.

Wes catches the slippery fish as though they have done this hundreds of times, bends over, and bashes a rock against its head. The catfish bleeds red, and the color leaks onto Wes's hands, a watery pink against his skin. "Finally." Tim wipes his brow with his hand, flinging drops of water onto his cheeks and eyelashes. "I thought we'd never get one."

"We can't cook it," I say. "No fire."

"We'll eat it raw." He pushes through the stream and climbs up onto the bank next to Wes. "Now that there's not as much pollution in the water it should be fine."

"Raw fish. Lovely."

"It's better than starving," Wes says softly.

"I'm not complaining." I don't look at him, staring down at the fish instead. The mouth is open, the eyes like small marbles. It died in the middle of gasping, struggling to breathe again.

"I'm not saying you were."

Tim pauses from wringing the water out of his pant leg. He looks between the two of us and clears his throat. "Why don't I take the fish back to the clearing? You can get water, or, you know, whatever."

"No, it's—"

"Yes," Wes cuts me off. "Take the fish back; we'll be there in a minute."

"Sure thing." Tim grabs the tail from Wes, then reaches

down to take the shotgun. As he straightens he winks at me. I frown, but he has already turned around, is already disappearing into the trees.

For the first time in days, I am left alone with Wes.

CHAPTER 9

*W*es kneels down to wash his hands in the stream, the blood slowly dissipating in the clear water. My feet itch to walk up the steep bank, to disappear while I can. But I can't seem to make myself move.

He stands again and slowly turns to face me. I stare at the bump on the bridge of his nose, at the long slope of his forehead. "Are you holding up okay?" he asks. "It's been a rough few days."

"I'm fine. Don't worry about me."

He steps forward on the rocky shore. We are almost close enough to touch, though I keep my hands near my sides. How can he smell so good after hiking for days without a shower? I am streaked with dirt, my heels are rubbed raw from the large boots, and my hair is looped in a knot on the top of my head that I've tied with the same type of string I'm using to hold my pants up. He is just as dirty, but somehow it looks good on him—the waves of his hair are more defined, his cheeks are tanner than usual. Only his eyes show how weary he is.

"I always worry about you."

He sounds sincere, but how do I know if it's real? Keeping my head down, I walk around him toward the water.

"You don't believe me." His voice is flat.

I lay the plastic jug in the stream and concentrate on the way the water rushes in, tumbling over itself. "I don't know what to believe."

"Lydia."

The jug grows heavy in my hands and I crouch to set it down on the rocks. "What do you want me to say?"

He runs his wet fingers through his hair, making the strands slick against his head. "Look at me. Please."

I stand up again. "I don't know what you want from me."

"I want us to be like how we used to be."

"Are you kidding?" I stare at him. "How could we ever go back to that?"

"I don't know. I don't know. But it's what I want."

I twist away until I'm facing downriver, the point where the water disappears into the trees. "I don't trust you anymore. I don't know who you are. Maybe I never did."

"You did, more than anyone."

"The Wes I knew never would have been capable of using me for a mission. I thought that I got through to you, that I changed you. I was an idiot. I should have listened when you told me you weren't capable of loving someone."

I feel him take a step forward.

"You did change me." His voice is pleading. "Let me explain, Lydia."

I shake my head. "I thought I wanted to hear your explanation. For months, I waited for you to find me, to tell me what happened. But you were never there. And now . . . I don't think I want to hear it anymore."

"What does that mean?"

I turn. He is closer than I thought, only a step or two away, and the weak light of early evening makes the angles of his face seem sharper. "It means that you broke my heart. And I'm not sure I want to trust you with it again."

He frowns, a deep line appearing between his eyes. "You don't mean that."

"I had to move on as much as I could, without you. The Project still has my grandfather locked up somewhere. That's all I'm focused on right now. I need to keep my head down so they don't kill him."

"Lydia—"

"It doesn't matter what happened nine months ago. You've been lying to me from the beginning."

"I haven't been."

"You have."

He looks away, staring down at the rocky shore. "It doesn't matter what I say, does it? You don't care what the truth is."

"I know what the truth is."

"You don't."

"Here's my truth, Wes." It is the first time I have said his name and I hear him take a ragged breath. "You always knew I was destined to be a recruit. You knew what the polypenamaether scar looked like, and you knew I had it on my arm. They sent you after me, and that was why you followed me to nineteen forty-four, not because you saw something special in me. Maybe it turned into something more, I don't know. Maybe you did have a good reason for giving me up to General Walker in the end. But remember that day with LJ?"

He runs his hand over his jaw and I know he is picturing that sweltering, small space in the East Village, LJ—Tag's roommate—leaning over his computer as he and I both realized we were always destined to become recruits.

"You were lying then. You were lying even before that. How do I separate the truths from the lies?"

"You're right." He raises his eyes to mine. "I always knew you were supposed to be a recruit." His voice is different now, resigned and soft. "I was tasked with bringing you in, and that's why I followed you to nineteen forty-four. I had been watching you for months, with your friends in school, with your grandfather when you visited Camp

Hero. I knew everything about you. When I first tried to get you out of the forties, it was because I knew you would screw up the time line by being there, and that would just make my mission harder."

I feel the acid rise in my throat. I knew I was his mission, but I had still hoped I was more than that, that maybe he felt the same immediate connection I did.

"But, Lydia." He puts his fingers under my chin, lifting my face when I would turn away. "I *did* change. In nineteen forty-four you were so defiant, so ready to protect your family, even at the risk of your own life. It changed me, seeing that devotion. All I wanted was to have this red-haired girl care about me, too. I was upset in LJ's room, because I never wanted you to know that you were supposed to become a recruit. I wanted to keep you away from this life. But I wasn't lying when I told you I fell in love with you. Everything I did after that was for you."

I pull my face away and his hand is suspended between us, grasping only air. "Turning me in was for me? All that lying was for me?"

"I was pro—"

But I cut him off. "Don't say you were protecting me. Don't say it. Loving someone means you trust them enough to deal with the truth together. It doesn't mean you shelter them with lies."

He is silent and the stream sounds impossibly loud, the water churning over the rocks and tiny waterfalls.

"There was a reason for what happened," he says softly. "For what I said that day, for why I turned you in."

"I can't hear it. Not now." It is getting closer to night, the treetops outlined black against the sky. My leg is throbbing and I shift my weight, aware of every cut and bruise on my body. "In the barn, when Twenty-two pressed the knife to my neck, I thought you had something to do with it."

He takes a step back, and even in the near dark I see the color drain from his face. "You really thought I would try to kill you?"

"I see the way you are together. You lied to me about not knowing her."

He shoves his hand through his hair again. "I . . . there was . . ."

It makes it worse, that he has no answer, that he has no good reason for lying. I picture the way they stood so close together, how she tilted her head back to stare at him, how he bent to hear her better. "She told me you were on missions together, before this. Why did you lie?"

"I didn't want you to think there was something between us. It doesn't matter."

"It does matter." I think of Twenty-two's face when she described the torture. "You know why she's scared of water."

But he doesn't understand what I mean. "I pulled her out of the water once. It was on a mission. She hasn't been able to handle it since."

"I thought it was—" I shake my head. "You saved her life?"

The recruits have been taught to hide all emotions, not to care about anything but the Project. It takes something huge to open them up, even in a small way. I can imagine Twenty-two on the bank of some faraway river, coughing and gasping as she relived the feeling of being tortured. And then there was Wes's face looming over her. She must have known, in that moment, that he was her key, that she was still capable of wanting.

But still.

"She pulled a knife on me."

"You know why she did that."

"Does that excuse it?"

He doesn't answer, just looks down at the rocks at our feet, and I realize that for him, it does. He is not on my side, even though Twenty-two threatened me. He understands her, maybe more than he ever understood me. "She won't do it again," he finally says.

"How comforting." I reach down and pick up the jug. The water sloshes against the lid and I struggle to keep it upright. Wes lifts his arm, then sees my expression and drops his hand to his side. "I'm going back."

He reaches out again and touches my shoulder. I flinch at the contact. "Lydia . . . I don't want to leave things this way."

"I need time."

He looks over my head to the north, where the Secret Service are probably scouring the dark woods to find us. "We don't have a lot of time."

"But I still need it."

He takes his fingers away from my arm and closes his eyes for a few seconds. I look away before he can open them again, afraid that I will give in if we stare at each other for long enough. Instead I grip the slippery plastic jug in both hands, holding it tight to my body as I make my way back up the bank.

Tim leans against the tree next to me, our legs stretched in front of us on the moss. It is spongy, almost as soft as a mattress, but we cannot sleep yet. We are scanning the forest, listening for a snapping branch, watching for a stray beam of light. After we ate the slimy catfish, Tim and I volunteered to stay awake for the first shift. Though Wes's expression darkened, he didn't protest, just lay down on the ground with his back to both of us. Twenty-two is not that far from him, her body curved in his direction. If they reached out they would be touching, and I stare at them more than I stare out at the trees, cringing every time one of them shifts in their sleep.

"He's not into her," Tim whispers.

I jerk my head away from the center of the clearing. "I don't know what you're talking about."

He snorts under his breath. "Yeah, right."

"I'm keeping watch, that's all."

"It's like you're in some daytime soap. Jealous over a pretty boy."

"I don't know a lot of soap operas where everyone's running for their lives."

"Then you don't watch enough TV."

"And you do?"

He shrugs. "My sister was obsessed. The trashier, the better. After my dad died, it was just her, my mom, and me. I always got outvoted."

"Your dad died?"

"When I was nine. It was a long time ago."

In the distance there is the hoot of an owl, and we both tense, our heads turning toward the noise. After that it is silent, and I feel Tim's body relax at the same time mine does. "You remember so much about your past," I say. "Most recruits forget, after the first stage of training."

"Yeah." The word is short, brusque, but I hear the emotion behind it. "I remember everything."

I stare at the dark silhouettes of Wes and Twenty-two, thinking of what she said will happen if we're captured by the Secret Service. "What was it like?"

Tim is quiet, and at first I think he won't tell me. But then he says, "It started small, with food and sleep deprivation. They threw me in a hole for days, maybe weeks. It was black in there, no light, no windows." He stops, resting his head against the rough bark of the tree behind him.

"You don't have to tell me," I say softly. "I'm sorry I asked."

"It's fine. I'd be curious too. I just try not to think about it. It didn't last that long anyway. I learned pretty quickly that if I told them what they wanted to hear, they'd speed it up. I think that's how I got out of it with . . . me still intact."

He is so different from Twenty-two, and even from Wes. They both turned inward, building walls around themselves for protection. But Tim did the opposite, reaching out for human contact to feel normal again.

"What did you mean, in the hotel room, about us helping each other?" I ask.

"I wanted to escape." His voice is just a little above a whisper. "I thought maybe we could work together. But there's no point in running now, not as fugitives. We'll have to get out of this time period first. Hopefully the Project will find us soon."

"How can you be so sure they will?"

"What good does it do to leave us in the woods? If we're caught we might talk. They won't risk that."

"Then why haven't they come yet? It doesn't make sense."

He doesn't answer and I turn to face him, feeling the moss give beneath my hand. "Did General Walker ever talk about your destiny with you?"

He shakes his head; I hear it scrape against the bark. "He

told me I was needed on this mission, but he never used that word. Why?"

"He kept telling me I had a destiny to stop this nuclear war. But I'm starting to think it wasn't true."

"Maybe it was. Maybe killing Sardosky meant you fulfilled it."

"If we did kill Sardosky. We might not have. We might have to repeat this mission again and again."

I hear him take a sharp breath. "If it had failed, they would have stopped us in the beginning, way back in that hotel room. But they let this mission play out. There's a reason for that."

"I just wish we knew what it was."

"If this mission wasn't your destiny, then why would Walker bring it up?"

"I don't know. But why wouldn't it be your destiny, too? Why is it just mine?" Above our heads, thin clouds create a veil that blocks the shape and texture of the moon. But there is enough light to see the shadow of Tim's face, the steady rise and fall of Wes's and Twenty-two's shoulders as they sleep. "Maybe he meant something else. Maybe this was just a cover for the real reason they made me a recruit."

"Like what?"

I have no answer and I stay quiet, turning my head to stare into the woods. There is no movement, no noise, and

I wonder how alone we are out here, how close the Secret Service truly are.

"Have you asked him about it?"

I follow Tim's chin jerk to where Wes is lying on the ground. "No. There's no point."

"What happened with you two, anyway?"

"It's complicated."

He swings one finger in a circle, encompassing the small clearing, the looming trees. "We've got hours."

I do not tell him about the moments when Wes kissed me or held me close, how his voice was so low when he said he loved me. But I describe my trip to 1944, changing the future by mistake, finding my grandfather again in 1989, and Wes's betrayal. I tell him about the Project holding my grandfather hostage, and why I wasn't brainwashed. By the time I am finished my throat is sore, and I reach for the jug of water—almost empty again—and tilt it back against my lips.

"That's insane," Tim says. "They just took me from my bed in the middle of the night. I didn't think I was lucky, but maybe I was."

"Lucky? You think this is lucky?"

"Well, not lucky, no. They tried to control me through physical torture, and that sucked, believe me. But it was like a Band-Aid being ripped off, not a long, slow, bleeding wound. Maybe that's why they never broke me."

Is that what I am, broken? I think back to the Lydia

I used to be: impulsive but still analytical, loyal, able to laugh and joke. If I had been pulled from my bed one night, would I still be that person, even after months in the cold Facility? Would I be like Tim, eager to reach out to anyone who seems receptive?

The Project did break something in me, but it was Wes who made those first, initial cracks. They only finished what he started, and now I'm in pieces, with no idea how to put myself back together again.

I stare at Tim's profile. His nose is wide, his mouth small for his face, but when he smiles he is almost as beautiful as Wes. I thought that shutting everything out was for my benefit, but maybe I was only playing into their hands, giving them what they wanted—a shell who would do their bidding. But they can't take everything from me. I won't let them. It's time I start remembering who I am.

"Tim," I whisper.

"Yeah?"

"It's Lydia. My name is Lydia."

I can just barely make out the sheen of his teeth as he smiles at me in the dark.

CHAPTER 10

A raindrop falls on my cheek, startling me awake. I sit up on the moss, already wet with dew, and more rain hits my head, my bare arms. Tim stirs next to me, his hand coming up to swat his neck, as though the water is a fly buzzing in his ear.

Wes emerges from the woods and stops short when he sees me awake. "Twenty-two circled back to see if we're being followed," he says after a minute. "She'll be here soon."

"We need to keep moving, don't we?"

He nods without looking at me. He hasn't met my eyes since our conversation by the stream. I wonder if he even remembers the way his hand curled around mine when I touched his shoulder to wake him in the middle of the night. He had whispered my name, too, but the sound made him jerk fully awake and he sat up, pushing away from me.

Now he walks over to Tim and nudges him with his boot, just as Twenty-two appears at the tree line. "Get up. It's time to go."

At first the hiking is like yesterday, and we trudge forward, the few raindrops that squeak through the leaves wetting our hair and our shoulders. But by midday it is pouring, and I am soaked to the skin, my shirt plastered to my chest, the oversized jeans threatening to fall down to my ankles with the weight of the water. The ground, once hard, becomes muddy and soft, and our feet slip and sink into it.

I keep thinking of what Tim said last night about helping each other escape. Right now we *need* the Project—it's the only way we'll get away from the Secret Service. But what about afterward?

I told Tim part of my story, but I didn't tell him about finding the list of future recruits with LJ in 1989, or about the mysterious Resistor. It's not that I don't trust Tim, but if a resistance movement does exist, then I don't want to unintentionally put him in danger.

Though I've wondered about the resistance, before now I've never considered what it could mean if it existed. But opening up to Tim allowed me to hope in a way I haven't been able to in months. If they're real, could they help us? Would they be willing? It's a long shot, but looking for them would give Tim and me a goal, a way to try and take back control of our futures.

Two hours, three hours pass, and the rain gets thicker, the mud deeper. And then Twenty-two takes a step, her foot sinks into the ground, and it doesn't stop until she is submerged to the knee. "Eleven!" she shouts. Wes pulls her out and the hole makes a sucking noise when her boot pops free.

"It's a marsh," Wes says. "We can't keep going forward. We'll need to turn back and find another path."

"It's too dangerous." I have to shout above the rain. "The Secret Service will have figured out that we're not moving north by now. They could be right behind us. And the water is rising. The whole forest might flood."

"We could climb up, wait it out in the trees," Tim suggests.

But the trunks are slick, and I see Wes eye my leg, still not fully healed.

"Who knows how long the rain will last." Twenty-two has her arms wrapped around her middle, her head bent low. "I don't want to be stranded out here, with no food and no shelter."

"We'll make our way west." Wes starts to move forward. "And try to find higher ground."

We walk until the rain is so heavy that everything around us is blurry and dim. The small streams that wind through the woods have flooded in the quick storm. Wes leads us to a hill, a tiny oasis surrounded by water on all sides. Twenty-two keeps her head down, her shoulders hunched. Her face is a pale sliver hidden by the heavy ropes of her dark hair.

At the top of the incline, I step forward, but Wes pulls me back, his hand sliding across the wet skin of my arm. "Watch out!" he yells into the rain.

I had been walking on autopilot, my feet sinking into the mud over and over, but now I focus on the ground in front of me. I am standing on the edge of a deep square hole, the bottom filled with a layer of water and grass—the dug-out cellar for a house that was swept away by the flooding years ago. "Thanks," I whisper to Wes, not sure he hears me above the endless falling water.

"There." Tim points to the other side of the hill. Tucked up against the side of a tree is the dark frame of an old car. As we get closer, I see that the body is rusted, but the roof is still there.

Wes reaches for the door handle, struggling with the warped metal. Tim helps and together they manage to pry open the driver's-side door with a low creaking noise.

We crawl in: Twenty-two and Tim in the back, Wes and me in front. The car has deep bucket seats, the leather faded and ripped. There are seeds on the ground near my feet, and I wonder how many animals have made this their home.

The rain pounding on the metal roof echoes through the small interior. It smells musty in here, like dirt and stale water. Twenty-two stays huddled, her arms wrapped around her middle. She will not lift her head, and her body is a shadow pressed against the door.

I am sitting in the driver's seat. In front of me the instruments are old and manual, with no digital screens like in newer cars. The steering wheel is still there, a thin circle of sharp metal. I grip it with both hands, trying to twist it back and forth. But it has long ago rusted in place, and the wheel won't budge.

"What are you doing?" Wes whispers. His voice is low enough that Tim and Twenty-two can't hear.

"Practicing my driving skills."

He doesn't smile, but his eyes crinkle at the corners and I know he's amused. It feels like he and I are alone in here, and I can imagine us in a different lifetime, a normal Wes and Lydia driving in a car like this, the window down and the radio on.

"The keys are in the ignition. Maybe it'll start."

It is the first time he has even attempted a joke in this time period. I'm still not sure how to feel about him and his betrayal, but I don't want to lose this moment. I reach over and turn the key.

The lights on the dashboard flicker on. I jerk back in surprise, the keys swinging in the air with the sudden movement.

"There's still juice in it." Tim leans forward into the space between the seats. "Listen."

I hear a faint humming noise. Wes reaches forward and

turns up the volume on the radio. A buzz of static fills the small car.

"It's too loud," Twenty-two says from the back. "Turn it off."

"Wait." I reach for the tuning dial and start to twist it slowly. "We might be able to hear the news. It could give us a clue about where the Secret Service is."

It is mostly static—this far from civilization it's hard to pick up any stations—but we finally hear the faint twang of a country song. I stop twisting and Wes turns the volume up. The song ends and a commercial starts, advertising for cars at a local dealership. Finally, the announcer's voice comes on.

We'll get back to the music in a sec, folks, but first we want to give you an update on the news that's rocking the nation. Here's the official report from Hill House.

The voice cuts out and a more professional-sounding woman begins speaking.

The suspects in the assassination of President Sardosky are still at large, and civilians along the East Coast are urged to wear their I-units at all times, so that any suspicious activity can be monitored by the FBI and the Secret Service. Officials believe the four have taken to the woods near the coastline, and northern states have been put on high alert as the suspects are most likely headed toward Canada. The four were initially identified as Michael Gallo, Samantha Greenwood, Bea Carlisle, and Paul Sherman, but the FBI has confirmed that those aliases were forged. We don't know yet who the suspects were working for, or if this was an independent act of terrorism, but we can tell you that when they are found they will be prosecuted to the highest extent of the law.

Meanwhile, the funeral services for President Sardosky will be held . . .

Wes turns down the volume until the voice is just a low hum.

"He's dead," I say flatly. "We killed him."

"Good." Twenty-two lifts her head for the first time since the rain started. Her eyes are brighter than normal, dark and shining in the dim light of the car. "That means the mission was a success. We won't have to do it again."

"But why hasn't the Project come for us yet?" Tim asks. "Why haven't they tracked and rescued us?"

"We've completed the mission," Twenty-two says. "But there were obvious complications. The Project will weigh the benefits of bringing us in versus the cost of leaving us out here. The odds are rarely in favor of the recruits."

"We're valuable to them." I cannot keep the frustration out of my voice. "They wouldn't just leave us here." I think of what Twenty-two said earlier about the Secret Service torturing us for information. If the Project knows that's a possibility, then they wouldn't risk us falling into the government's hands.

"Some of us are more valuable than others," Twenty-two mumbles, and I think of what she said about me being special to General Walker in some way. "But I guess not valuable enough, huh? Not if they don't come for you."

"Maybe they can't get to us." Tim keeps his voice even, but he slumps back against the battered seat, his shoulders low. "Maybe the manhunt is too big for them to rescue us without drawing too much attention to themselves."

"The size doesn't matter. They could still find a way," Wes says. "There might be another reason they haven't come yet. The time line could have changed."

No one speaks. Right now, the four of us are outside our normal times. If the past, and therefore the present, were altered, we would be completely unaware of it.

"But the president is dead," I say. "So the time line couldn't have changed that much. They know we're out here. But we can't count on them coming. We need to stick to the plan and make our way to Montauk before the Secret Service finds us."

"You heard the radio," Tim says. "They still think we're going north. They have no idea where we are."

"We can't trust that." Wes stares out the windshield at the water beating against the smudged glass. "They wouldn't leak their military strategy to the local media. I bet they know we've changed direction by now. We need to try and steal a car. Quickly."

I lay my palm against the steering wheel. This car might have a tiny bit of power left in the battery, but it isn't going to take us anywhere.

"Turn the radio up." Tim says. "They can't track us in the

rain, and we're not going anywhere until it stops."

Wes turns the knob and the announcer's scratchy voice fills the car again, cut here and there by patches of static. We sit in silence, listening. Every once in a while they will play a song, or sometimes an advertisement, but mostly it is a constant, repetitive loop of the media's reportage of the national manhunt to find the four people who assassinated the president.

The rain outside slows, then stops, until all that's left are fat drops of water that fall from the branches overhead to splat against the roof of the car. The sun starts to shine again, runny and thin.

"Time to keep moving." Wes reaches for his door handle, but I put my hand on his arm as something on the radio catches my attention.

"Wait. Listen."

So come on down to Bentley's Hardware where you'll find half-price Peter-brand shovels and discounted mowers for the summer season. Sale ends Friday. That's Bentley's Hardware, one-six-seven Eleventh Avenue, New York, New York.

"Did that just say . . ." I whisper.

Wes frowns. "Bentley's Hardware."

"What does it mean?" I turn to look at him. "Is it a coincidence? Is there another Bentley's Hardware?"

"It must be." But I hear the doubt in Wes's voice. "This is the future. Maybe your family moved to New York City after Montauk was flooded."

"It said *Peter-brand* shovels. There are no Peter-brand shovels. And Peter is my grandfather's name."

"You can't know all the brands of shovels, not in twenty forty-nine." Wes turns down the radio, but I am breathing too hard to hear the silence. "Lydia, don't jump to conclusions. I'm sure it doesn't mean anything."

"Then why was it on a New Washington radio station? It's a New York store. It doesn't make sense. Someone knows we're here and is trying to send us a message."

"You can't know that."

"You're the one who said you don't believe in coincidences, remember? And that far south, Eleventh Avenue is basically the West Side Highway. There are no family-owned hardware stores over there."

Wes leans toward me, resting his hand on the gearshift between us. "Lydia, the city could have changed."

"In just thirty years?"

It is Twenty-two who answers, the edge in her voice even sharper than normal. "It's not likely that a small hardware store would be in that area." She waits a beat. "I take it this name means something to you . . . Lydia?"

Wes opens and closes his mouth, realizing his mistake. He turns to face her in the cramped space. "Twenty-two. We, Seventeen and I—"

"Knew each other before? I'm getting that." She gestures

at Tim. "What about you? You don't seem surprised."

"Leave Lydia alone," he says. "Can't you see how much this is affecting her?"

Wes looks at Tim. "You know her name. She told you her name."

"She—"

"Can we please concentrate on what's important here?" I raise my voice a little and they all fall silent. "I think this is a message for us. A location and a date. It might be from the Project. It says the sale ends on Friday. That's in two days. We have to get there before then."

"Lydia . . ." Tim leans forward between the seats and Wes pulls back, pressing into the side window. "You don't know this was for you. There are a lot of Bentleys in the world. It could just be an advertisement, picked up by another channel. A coincidence."

"It's meant for me, for all of us. I can feel it."

"You're tired," Wes cuts in. "We all are. We'll keep moving, we'll find a car, but it'd be impossible to get to New York in two days."

"What if I went alone? What if I found help for us and came back for you guys?"

Tim is shaking his head before I even finish the words. "You have no proof this means anything. We can't let you do it."

"If they capture you, then we'll all be at risk," Twenty-two adds.

I catch Wes's eye. He looks tired in the pale sunlight, a streak of dirt painted on the side of his cheek. "I can't just sit here, doing nothing, waiting for those swarms of soldiers to find us," I say. "This could be what we've been waiting for, the Project reaching out to us. This might be the only chance we have. Can't you see that we have to try?"

Wes sighs, and I know he wants to agree with me, wants to give me something in exchange for what he took. But then he says, "It's too dangerous, Lydia. And too much of a risk for something that's probably a fluke."

I take in their set expressions. They will never agree. But it isn't a fluke. There is no such thing as a coincidence when you're a recruit for the Montauk Project. Wes was the one who taught me that, almost a year ago.

No matter what happens, I have to make it to New York.

CHAPTER 11

I push my way between the gnarled branches. From somewhere through the trees I hear the highway, the soft whoosh of cars as they pass. I just need to find a house, or a small town, anyplace where I can steal a vehicle to take me north.

It wasn't easy leaving Wes and Tim behind in the clearing. The rain had sent us west, close to the edge of the woods. I left them sleeping, grabbing the last few minutes of rest before we tried to steal a car from a nearby home. But we all knew how small our odds were and were silent as we made camp earlier. Twenty-two went out to scout again, to see how close the Secret Service was. I was supposed to be on patrol, but I decided I would leave as soon as the two boys closed their eyes. I am tired of looking for ghosts in the trees, of wondering how we will be tortured if we're caught. The others might not believe this message meant anything, but I know it did. It has to be from the Project. If I can get to New York in two days, then I can come back with a new team and save everyone else. It's the only chance we have of making it out of here alive.

I am stepping past the black trunk of a tree when a hand reaches out and yanks me against something solid. I do not scream. I grab the arm across my waist and use it as leverage to swing my body to the left, hard enough to break the unknown hold and twist myself around. I lunge at the dark figure from behind, but he locks onto my arm, flipping me through the air. I land on my back on the forest floor and before I can move the figure straddles my body, pinning my arms up over my head.

"It's me."

Wes. I pant under him, my chest rising and falling against his. "Let me go."

"Are you going to attack me again?"

"You were the one who attacked me."

"Yeah, but I wasn't the one who snuck off alone. Jesus, Lydia. What the hell were you thinking?" Instead of getting up, his fingers flex against my wrists, pushing my hands into the dirt. I am suddenly aware of how close his face is, of how heavy his body is against mine.

I clear my throat and turn my head away. "I have to get to New York."

"At the risk of your life? Just to follow a hunch?"

"It's not a hunch."

He lets go and twists his body until he's sitting next to me. "I forgot how stubborn you are."

I sit up, brushing a crumpled leaf from my hair. "I thought you were asleep. You weren't supposed to follow me."

"I knew you'd try something like this. I was just waiting."

"I have to go. I know it's a long shot. I know it's almost ridiculous to attempt, but the Project isn't coming. The four of us trying to steal a car together is too dangerous. We have a better chance if we split up. This is the only hope we have. I had to do something."

"I would have come with you."

I shake my head. "You wouldn't have agreed. None of you would. But I *know* the ad means something. Just let me go."

He is silent for a minute, watching me. Then he leans forward, resting his arms on his bent knees. "Your face in that cell, the moment you started to believe I didn't love you, it was the worst thing I've ever seen. Worse than all those dead recruits. Worse than the years of brainwashing. I'll never forget how pale you were. Your eyes were so big and green. I watched a light go out in them."

I push back, away from him. "I can't—"

"If you insist on this suicide mission, you need to know

the truth first. You have to listen."

"Please." But even I don't know what I'm begging for anymore.

"It killed me to hurt you. You have to know that, Lydia. It was the hardest thing I've ever done."

"Then why did you?"

"The Project knew everything and they were coming for you." His voice lowers. "I thought if I could control the situation then I could protect you."

"You keep saying that, *protect me*; you've said it since the beginning."

I let the words hang there, and Wes frowns. "I never did a very good job of it, did I?"

I don't answer. It is not fully dark yet and around us the forest is so still. The usual sounds of night—crickets chirping, frogs in a faraway bog, the screech of a bird—have disappeared.

"I was supposed to check in with General Walker that morning." Wes watches me closely, as though he's afraid I will launch to my feet and start sprinting away at any moment. "When I did he told me they were coming for you and that you'd start the first stage of training as soon as they brought you in. I wouldn't let that happen to you, but I knew they would reach you before I could. So I made a deal."

"You gave me up so I wouldn't be brainwashed," I whisper.

"It wasn't just you." He moves his body until he's turned

toward me, but I cannot bear to see his face right now, even if it is hidden in the deep blue of twilight. "They were going to kill your grandfather. I told Walker he'd have an easier time with you if they used him as collateral, that it would get you into the field faster."

"You saved us both." I take a slow breath, feeling the knowledge sink in. He didn't betray me for no reason. He was trying to keep both my grandfather and me safe.

But now I'm trapped by the Project, and Grandpa is in a cell, sick and alone. Is this life better for him, even if the alternative was death?

No. I won't let myself think like that. Wes knew that I would always pick the option with hope. He was trying to help, regardless of the outcome.

"Walker was eager to start the assassination mission, so he agreed," Wes says. "But he was suspicious that maybe I had . . . crossed a line with you."

I bury my face in my hands. "He made you come to the cell. He made you tell me those things." My voice comes out muffled.

"I had to prove you meant nothing to me."

He rises until he's kneeling. I feel him move closer. His fingers curl around my bare arms. "Lydia, I'm sorry. This isn't what I wanted for you."

I let him pull my hands away, let him see the tears that are sliding down my face.

"But they did break me, Wes. I've been broken for months."

"You're not." He reaches up and rubs his thumbs across my cheeks and I feel the wetness there, seeping into his skin too. "You're stronger than you think."

"I thought I could learn how to block it all out, but I can't. It's too much. I hate this life."

"We'll get away from it; I swear we will, Lydia."

"How? We're being hunted. When we're not, the Project is everywhere, controlling everything. I don't even know if that resistance movement is real, if they can help us. There's no way out."

His brows are narrowed. "There has to be. I don't know how we'll break away. But we will. If we're together, we can do anything."

I think of the lies he told from the beginning, what he kept from me. It has haunted me for months, his betrayal, and I do not know if this confession is enough to erase that.

I open my mouth to say something, but then I hear a sharp, sudden noise that cuts into the night. Wes is solid beside me. "Gunshots," I gasp.

"The clearing."

We both jump to our feet and run through the woods, back toward Tim and Twenty-two. I wipe the tears from my eyes, chasing after Wes's black form as he ducks below branches, leaps over rocks. When he gets near our makeshift campsite he slows a bit, and I see what he does—Tim and Twenty-two tucked behind separate trees.

Tim raises the shotgun and points it into the opposite woods. He fires and the noise is as shocking as thunder, ringing in my ears long after the bullet has disappeared. I duck behind a tree as the other side opens fire—quick, relentless blasts. Small pieces of bark explode around me in a shower of dust and wood.

This is the FBI. Surrender, a booming voice calls out through a megaphone. It is closer than I thought, maybe only twenty feet away. In the near dark it is impossible to tell how many agents there are, and I picture body after body hidden in the trees, armed and ready.

"Move back!" Wes shouts as soon as the shooting stops. Twenty-two sprints away, darting from tree to tree to maintain cover as she makes her way toward us. Tim does the same but he is slower, clumsier. When they reach us we fall into one of the formations I learned in training—a rough square with Twenty-two and Tim on point, Wes and I behind.

I can hear them out there, twigs snapping under their feet, guns jostling as they move forward, coming for us. The sulfur from Tim's shotgun burns at my nose, and I struggle to take a breath.

Wes taps his head twice with his index finger, the code for *retreat.* Our only choice now is to run.

Suddenly a yellow light erupts through the forest, so

bright I blink and cover my eyes with my hands. They have a spotlight on us, and our cover behind the trees is now almost worthless.

"Now!" I shout. "Go now!"

Twenty-two is already moving, but Tim winces, doubling over to clutch his side. I grab his arm, ready to pull him after me, when I feel it, wet and hot and red.

Blood. He's covered in blood.

"Oh God, Tim." I wrap my arm around his waist and he falls into me. "Wes, he's been shot."

Wes grabs the shotgun from Tim's hand, pumping the barrel once. As he winds one arm around Tim's body, he turns and fires the weapon into the woods. The bright light disappears, shattered by his bullet.

We run as fast as we can, Wes on Tim's left side, me on his right. Twenty-two is up ahead, darting from tree to tree, her small body almost invisible in the darkened forest.

Tim is moaning, his head lolling back and forth, and even with Wes's help I struggle under his weight. He was shot on the right side, under his ribs. The bullet pierced his lung; I can hear it in every gargled, jagged breath he takes. Blood pours out of the hole, staining my T-shirt as well as his.

"He has to lie down," I yell at Wes. "I need to stop the bleeding or he'll die."

Wes's face is grim as he steers us around a large fallen tree. He lifts the shotgun, pumps the chamber again, and points it into the woods. "Lydia . . . we won't have long."

"Just let me stop the bleeding." I help Tim lie back against the old, rotting wood. He closes his eyes and tries to lift his arm, but his hand just spasms in the air before it falls limply back to his side. It reminds me of him in the stream at dusk, slowly moving his fingers through the dark water and waiting, waiting for the moment the fish would swim close enough to touch.

I grab the edge of my shirt and rip a long strip off, then press it down onto the wound. The cloth is almost instantly soaked through with blood. I press down harder and he moans again, low and raspy. "Open your eyes, Tim."

He does, but they are glassy and unfocused. "Me," I say, "look at me."

He swings his gaze wildly, but finally his eyes settle on my face. "Lydia. Is it bad?" The words sound like they are spoken through liquid.

"No," I lie, shaking my head so hard my teeth rattle. "You'll be fine. Just keep your eyes open."

I hear Wes fire from above, see Twenty-two crouch behind a boulder in front of us. The men in the trees are coming closer, with their larger guns, their endless ammo.

"I thought the Project would come for us—" Tim gasps and his body goes tight. He bares his teeth and blood slides out the corner of his mouth.

"Don't think about that. We'll make it out of this. The

Project will find us and we'll go back in time and erase this whole night. You just have to hold on for a little longer." I fight to keep my voice even.

"You told me your name."

"Because I trust you." I didn't know a body could have this much blood, and my hands are slick with it. I press down again. Tim doesn't even moan this time. There's a large bruise blossoming on his neck in shades of blue. His skin is turning to rice paper, translucent and fragile.

I can stop it. I have to stop it.

"Lydia." He sounds so faint, and I lean in close to hear him. "Get out. Promise me you'll get out."

"We'll both get out." Tears are clouding my vision, making it hard to see. A sob rips at my throat but I swallow it down. "Don't give up."

"Please." The word is less than a whisper.

"No, no, no, no," I chant. I feel Wes squat down beside me, his hand heavy on my shoulder.

Tim takes a splintered, shallow breath, and then his chest stops moving. The seeping blood slows. His eyes are open and unseeing.

"Wake up. Tim, wake up." I shake him, but he doesn't blink or move. *"Wake up, Tim."*

"Lydia." Wes's arms wrap around my middle, trying to pull me back. Away.

I fight against his hold. "I have to stop the bleeding. I have to stop it. I have to—"

"Shh." I feel Wes breathe into my hair. "He's gone. Lydia, he's gone."

"No." I close my eyes. If I keep my eyes closed then it didn't happen. "This isn't real; this isn't real."

New bullets burst through the woods in a torrent of gunfire. Wes pushes my body down until we're both hidden behind the fallen tree. I keep my eyes closed so that I won't have to see Tim lying dead next to me. The bullets seem like they will never end and I know we need to get up and keep moving. I cannot fall apart now. There is no time for grief.

"Let's go," I whisper.

There's a pause in the shooting and Wes pulls me to my feet, keeping me angled away from the log. His hand clutches mine; he signals to Twenty-two and then we are running. I do not look back at the soldiers hunting us, at Tim's body, bloody and still.

We rush through the trees and the gunfire is everywhere, never stopping. I feel a burning on my arm and know that a bullet has nicked my skin. "We're not going to make it!" I yell. Wes hears me but doesn't say anything, just pulls at my arm, speeding up the smallest bit.

They keep coming and coming. I hear a thud and turn to see Twenty-two's body facedown in the dirt, a dark spot spreading on her back.

"Twenty-two." I tug at Wes's arm. He stops, dropping my hand. I start to move toward her, but bullets rain down again, forcing us behind two trees.

"There's no way to reach her." His voice is still calm, the same way it was during that car chase so many days ago, and this time I find it comforting. Maybe he thinks we have a chance, however small it is.

"We can't just leave her here."

"There's no choice, Lydia." His voice is drowned out by the constant shooting. It lights up the woods on their side, and behind the sparks I see the shadows of hundreds of bodies, the long barrels of their rifles.

Twenty-two's arm trembles on the ground. She's still alive, but I can picture her bleeding out, her olive skin turning chalky, her small body racking as she struggles for breath. Even if we can get her away from here, she will die just like Tim did. We have no medicine, no ambulance. Maybe she has a better chance with the FBI, who will at least keep her alive so they can interrogate her.

I turn away from her twitching form. The minute there is a pause in the gunfire Wes takes my hand and we are running through the woods again, the bullets flying all around us.

In the space between two rounds of gunfire, I hear it again—the quick rise and fall of cars passing on a highway. I yank on Wes's arm, changing our direction until we are running toward the sound. He squeezes my hand in his, and then he falters, stumbles, and I turn to see him grab his leg. "Wes!"

"I'm fine." He says the words through gritted teeth. "It's just my thigh. I can keep going."

We are so close to the road, to escape. I tighten my grip on his hand and pull him forward. He is slower, limping, but he doesn't stop running.

"Just hold on," I whisper. "We're almost there."

We break through the edge of the trees and onto an open stretch of land. Sometime in the past few minutes night has fallen, and the moon is a low ball on the horizon. Ahead of us is the highway, the cars rushing back and forth, their headlights a slash against the black tar.

We are too exposed in this open space, but we do not hesitate, running forward and hunching down to make our bodies small. When we are halfway to the road, the agents emerge from the woods behind us and I glance back, startled by how many there are, hundreds of black uniforms stretching out, their bulletproof vests bulky against their dark silhouettes. "Keep down," I shout to Wes. He is sweating, the drops beading like dew on his forehead, but he curves his back over, keeping as low as he can with a bullet in his thigh.

We are only a few feet from the road when I feel him jerk forward. This time he clutches his shoulder and falls to his knees.

"Wes. Wes. No." I kneel beside him in the tall grass. "Get up. You can do this. Get up."

His hand wraps around my arm, his grip still strong.

"You'll be okay. Just get up."

The gunfire stops. I imagine they do not want to hit a civilian car, or maybe they think we are defeated, that we have nowhere left to run.

"Lydia. Go. This is your chance."

"Not without you."

He shakes his head, swallows hard against the pain. "We both know I can't jump on the back of a car right now."

I look over his bleeding shoulder. The highway is on the grid and the cars fly past at seventy miles an hour, maybe more. If we're going to make it, we have to be quick and strong and ready to hold on for hours.

"Go," he repeats. "I'll be fine."

"I can't leave you here." It was hard enough watching Tim die, abandoning Twenty-two. I cannot lose Wes.

"You have to."

The soldiers are coming closer, moving quickly, their bodies angled to the side, their guns cocked and pointed at us. Wes abandoned the shotgun after Twenty-two fell. He still has the knife that she found in the barn, but it is no match against all these agents. We are helpless now, with no way to defend ourselves, no way to fight back.

"Get to New York, find out who was trying to contact you. If it's the Project, then you might be able to change our fate. You can fix this, Lydia."

If I am caught too, we will both be prisoners, waiting for a rescue that may never come, or a death sentence that definitely will. Chasing after the radio advertisement is a long shot, and odds are it won't lead to anything. But there's the smallest bead of hope inside of me—hope that I can save Wes and Tim and even Twenty-two. And right now that's all we have.

I reach out and touch his hair, his cheek, his lips. "I'll make this right," I whisper. "Believe in me."

"I always do." He gives me that lopsided smile of his, the one I haven't seen in months, and I do not think; I just press my lips hard against his, pulling away before he can react.

It only takes a second to stand, to sprint toward the road. I do not turn around as I leap onto the back of a pickup truck and swing myself into the low bed, falling heavily onto my side. I lay my body flat on the cold metal, listening to the gunshots ring out, fade, and fall away, until all that's left is the screaming of the wind.

CHAPTER 12

As soon as the truck stops, I crawl out from the back of the pickup. We are in the parking lot of a convenience store, though I don't know what state this is. The truck was headed north when I jumped on it, but I couldn't recognize any of the landmarks we passed, with the landscape altered so drastically since my own time. I can only trust we were moving in the right direction.

It is barely morning, the light caught somewhere between black and gray, and the lot is deserted except for a large semitruck. During the drive here, I lay on my back and stare up at the stars, waiting for the moment the government would shut down the grid and grind the cars on the highway to a halt—but it never happened. The FBI and Secret Service must have been too far away to see which vehicle I escaped on, and they couldn't justify stalling transportation across several states.

The driver of the pickup never even knew I was in the bed of his truck as he automatically drove down the dark highway. Now he is inside the gas station, buying food or using the restroom. The old gas pumps, abandoned and no longer functional, aren't far from where we're parked. Cars run on solar power, and the grid provides the electricity. Drivers pay for their vehicles, they pay to use the roads, but they do not need to fill up their tanks anymore.

The semitruck has New Jersey plates and an *I Love New York* sticker on the bumper. I hop up onto the back and crouch down, steadying myself as I lift up the unlocked back door. It's heavy. I only manage a few feet—just enough for me to crawl inside. In the semidarkness, I shut the door again. Now the only light is a thin strip near the floor. The driver comes back within minutes. I hear him start the engine, the ground vibrates beneath me, and soon we are on the road. He is carrying bananas, hundreds of them, stacked in wooden crates all around me.

When I am hungry I eat the underripe, still-green fruit. I try to sleep a little, my head resting on a crate, but I keep jerking awake, feeling Tim's blood hot on my hands, seeing Wes kneeling in the dirt, his fingers white as he pressed them to his shoulder.

Because the truck drives so smoothly, I barely feel it when we stop. A door opens and closes, and I crouch behind a box of bananas, waiting. I only hear silence.

I lift the back door up a fraction of an inch and peer out the small sliver of space to see red brick and a stack of wooden frames. I push the door up farther, slide out, and close it again quickly.

I am in a narrow alleyway, so tight that I have to squeeze against the side of the truck to inch my way forward. Up ahead I see light, white and blazing and preventing me from seeing the street. The closer I get to the sidewalk the more I make out: the long shape of a building, cars moving past in quick, efficient rows. It is a city, and I cross my fingers as I emerge from the alley. Someone bumps into me and I back up, watching the streams of people hurry past, speaking English, Chinese, Russian. The lights above are flashing neon, even though it's midday. Times Square, New York.

I've been to New York countless times with my grandfather, but I've never seen Times Square like this. The advertisements are holograms, three-dimensional images that pop out of their frames and fly into the air. The city is quieter, no horns honking, no brakes screeching. The cars move forward on the grid, orderly lines that stop and start on invisible magnetic tracks that are hidden in the concrete. The streetlights are gone, but the walking signs remain and pedestrians push forward as soon as the lights turn green.

The heat is overwhelming, making the back of my shirt stick to my skin. I keep my head down, one hand pressed to my forehead like a visor. I had not thought past the initial rush to get to New York, but now I realize how exposed I am here in this massive crowd. If anyone scans my face with an I-unit I could be instantly detained. But maybe a crowd is the best place to be—most people ignore me, too busy looking at the gleaming metal towers that stretch up and up, the flickering images that move and dance in the open sky.

I see my own image on one of the overhead screens, a 3-D projection of my face spinning around and around. Next to me are Wes and Twenty-two and Tim, a red *Wanted* sign over all our heads. They are pictures from the fund-raiser, and it is odd to see all of us dressed up in our gowns and tuxes again, especially now, when I'm covered in dirt and blood.

I start to make my way south, toward where I think I'll find 167 Eleventh Avenue. An older man bumps into me and apologizes, and I murmur a response. The crowd is thick, with people pushing in from all sides. I am jostled back and forth, and I hear the woman next to me whispering about my dirty clothes: the stained black T-shirt, the filthy jeans. Suddenly she disappears, and in her place is a tall, dark-haired boy who can't be more than fifteen. He grabs my arm and I tense, afraid that if I fight against his hold it will bring too much attention. He leans down, his lips close to my ear. "There are seventeen shells where the water ends."

I freeze. "But the rocks are too sharp," I whisper back.

"I'll take you to a place where they're smooth."

Another code. He's wants me to go somewhere with him.

"The ocean or the lake?"

"The lake."

The Center in New York City, an outpost where the Project trains and houses recruits. "The ocean" is the main Facility in Montauk.

I nod, and keep my head bent as the boy leads me down a side street, away from the bustle of Times Square. The buildings close in tighter here, the holograms are gone, and somehow it feels even hotter—ever since the temperatures rose, New York is over 100 degrees every day in the summer.

There's a white van with sleek lines parked halfway down the block. I head toward it, not surprised when the boy presses a button on a key that opens the door.

Inside, the vehicle is white, clean, and large. There's no steering wheel. The boy sits in the driver's side and presses a button near the dashboard. A screen flickers on in front of him. *Destination?* a soft female voice asks.

"Sixth Avenue and Fifty-Sixth Street," the boy answers. I recognize it as the address for the new Center.

Before the waters rose, the Center was hidden hundreds of feet below Central Park. It was massive, meant to house all the recruits, as well as the Project's prison cells. But though the Facility in Montauk wasn't flooded, the Center was, and the Project had to move it in 2029. Instead of going down, it now goes up, spanning an entire hundred-story skyscraper.

"Activate air conditioning." The boy's voice is a little high, and I notice that he's rail thin, with very little muscle tone. His slight build is unusual for a recruit, and I wonder how new he is, how raw.

A blast of cool air hits me from vents in the dashboard as the van hums on, the engine smooth and quiet. We pull out onto the grid, slipping between two cars in an orderly fashion. I think of how New York used to be—the beeping of horns, the fighting over parking spots. The grid has taken that away, and it feels like a different place with all this quiet.

We're headed uptown and I stare at the buildings as we pass. Everything is brighter and cleaner than I remember; there is no trash lining the gutters, and the buildings gleam with glass and metal. Wes and I were here just last year, but that was 1989, and then the streets were splashed with graffiti, the buildings run down and boarded up, drug dealers shouting at us as we walked. These days, it is impossible to live on the island of Manhattan unless you are a millionaire, and it shows—the city's dark corners and edges have been wiped clean.

Now that the Project has found me, the knot that has been sitting in the base of my stomach for days is slowly unraveling. They must have sent the radio message. We weren't abandoned, not as completely as we'd feared. And now, with access to a TM, I'll be able to go back in time to save Tim, Wes, and Twenty-two.

The van stops at the Fifty-Sixth Street address, not far from the base of Central Park. The Center is in a new building, one that was constructed after a recent hurricane tore through the city. It has mirrored windows that act as solar panels, and reinforced steel columns embedded in every corner.

From the outside it looks like any other office building on the block. The people on the street walk quickly with their eyes straight ahead. No one notices me and the dark-haired boy as we cross the busy sidewalk. As soon as we approach the building, a keypad appears on the wall and the boy types in a ten-digit code. The door slides open and we enter a narrow lobby.

A young woman sits at a metal desk that's perched in front of an elevator. Her dirty-blond hair falls in waves over her shoulders, and she's wearing a simple beige dress. "May I help you?"

"We have a meeting with Fortitude."

Her smile fades and she holds out her hand. In it is a small, round plastic disk. The dark-haired boy lifts his arm and passes his wrist over it like a scanner at the grocery store. It beeps. The girl moves it toward me. As I raise my hand, I see that she has a silver scar on her wrist where her tracker was installed. She is a recruit, just like the two of us.

The device scans me and gives an identical beep. The girl sits back, staring ahead blankly as we skirt the desk and walk toward the elevators. This time we have to press our thumbs to a small keypad next to the door, and then look into a tiny hole for a retina scan. It is only after we are both cleared that the elevator door opens.

The dark-haired boy and I do not speak as he pushes the button for the fifty-third floor. Before the elevator moves the light dims, and a red beam sweeps from the ceiling to our feet, covering our entire bodies. It is scanning for weapons, for tracking chips, and using facial recognition software to confirm our identities. When we are clear, the elevator jolts, moving so quickly that my stomach turns over.

On the fifty-third floor, the door opens, and a guard in a black uniform gestures me forward. The dark-haired boy does not leave the elevator as I follow the guard into a long, mirrored hallway. Every surface is reflective, and the white lights in the floor bounce off the walls and ceilings, making it feel as though I am in the TM again, waiting for the moment that my body disintegrates.

We pass through two hallways before the guard opens a door on the right and shoves me inside. The room is small with a desk in the middle and curved metal chairs on either side. One wall is a floor-to-ceiling window that looks out over the city. I see the rise and fall of the buildings—the sky-scrapers downtown, the Empire State Building not far from here. The traffic on the grid looks like a choreographed ballet, cars starting and stopping in neat lines. Down by the water, a thick wall stretches along the shore, and I watch the waves crash against the opposite side, the sea spray dark and foaming as it coats the top of the concrete structure.

When hurricanes tore through New York in the late 2020s, all of downtown was flooded, and thousands of people were forced to evacuate. But instead of abandoning the city, the mayor decided to build an eighteen-foot seawall around all of Manhattan and parts of Brooklyn and Queens. He implemented a wall tax that drove out the poorer residents, closed the ferries, and in 2032 dug up Battery Park and knocked down structures closest to the water's edge, making the beaches deeper and higher.

I learned about the new wall in training, but seeing it in person is like looking at an ancient moat that encloses the city, as though we are always awaiting an attack by sea.

The door opens again and another black-uniformed guard moves to stand near the far wall. I take a step toward the desk as an officer walks in, his salt-and-pepper hair familiar in a way that makes my heart start to pound. General Walker.

But then a woman with dark-red hair enters, and I fall

CHAPTER 13

"*Seventeen*," the older man says.

My mouth is open, but nothing comes out.

"We are aware that this may be a shock." Future me's voice sounds familiar, but it is deeper than mine. Colder. She continues, "Regardless, you'll need to debrief both of us on the events of the mission."

"You're . . ."

"You. Yes." She wears a slim beige dress that clings to her thin frame, and her dark-red hair is pulled back in a tight bun. Her skin is as pale as mine. She looks like she's in her late thirties, but I wonder how old she really is, in this age of stem-cell technology. Fifty? Sixty?

She crosses the room and sits down at the desk, her

movements quick and efficient, with a grace I've never been able to possess.

The older man moves to sit next to her.

"General Walker?" I whisper.

"Colonel Walker. General Walker was my father."

The two men look startlingly similar, with the same graying hair, square jaw, and straight nose.

"You can call me Agent Bentley." This future version watches me closely as she speaks. Her voice isn't as cold as the colonel's, but it's not exactly warm either. She seems . . . blank. Like a recruit.

"Agent Bentley?" I glance between her and Walker. She's not just a recruit—they're using my last name, with a title I've never heard before in the Project. "What does that mean?"

"Agent Bentley is here as a consultant. The mission you were on was significant. Since Bentley lived through it, she came back here as a favor to help us out. Now we're especially thankful she did, since something in the time line was altered." Colonel Walker gestures at the chair across from the desk. "Sit down, Seventeen."

But I cannot move away from the window, my muscles locked tight. "I would never help—"

"Things change." Colonel Walker raises his thick brows. "Sit, Seventeen."

This time it is a command, and I automatically cross the

room and sink down into one of the sleek chrome chairs.

"Tell us what happened in the woods," Walker says.

"Don't you know already?" I glance at the future version of me—Agent Bentley. While Colonel Walker slouches, she sits perfectly still, her back straight. He isn't treating her like a subordinate, which means she must have some power here.

"The time line has changed," she says. "You were supposed to be found in Times Square with Recruit Eleven, but this time you're alone. Colonel Walker and I want to know why that shift occurred." Her voice stays cool, but as she says Wes's number, a muscle twitches in her cheek.

"I . . . I don't know." I have a hard time looking into her—*my*—face, and I stare down at the silver metal desk as I answer. "This is my first time in the future. I didn't even know something was different. Eleven . . . he couldn't come with me."

"The president is dead, which means the mission was a success." Colonel Walker reaches into his pocket and pulls out a pack of cigarettes. They are the new nontoxic, non-tar kind that burn clean. He lights one, blowing the smoke out into the room. "But we're concerned about what this shift means. Eleven isn't our priority, but if he's dead, then it could affect the time line in other ways in the future. We want to be prepared."

He speaks of Wes's death so casually, and I struggle to

keep calm. Agent Bentley is better at it, though I see the slight way she flinches at the colonel's words.

"Ti—" I stop. If Agent Bentley still has my memories, then she knows what name I was about to say, but she makes no comment. "Thirty-one was killed in the field. I was forced to abandon Eleven and Twenty-two when they were shot to come here. I'd like permission to go back to the start of this mission and change what happened, so they'll survive."

"Now why would we authorize that?" Colonel Walker takes a long drag of the cigarette. It still smells like the old ones, sharp and acrid, and Agent Bentley scrunches up her nose as the smoke curls in front of her face. "Sardosky is dead. The nuclear war we've been trying to stop will never occur now. Except for the time line shift, the mission was a success. We don't know yet how Eleven's disappearance will affect the future time line, but it might be insignificant. He was an older recruit, right?" He looks over at Agent Bentley, who nods stiffly. "Then he probably wouldn't have lived for much longer anyway."

I push forward in my chair until I'm sitting on the very edge. "Eleven *is* significant to the time line." I know my voice is desperate, but I can't help it. "I can go back to the woods. I can find them there before the Secret Service finds us. Sardosky will still be dead."

Colonel Walker is already shaking his head. "There's no

point. Maybe later, if we find out that Eleven was important in some way. Right now we'll try to pinpoint the exact moment of the change, using Agent Bentley's knowledge of what happened. But I suspect those three recruits are expendable."

"Expendable?" I whisper the word. A shadow passes over Agent Bentley's face, but she makes no outward movement. I've always known that the Project felt that way about recruits, but this is Wes. And Tim. They don't deserve to be treated like this.

The colonel takes a drag of his cigarette. "Recruits come and go."

"Is that why you didn't try to get us out after we completed our mission? Is that why you left us in the woods, being hunted like animals?" I sound like I'm being strangled, and I swallow hard.

"We knew you would make it to New York. It's what was originally supposed to happen," the future me says, her voice softer than it was before.

"Why didn't you tell us that when we were prepping for the mission? Why did you just let us wait in the woods for days?"

"We only knew for sure that you and Eleven would live, at least in that version of the time line. We couldn't tell your whole team about the outcome, not when half of them were destined to die. And besides, there were too many eyes on the woods. There was no way to do a safe extraction." Colonel Walker puts out his cigarette on the table, grinding the red tip into the metal until it is just ash. "But you made it out in the end. That's what really matters."

I lay my hands on the desk, feeling the cold sink into my fingers, and I ask the question that has been plaguing me for days. "Why does it matter that I was the one who lived?"

"Isn't it obvious?" He tilts his head toward Agent Bentley. "She might be an agent now, but in a few years her title changes to Director Bentley."

I look at her—at myself—in horror. "Director?"

"In about twenty years, you'll be running things," the colonel says.

I was always different from the others. General Walker must have been lying when he said my destiny was to kill Sardosky. Or maybe that was part of it, but not the whole story. *This* is what they saw as my destiny—running an organization that stole everything from me. Becoming something I hate.

"No." I shake my head violently back and forth. "It isn't true. I don't believe it."

"It'll happen, whether you believe in it now or not," Agent Bentley says. Walker smiles at her, but she does not acknowledge him.

"If you're so powerful, then let me go back. Let me save them."

She doesn't answer.

"How could I have become like you?" I whisper the words. "Someone who would leave them out there to die? What about Thirty-one? Eleven?"

I stare at the older version of myself, willing her to say something, to fight for Wes. I need her to show me that I still exist inside of her, that I haven't become exactly like Colonel Walker. But she just sits there, her hands folded neatly on the table in front of her.

Through it all, even during my training, even when I felt so lost inside the Facility, I never stopped trying to save the people I love. If she won't even speak up for Wes, then I know that I am gone, that the Project has won.

I hunch over the desk, needing to hide my face from them. Tears fall onto the scarred metal, small drops that slowly start to form a pool.

"What are you doing?" I hear a scrape as the colonel pushes back his chair. "Show some respect in front of your officers."

He is standing over me, hovering, but I still don't look up.

"Put your arm down, Colonel." Agent Bentley's voice is quietly commanding. "Remember that when you hit her, you're hitting me."

I lift my head to see him standing over me, his hand raised in the air, his face turning red. It is the first time an officer from the Project would have physically struck me.

There's something personal about hitting someone in anger that doesn't quite match my experience with the Montauk Project, and I wonder if Colonel Walker is taking some frustration with Agent Bentley out on me.

He slowly lowers his arm, though he doesn't stop glaring at me. "I apologize, Bentley. But remember that you're not in charge yet. Not in this time period."

She stands without looking at him. "We'll continue the debrief when you're ready to cooperate, Seventeen."

Hearing her say my number instead of my name is a physical blow. I suck in air, but I cannot catch my breath. She has stolen everything.

I lie back on the hard mattress, staring up at the mirrored ceiling. My face looks back, tired and pale and small. I am dressed in the all-black uniform of the recruits, after showering in the small bathroom off the side of this room. I'm clean for the first time in days, but I still feel as dirty as I did before, like I'm forever covered in dirt and grime—in blood.

I turn over onto my side and face another white wall. This room is a small square box designed to feel like a prison cell. I don't know how long they'll keep me here, but I know that it's only a matter of time before I'm sent out into the field again, forced to do mission after mission until I end up as cold and empty as her.

I won't accept this future. I cannot become something I hate, willing to put the Montauk Project in front of the lives of my friends and family. What will happen to my grandfather? To Tim and Wes?

But how will I get out of this place? I need to go back to the beginning. I have to find some way to make it right.

The bright lights overhead suddenly disappear. I sit up on the bed, fuzzy spots moving in front of my eyes. The Center never gets dark. Not unless something is wrong.

They flicker once, then come back on again, burning white. It takes a moment for my eyes to adjust, and then I see myself—Agent Bentley—standing in the middle of the room.

"What are you—?"

She puts her hand up. "I've cut the camera feed to this room, but we don't have much time. You need to listen to me."

I scramble up from the bed, my boots falling heavily on the slick tile floor. I want to trust that she's here to help me, but I cannot get her vacant expression out of my head. Was it all just an act? Is this the act now?

"What do you want?"

"I know you, Lydia." She takes a step forward, her hand still stretched between us. "I *am* you. You're curious about me, and you know that you could never have changed as much as the woman in that meeting had."

I stare at her for a beat before I nod. She smiles slightly and it transforms her face, making her look softer, more human. More like me.

I cross my arms over my chest as I wait for her to speak. I'm willing to listen to what she has to say, but I'm guarded, wary. Still, I feel relief start to unfurl inside of me. Coming to this room is something I would have done, which means Director Bentley couldn't have changed that much.

"When I did this mission, We—" She blinks rapidly and looks down at the ground. I wonder why she can't bring herself to say Wes's name. "Eleven and I were the only ones who made it. We came to New York to try and find out who was behind the radio advertisement. The Project found us in Times Square and had a recruit deliver us to the Facility. They wouldn't let us go back in time to try and save Thirty-one and Twenty-two, but I eventually accepted their decision, because . . ."

"Because you had Wes," I say.

She nods. She seems like a different person now, her face more expressive, her hands moving as she speaks.

"We stayed with the Project. We couldn't find a way out. And then General Walker told me that my destiny was to run everything one day. It's true that I was supposed to be on the Sardosky mission, so in a way it was *a* fate, but it wasn't why I was recruited. My true destiny was to eventually become the director. That's why they picked me. That's why they didn't push me as hard as the other recruits."

I shake my head, but she keeps going. "At first I fought against it, too, but Eleven helped me see how it could be a good thing. I could create change. I could make the Project a better place."

I take a step backward until my knees hit the edge of the bed. *Wes* helped her see that? "But nothing has changed. You heard Colonel Walker in that meeting. He didn't care if any of the recruits but me made it out alive."

"Change doesn't happen all at once. There are still men like Walker, who learned from his father how to run this organization without mercy. He might be in charge in twenty forty-nine, but in twenty seventy-seven, I'll run everything. Right now the Project has vague ideas about controlling the time line, with no real organization or communication across different eras. Sometimes they do good, but more often they are changing history so frequently that no one remembers what the original time line was in the first place. And the recruits are dying young." Her hands fall, and she suddenly seems smaller, frailer. She drags her fingers across her face before she speaks again. "In the future, you and I fix all that, starting by disbanding the Recruitment Initiative and sending fewer recruits through time. There are no more children taken from the streets or from their families. The recruits are all volunteers, and are trained with safer TMs. The days of the Montauk Project's reign of terror are over. Our job is still to watch over the time line, to save people when we can, but we'll be smarter about it. More careful."

A safer Montauk Project? Is that even possible? Could she, could *I*, really make a difference? I can tell this future Lydia believes what she's saying. But— "That's years from now. How many people have to die in the meantime? What happens to Wes and Tim? To Twenty-two?"

She looks away. "You have to think of the bigger picture."

I sit down on the bed, the mattress like stone beneath me. "Wes dies, doesn't he?"

She doesn't respond.

"Tell me. Please."

When she speaks her voice is as blank as it was in the meeting. "Eleven makes it a few more years before his body gives out. But that was in my time line. Things could be different now."

"You mean he could already be dead."

"I don't know."

"Let me go back and save him." My voice is higher, pleading. "Don't let Wes and Tim die like this."

"I can't." She still won't look at me. "This is happening during Walker's command, so it's his choice. If I fight too hard for you, then they'll think I'm attached, and I won't be able to do any good in the future. It's important that Walker believes I'm like them."

"Then why are you even here talking to me? What's the point?"

She comes forward until she's right in front of me, and then she kneels, her beige dress molding to her body as it stretches across her legs. Our faces are only inches apart.

"I want to give you what I didn't have, Lydia. I want to give you a choice."

CHAPTER 14

Agent Bentley sits back on her heels, watching me. I want to turn away, but I force myself to meet her eyes. "Is this like the choice General Walker gave me in that cell months ago? My grandfather's life in exchange for my cooperation? Because I'm not interested in another deal like that."

"No." She frowns, and I wonder if she's angry that I don't immediately trust her. "I'm giving you a real choice."

"How?"

She sighs and pushes to her feet in one fluid movement. "I know you're skeptical, but we don't have much time, so I'll lay out your options. You can stay here and give in to the destiny the Project has planned for us, or you can leave. It's Friday afternoon, which means you still have time to find out if the Bentley's Hardware advertisement meant anything."

I sit up a little straighter. "You're saying the Project didn't send the message?"

She shakes her head. "I never found out who did send it, though I have my guesses."

"Who?"

But she doesn't answer. "It might seem simple to you—if you leave, you have a chance to escape the Project and maybe even save Wes. If you stay, then you'll become like me. But this life isn't all bad, Lydia. I'm not unhappy."

"You've lost everything and everyone you love. How can you even be a little happy?"

"Not everyone. Grandpa survived."

"What?" I stand up and reach out, curling my fingers around her wrist. "Grandpa makes it? Is he still alive?"

She smiles slightly and rests her hand on my fingers. At her touch I pull away. "It would be impossible for him to still be alive in this time period. But I made sure he was safe. As soon as I had enough authority, I sent someone back in time to have him released, in the nineteen eighties. He lived a normal life."

"Grandpa," I whisper. "He's all I've been fighting for."

"I know."

She steps toward me, but I step back again until I'm pressed to the side of the bed. "If you choose this life, you won't be helpless anymore," she says. "You'll create a better system, where time is treated as sacred, and the butterfly effect is risked only in extreme circumstances."

I think of her face in that meeting, emotionless and stark. It may not have been real, she may have been acting, but isn't that just another form of helplessness, hiding her true self from everyone around her?

"Why?" I ask. "Why are you giving me a choice at all, if you think this destiny is the best option?"

I watch her shoulders grow stiff under the thin silk of her dress. "Eleven . . ." She takes a long, slow breath. "Wes and I had a few good years together, even in hiding. You remember that moment you saw in the hallway. Those memories have kept me going, even though he's gone now. But he was supposed to come back with you, and I know Colonel Walker will never allow us to rescue Wes. And that means that Wes and you won't have the life that he and I had together. You won't have any of those memories." She lifts her hand and touches my shoulder. In her heels she is taller than me, and I have to look up to meet her eyes. "I'm not saying which life you should choose. And I'm not doing this because of Wes, not really. I don't even know what will happen to me if you choose to leave here. Maybe I'll disappear when the time line changes. Or I might still be alive, but the world I know won't exist anymore. But I can live with that. I made the most of a life that was handed to me because I never had any other options. I want you to decide your own fate."

I bite my lip but don't respond.

She squeezes my arm lightly. "I know you see the Project as evil, but just a few days ago you were a part of preventing an all-out nuclear war. That's noble, regardless of how it happened. And there's more good that can be done. Remember that."

She steps back, dropping her hand. I can still feel her fingers pressed into my skin. "If you're going to leave, then go out through the elevators where you entered. I've made sure that you have clearance to leave for the next half hour, so decide quickly."

She starts walking toward the door. I lean forward before she can reach it. "Don't you already know what I'm going to do?"

She stops, turns. "Maybe." When she smiles it makes her cheeks fuller, the lines around her eyes softer. "But the point is that it's your decision. I trust you, Lydia."

The door makes almost no sound as it opens and shuts.

I move toward the door, then back to the bed, thinking of everything the future me just said. I want to walk, to run from this room, but something makes me hesitate.

I have been living with the unknown for months—worrying about my grandfather and wondering what my future might hold. There is a strange comfort in seeing how your life plays out, even if it's not what you dreamed of.

In my mind, the Montauk Project represents evil.

Logically, I know it is more complicated than that. But they stole my life from me. By choosing this future, I could prevent them from doing that to someone else.

But the cost will be Wes, and any hope I have left of breaking free from the Project.

This future me said that my grandfather will be safe. Everything I've done has been for him. But how far am I willing to go? There must be some way to ensure that we can both have the future we want.

How can I make this decision? How can I not?

I turn and take a step toward the door. And then another one. And another. Before I know what is happening, I am in the hallway, the mirrors glittering all around me, light and my own image reflected over and over.

The future me may have accepted the Project's destiny, but I can't bring myself to do the same. I do not want to live a life that's already laid out in front of me. If I go to the address on Eleventh Avenue, then I know I will have tried everything. I will not have accepted a preordained path where Wes is meant to die, where Tim will never have another chance, where I am meant to be in charge of the Montauk Project.

And now I know the ad wasn't planted by the Project, which means someone else is trying to contact me. I have no idea who it could be, but maybe they can help me save Wes.

——

I do not pass anyone as I move through the hallways, go down the elevator, and walk out into the lobby. The blond-haired girl looks up at me with her vacant expression, but she doesn't say a word, and I silently thank the older Lydia for giving me clearance. As soon as I'm out of the building, I start walking south, counting as the street numbers slowly descend.

It takes me over an hour to walk the sixty blocks to 167 Eleventh Avenue. Every once in a while I think I feel someone watching me, but I keep my face turned down. It helps that I'm wearing all black, that I'm no longer caked in dirt and blood.

The address brings me to the edge of the city where the Westside Highway runs parallel with the Hudson. The new wall is in between them, blocking the river and the view of New Jersey. In my time, the strip of land by the waterfront held buildings, harbors with boats docked in the Hudson, and sometimes a park or a bike path. Now it is all gone, the thick wall almost reaching the edge of the highway.

In Times Square I was in a cave of buildings, unable to see the water's edge. In the Center, we were high enough that the city below appeared spread out and open. But now, with the wall towering over me, the concrete already faded and rough, I feel like a rat in a maze, bumping against the sides as I try to find my way out.

I stare at the descending numbers on the buildings and realize that 167 would be across the street, between the highway and the wall. But there are no buildings now, only a thin length of sidewalk.

How can it not exist? Is this a dead end, or even more of a clue that someone was trying to reach me?

I cross the highway when the cars on the grid glide to a smooth stop and stare at where the address should be. All that's left is the remnant of a small park that was cut in half by the seawall. Now there is only a tiny patch of green with a rusted bench. An older black man is sitting on it reading a book.

When I get closer, he lifts his head. He looks right at me and I quickly turn, hoping he didn't have time to scan me. But I hear his book shut as he sets it aside, hear him get to his feet. I start to walk in the opposite direction, wondering if I should run, or if that will give me away too quickly. He clears his throat loudly. "Nikki says hi."

I stop moving. How does he know that name?

"So does LJ. He wanted to come, but we thought it would be best if it was just me."

The cars on the highway rush past. They are right next to us, but the sound cannot drown out my heartbeat, ringing in my ears. I slowly turn. He grins and I recognize him then, his wide smile, his broad, blunt features. "Tag?" I whisper.

The last time I saw him—only nine months ago—he was a skinny eighteen-year-old orphan who loved to paint.

But this person is a man, his chest is filled out, his hair mostly gray.

"How did you find me?"

"It wasn't easy. You're a hard girl to track down." He turns his head, taking in the busy streets. "It's not safe here. Will you come with me?"

I do not hesitate. "Yes."

CHAPTER 15

$\mathcal{I}$ *sit* up on the narrow bed. Above me is a single naked bulb hanging on a swinging cord. Tag brought me into this room before he took off the blindfold that he asked me to wear. "It's not because we don't trust you," he said as he tied it around my head in his car. "We just need to keep this place a secret from everyone. It's safer that way." In the blackness it was impossible to tell where we were going, but we couldn't have traveled for more than half an hour.

There is a knock on the door, and it opens before I can respond.

"Lydia. You're here."

A man enters the room, his honey-colored skin glowing even in the faint light. Like Tag, he looks to be in his sixties. But that doesn't keep me from recognizing him.

He smiles, and I remember that day in my father's hardware store when this man came looking for me, how my hand hovered over the plastic phone, ready to call for help.

He sits down in a chair next to the bed. The walls in here are gray concrete, and there are no windows. The room reminds me of the cells in the Montauk Facility, though it isn't as clean. There is dirt and dust collecting in the corners, and the metal bed frame is chipped and creaking underneath me.

We are silent for a minute, watching each other. From somewhere outside the room I hear a banging noise, then muted voices. Finally I say, "I know who you are."

"Jay? Or maybe you remember the Resistor?"

But I shake my head. "Jay. Little Jesse. LJ. The Resistor. It all makes sense now."

"You were always quick, Lydia." His smile widens.

"That day in the hardware store. Why didn't you tell me it was you?"

He shrugs his thin shoulders. Unlike Tag, LJ has not filled out as much, and I can see the fourteen-year-old boy in his round face, his large brown eyes. "You didn't know me yet. I thought you had already been back to the eighties, that you had already met me in the past. But you were confused and scared. I figured it was best to leave it."

"I can't believe it was always you." I shake my head. "You contacted us from the future, fed us information when we needed it. Warned us both that we were meant to become recruits. You started a *resistance*." I push forward on the bed, but my arm buckles under me as pain radiates up my wrist. I lift my hand and stare down at it. The skin near my wrist is red and puffy.

"We used an EMP device to short-circuit your tracker."

"What?"

"Didn't you feel it, in the car?"

I remember Tag taking my arm as he led me down the street. I thought I felt the sting of something, but I couldn't be sure, not with all the other cuts and scrapes all over my body.

I flex my wrist. Without my tracking chip, the Project will never know where I am again. The future Lydia told me to make my own choice, but there is something very final about deactivating my chip. I can't go back now, and I'm not sure what that decision means for me, Wes, or my grandfather.

"You should have asked me first," I say.

The smile fades from his face and he runs his hand over his head, his buzz cut not quite hiding his balding head. "Don't you want to be free from the Project, Lydia? It's time their hold was officially broken. Not just over you, but over everyone."

I clutch my wrist to my chest. My skin feels raw, heavy and irritating. "What does that mean?"

But he just slaps his hands against his knees and pushes up from his chair. "Let's talk after you've had a minute to process all this. There's a bathroom through there, if you want to splash cold water on your face."

I see the battered metal door across from the bed, the edge of a chipped sink visible through the opening.

"I'm glad you're here, Lydia. We have a lot to discuss, when you're ready."

I stare into the cracked mirror above the sink. It is lined with green and black mold, and the basin below is rusted brown. I turn on the faucet and hear the pipes whine. A thin trickle of water comes out and I cup it in my hands, splashing it onto my face.

I step back and stare down at my body. The wound on my leg has scabbed over, but I have new injuries—the scrape on my arm where a bullet grazed me, the raw bruise on my wrist. My eyes have purple smudges underneath, and my cheekbones are even sharper, too thin after almost a week with constant hiking and little food.

The resistance movement is real. It wasn't a fantasy, a lost hope. And now the sacrifices I made to leave the Center— not knowing what would happen to my grandfather, a future where I might have done good—feel less scary. A resistance could have resources. They could help me.

A knock on the bathroom door interrupts my thoughts. "Come in."

The door opens to reveal a middle-aged woman with dark curly hair and a round, plump face. "Oh, Lydia," she whispers. "You look exactly the same as I remember."

"Nikki." I breathe her name and then I am in her arms and she is laughing into my hair.

"We didn't think we'd see you again. LJ tried to find you years ago, but we couldn't pin down your location, and we figured the Project had you. But then we saw your face plastered all over the news, and we knew we had to find a way to bring you in. I'm so glad you heard the radio message. It was the only way we could think of to contact you."

She smells like soap and freshly baked bread. I slowly, tentatively lift my hands and press them to her back. This is the first time anyone has embraced me in months, and somehow it means even more coming from Nikki, the tough girl from the streets of New York who used to call me Princess. She tightens her hold and I feel the tears threatening to spill over. I could handle it—fearing for my grandfather, Tim's death, abandoning Wes in the dark field—if I didn't have comfort, if I could force myself to stay strong. But being held by her is making me come undone.

I pull away, staring up at the harsh bulb overhead until my eyes are dry and itchy.

"How are you feeling?"

"Like hell."

She laughs, the sound high and bright. "I can imagine. Come out of this bathroom. There's someone I want you to meet."

We enter the bedroom. A teenage girl with Nikki's

sharp features and Tag's dark skin is standing near the door. "This is my daughter, Angela," Nikki says.

"Hi," the girl whispers. She can't be more than thirteen, and her legs and arms look too long for her body.

"I'm Lydia."

"I know. Mom talks about you a lot."

"Stop it." Nikki moves to hook her arm over Angela's bony shoulder. "She'll think I've gotten all soft in my old age."

I study Nikki's face, trying to match this older woman with the teenager I knew a few months ago. She still has the same squeaky voice, the pointed nose, but she *is* softer, less rough and abrasive. "I can't believe you have a kid."

"I have two kids. Chris, our son, is with Tag right now." She pulls Angela in closer and I turn away from the easy affection between them. I haven't seen my mom in so long, and I am afraid that soon I will start to forget how her blond hair felt after she brushed it, or how her pancakes tasted like almonds and butter.

"I thought we'd never see you again, after you left the squat that day," Nikki says.

I sit down on the mattress, the iron frame squeaking under me as I stare up at them. "How did you end up here? What happened to the three of you?"

"LJ told Tag and me about the Montauk Project as soon as we realized you were missing. We didn't believe LJ at first, but he convinced us it was real. I knew we needed to leave, and luckily Tag wanted to come with us." She squeezes Angela's side and smiles down at her. The girl has clearly heard the story before and lifts her hand to pick at her cuticles as we talk. "We went to Mexico and stayed with some family for about five years, but then LJ wanted to come back. He had a lead online that he thought could help him learn more about the Project. He was tired of running and decided to fight instead. The three of us changed our names and hopped cities for a few years. LJ was always into computers, you remember?"

I nod.

"He created a few safe places online where people could share information. A lot of them were just conspiracy theorists, but a few former soldiers stepped forward with their stories. At first the Project didn't seem to notice, but then LJ realized he had a ghost tracing his message boards. That's when we went off-line. It took a few more years to create all this." She waves her free hand through the air at the room around us. "We were the first base of operations. But the resistance is spreading. There are two other organizations across the country doing the same thing now."

When I imagined the resistance, it was one man in a room with a computer. Maybe two. This is more than I could have hoped for.

"What exactly does the resistance do?" I ask.

She frowns, and I wonder if she has told me more than she was supposed to. "LJ should tell you the rest. We'll show you the control center. It's just outside."

She pushes open the bedroom door. The windowless space beyond has high ceilings and rusted pipes that run from corner to corner in crisscrossing lines. There are computers on tables crowded in the center of the room, though none of them are the modern, holographic kinds. Some are even old desktops with wide frames.

Tag is sitting in front of one, with a younger version of him leaning over his shoulder. The boy looks so much like eighteen-year-old Tag that I jerk back when I see him. Nikki smiles. "It's uncanny, right?"

There are maybe twenty other people here, some bent over desks, some sitting on battered couches that line the water-stained cement walls or clustered in groups, in quiet conversations.

"Are you underground here?" I ask.

Tag and Nikki exchange a look, but it is LJ who answers, stepping out from a connecting hallway. "Yes. But we can't tell you anything else."

"You don't trust me?"

"We don't trust the Project."

I don't like the way he is lumping me in with them, but before I can protest, he motions me forward. "There's something I want to show you."

I follow him into a dark hallway. The ceilings are lower, the walls narrow. It feels like a tunnel, and even the lights are dimmer, as if the hallway was designed to conserve energy for the main spaces.

"How did you find this place?"

I don't expect him to answer, but he says, "I built it not long after I started the resistance."

"I thought it was just chat rooms and secret messages."

He looks over his shoulder at me, raising his dark eyebrows. "It's a little more than that."

He stops and opens a door on the left. Inside an older woman is sitting in a rocking chair. In her arms is a small baby, its pink face scrunched up in sleep, a fist pressed to its tiny mouth. I glance around the brightly lit room. It is filled with cribs and cots, and dozens of children are sleeping or playing quietly in the corners.

"You have a nursery?" I ask.

The woman makes a shushing noise and LJ shuts the door again.

"We've been hacking into the Project's mainframe to get updated copies of The List."

"Those kids are supposed to become recruits," I realize. "You're getting them before the Project can."

He nods. "We've been rescuing prospective recruits for years, as early as we can. It's become the core of what the resistance does. Those people you saw out in the main room were all once targeted by the Project, too."

The resistance is saving these kids from the short, brutal life of a recruit, but he's still kidnapping them, stealing them away from whatever families they may have.

"Aren't you worried you're doing the same thing the Project is, taking them from the only lives they know?"

He starts walking down the hallway again. "What life did they have if we just let the Project take them? Most of them were abandoned, homeless, or about to be swallowed up by the system. We're rescuing them."

I think of Tim, who lived for years with his family before the Project came for him. Would he have been better off if someone like LJ had taken him as a child?

We have reached the end of the twisting corridor. "This is what I really wanted to show you, Lydia."

He pushes the door open, and I feel myself go white, the blood draining from my cheeks.

There, in the middle of the room, gleaming silver under fluorescent light, is a TM.

CHAPTER 16

$\mathcal{I}$ *stare* up at the large, circular structure. Modern TMs have clouded glass on top, with slick silver on the bottom, but this one is made of interlocking pieces of scrap metal, like an oversize steam pipe. Long wires connect it to a computer mainframe that sits on a broad desk.

I walk closer to the machine, my footsteps loud against the concrete floor.

"Early on we made contact with one of the Project's engineers, and brought him into the resistance. It took a few years, but he and I were able to use Tesla's alternating current theory to create this. We made sure to build it in an area with a lot of magnetic energy."

I move until I'm standing next to the TM. The top

reaches all the way to the high cement ceiling, disappearing into it like a tube. "Does it work?"

"Fairly well."

The room isn't large, and the TM dominates its space. Overhead a metal catwalk curves between two walls. LJ moves to sit down at the desk. "This is why we live so simply. All our resources go into this."

I run my hand down the metal side, my fingers catching on the exposed bolts. With a TM, I do not need the Project to help me rescue Tim and Wes. I can go back to the start of the mission myself and change our future. I can save all of us, without having to embrace the destiny that Walker laid out for me. Hope is like a vine growing inside of me, spreading through my stomach, my chest, my heart.

"You've sent people back already?" I work to keep the eagerness out of my voice. Nikki said they saw my picture on the news and knew they needed to bring me in, but there must be more to it. LJ would not be watching me so closely if he didn't want something.

"I was the first to travel," he says. "I went to nineteen eighty-nine."

He is silent while I piece it together. "That's how you sent us those messages. They weren't from the future. You had just timed it perfectly to be in nineteen eighty-nine when we were connecting the dots."

He picks up a pen from the desk, tapping it on the

wooden surface. It is a careless action, but I see the tension in his lined forehead, the rigid set of his shoulders. "I was also the one who gave your grandfather the disk with the list of recruits."

I turn until my back is to the TM. "Why didn't you just tell us the truth? Why the message boards and the floppy disk? You know how scared we were when we found our names on that list."

"I couldn't. Things had to happen exactly as I remembered them happening. Otherwise the butterfly effect could have ruined everything."

"The butterfly effect." I slump back against the metal, sliding down until I'm sitting on the ground. "I am so sick of those words."

It feels odd to be leaning so casually against a TM. In the Facility it is treated like a god, something to fear and worship, despite knowing it will ultimately destroy us.

"But the butterfly effect is true. I know, better than anyone." He sighs, and suddenly he seems years older, his chin dipping into his jowls, his eyelids heavy and red. "I tried to save Maria. It didn't work."

Maria. The pretty dark-haired girl we tried to rescue from a club after LJ saw her name on the list. "I'm sorry."

He looks away, concentrating on the desk in front of him. "I've been through time a lot now. You know how hard it is on your body. I don't know how the recruits can last for so many years."

I think of Wes's hand shaking against the white linens of the dinner table, Twenty-two's body facedown in the dirt. "I don't think many of them do."

"That's why we have to stop them for good, Lydia." He gets up from his chair and walks closer to me. I have to tilt my head back against the TM to look into his face. "And we need your help."

"What can I do?"

"Go back to the beginning. Stop the Montauk Project from ever existing in the first place."

I sit in the small bedroom, staring at a poster of a shirtless singer I don't recognize, one of those baby-faced teens who never seem to go out of style no matter the decade. Angela is sheltered down here—LJ says he keeps them off the grid as much as possible, no I-units, no government-run internet, only an old television—but she is still a teenage girl. Sitting on her narrow bed, staring at her dresser crammed with knickknacks, her books stacked on the floor, I am jealous of her space, of the tiny corner of the world that belongs only to her. It was something I took for granted when I had it, and miss it now that I don't.

"I brought you these." Tag is standing in the doorway holding up a pink cotton dress and a pair of scuffed leather oxfords. They will be perfect for 1943, the year the Project started, the year the TM was first built.

"Thanks," I whisper.

Tag steps forward, handing me the clothes. I take them from him, dropping the shoes onto the floor with a dull thud. I do not look up.

"LJ tells me you're not sure what to do."

"I know there are benefits to stopping the Project. But there are also negatives. So much about the world could change. More than we can even imagine."

He moves to sit next to me on the bed and I feel the soft mattress tilt under his weight. "But you would finally be free."

"And stuck in the forties. Alone. Mary and Lucas and the Bentleys would have no idea who I was, and Wes—"

I cannot bring myself to finish the thought. Tag is watching the thin line of my lips, the way my shoulders fall.

"What happened to Wes?" he asks softly.

I shake my head but don't answer, and I hear him sigh.

"Did LJ tell you why he wants you to go back?"

"He said they've been waiting for the chance to find the right person to attempt it."

"He also knows that you understand how much the Project can steal from a person." He leans forward, clasping his hands together at his knees. It is a mimic of my pose and I wonder if it's deliberate, if he thinks he can win me over through body language.

"We named our son Chris for LJ and Nikki's older brother. He was taken by the Project too."

"I remember."

"Did LJ tell you that he contacted him?"

"No." I turn to look at his profile. "How did he do it?"

"He hacked into the Montauk Project's mainframe, and somehow located the files on where a group of recruits had been sent. He eventually figured out some mission Chris was on and met him there. LJ said Chris was like a zombie, and barely recognized him. But he kept at it until Chris finally cracked. That was around two thousand twelve."

In the hardware store, that same year, LJ told me he was close to contacting a recruit. He must have meant Chris. "What happened?"

"As soon as LJ broke through to him, the Project figured out what was going on, and Chris just disappeared. He was supposed to meet LJ in New York, and he never showed. We couldn't find a trace of him after that."

"They killed him."

Tag shrugs. "Maybe. Probably. By that point LJ had told Nikki and me what was going on, and we were all living down here in hiding. Since then, he's been able to rescue a few more recruits and get them out . . ."

His voice hangs there, and I finish the thought. "But it's not enough to make up for what happened to Chris."

"No. It's not."

I stand up from the bed and pace to the opposite side of the room. There are water stains on the wall, dark lines that drip from the ceiling to the floor. "I know all this, Tag. I know what they do. I know how horrible they can be."

"Then why don't you want to stop them?"

"Because . . . because I left Wes on the side of the road with the FBI surrounding him. I swore that I would go back to the beginning of the mission and fix it. With access to a TM I could do that."

Tag stands too and when I pace back toward him he grabs my shoulders, holding me in place. "Lydia, this *is* the best way to save him. I knew Wes for a long time. When we were living on the streets together, before the Project snatched him away, we were happy. It was tough, yeah, but we had each other, we had a gang we ran with. Wes was smart and he was handsome and everyone knew he would get out of that life eventually. After I saw him again when you both came to the eighties, he was like a shell of what he used to be. Shaking all the time like his body was falling apart. Constantly staring over his shoulder. Cold. The Project did that to him. The only time I even saw a spark of the old Wes was when he was with you."

I try to pull away but he tightens his grip, locking me in place. It's not anything I didn't know, but hearing Tag's words feels like I'm living that car crash all over again, thrust up in the air with no way to anchor myself, the sharp metal ripping into my skin.

"Even if you can go back and save Wes, then what happens? You keep working as slaves for the Project until you both die, maybe on a mission, or maybe from the TM breaking you down? That's the life you want for yourself, for Wes?"

"No," I whisper. "No. I want us to be free."

"Then set him free, Lydia. Set him free and let him go."

After Tag leaves, I sit on the bed, holding the pink dress in my hands. Seeing the future me and meeting LJ again has all led to this moment—I finally have to decide how my future will be tied to the Montauk Project.

If I destroy the Project, Wes and I would never meet. My family and friends might know a different Lydia, but it wouldn't be me. Any good the Project has done will never have happened, and the time line will be a mystery, with no one left to stand guard or protect the world from future mistakes.

But the Project has stolen so many lives, including mine. They control and manipulate the time line, and no one even knows that it's happening. It's the kind of power that is too great, especially when it falls into the hands of someone like Colonel Walker.

If I end the Montauk Project, Wes and Tim and my grandfather could have a chance at a normal life. I wouldn't be in it, but is that the sacrifice I have to make?

I walked away from the destiny that future me presented. I can't go back now. If I don't stop the Project, then it will control me for the rest of my life, either as its leader, or as a fugitive, forever looking over my shoulder. I don't want to run away anymore, or put my head down and live the life of a recruit, moving blindly forward, only surviving by hiding my true self from everyone around me.

I have to stop the Project. It's the only choice left.

The door opens again. This time it is LJ, and he's carrying a heavy folder. "The plan," he says, waving it in front of me. "You can look through it on your own, though the gist of it is simple. We send you to the spring of nineteen forty-three, and you infiltrate the new Facility. The heads of the Project are looking for personnel in the early forties. It's a secret, of course. They plant fake advertisements in major newspapers and conduct an intensive screening process until they find candidates who match their criteria. They like people who don't have strong family ties, who will make analytical choices instead of emotional ones. It takes months for the Project to weed out people, but we know you'll be able to pass their tests. You can apply for an assistant position. It'll give you close access to the head scientist, Dr. Faust. Then you'll have to kill him before he discovers how to employ Tesla's research to create the first TM. You'll also have to destroy his notes and research, but that shouldn't be too hard; apparently he's always been suspicious, and only has the originals. There's a picture of him in there."

"I know who he is. I've met him before." Faust's face, his thin brown hair, flashes through my head. He becomes responsible for so much destruction, but can I really murder him in cold blood?

"The folder also has backup plans in case you end up in the wrong time."

"The wrong time? What does that mean?"

He lifts one shoulder. "I've never been able to get the same accuracy out of the TM that the Project does. It's better than it used to be. When I first went through, I was two years earlier than what I'd intended. But don't worry. We've thought of every scenario and offer solutions in here. Do you want to see?"

He holds the folder out.

I take it from his grasp. It is a thick file, and I open it to see a blueprint of the Facility on top. Underneath is a blurry photo of Faust, standing in the woods of Camp Hero. Below are pages and pages of notes. LJ must have gone through time over and over to pull together all this information.

"A lot of it will be old hat to you," he says. "But I hope some of it will be helpful."

"No, this is great. Thorough."

He lets out a slow breath. "So you want to help us?"

"Yes." I shut it again, weighing the thick folder in my hands. "The Project has to be stopped."

A few minutes later I walk into the TM chamber wearing the pink dress, the folder tucked under the cotton fabric, taped against my back to keep it in place. LJ is already seated at the desk, Tag and Nikki standing next to him.

Their son, Chris, is across the room, standing next to a large wheel that's attached to a generator. At LJ's signal he pulls at the round metal, his biceps tightening under the strain. A humming, grinding noise fills the room, echoing off the high ceilings and empty spaces.

LJ taps a few buttons on his keyboard while Chris spins and spins the wheel of the generator. The base of the TM starts to flicker. He is powering it slowly, and the large machine responds, thin light traveling up the sides and streaming out of the cracks in the sheets of metal. In a few seconds it is lit up from within, as if it is glowing, as if it is alive on its own.

"Where will it send me?" I ask LJ. Without another TM to catch my body as I hurtle through space and time, I will emerge from the wormhole as soon as I meet a solid surface.

"I've programmed you for the woods in Camp Hero. Montauk will use the natural magnetic forces there to pull your body to it. You should land harmlessly in the woods, right where Dr. Faust will eventually create his time machine."

The generator hums, and now the TM has added to the sound, a low, constant buzz that vibrates through my body, my bones. I have heard that noise so many times, and it's hard not to shudder as it calls out for me.

Nikki steps over to where I'm standing near the doorway. Her arms close around mine again. "Thank you for doing this."

I allow myself to press against her for just a minute, to feel the comfort of her arms. But I need to stay focused in order to get through this, and I step away quickly.

LJ straightens from behind the desk. "It's time."

I open my mouth to respond but I'm cut off by the shriek of a loud siren. It sounds like an old-fashioned fire truck, dipping down then louder again. I cover my ears with my hands, but cannot block out the noise.

"The alarm. Someone's breached the perimeter." Jay rushes back to the computer. His fingers move so quickly they blur as he jabs at the keys. "There's a break near the southwest corridor."

"The Project," Nikki whispers, her hands pressed to her face. "They've found us."

"I'm on it." Tag moves toward the door, pausing at the last minute to look at me over his shoulder. "Good luck, Lydia."

"Wait." I put my hand out to stop him. "I know you won't remember this, once the time line changes, but take care of Wes for me."

"I will." His wide mouth is set in a grim line. "I promise."

I do not watch him leave, just stride across the room to the TM the resistance created. I pry open the makeshift pieces of metal that have been tacked together to create a door. The light inside is impossibly bright, and I blink, my eyes tearing as I enter the machine. I turn to pull the heavy door shut. Nikki and Chris are already gone, and only LJ remains, tapping on the keyboard, his eyes darting toward the hallway and the shrieking alarm. On the monitor in front of him I see a pulsing red dot on a black screen map. It is moving rapidly to the right.

I hesitate before closing myself into the TM. When I do this, everything changes. I will never see my parents, or Wes, or my grandfather again. My memories will be all I have, and over time, they will fade until I will be left wondering if they ever happened at all.

But I will not let the Project steal any more lives, especially from those I love, and so I pull the door closed, the metal slowly grinding as it shuts. Light is all around me, throbbing, shifting, so hot that my skin burns against the fabric of my dress. I can only hear the faint sound of the alarm outside, the TM buzzing louder and louder, a constant drone that rattles through my body. I sink down to my knees, pressing my hands to my ears again. The light around me starts to change colors, first red, then blue, then green. I tilt my head back to see that the ceiling has disappeared. In its place is smoke and sparks, a churning mass.

As my body slowly melts away I hear a noise, an echo, a flickering sound.

"Lydia!" it screams. At least I think it does. Or maybe I just imagine it in that final moment before I am torn apart, before I am gone.

CHAPTER 17

I come to on the floor, feeling metal beneath me, not dirt. This can't be right. I'm supposed to be in the woods.

I crawl to my feet, touching those familiar smooth walls, the manual control panel built into the side. My fingers shake against the still warm metal. I'm in another TM.

The door slides open. A man in a white lab coat is standing there, his light hair slicked to one side, his pale eyes wide behind thick, black-rimmed glasses.

"You're not one of our s-subjects," he stammers.

I straighten fully, ignoring the way my back spasms, my arms tremble, the lingering effects of the TM tearing through my body. "What's the date?"

"W-what?"

"The date. What is it?"

"May fourth, nineteen forty-five."

My stomach dips as though I'm standing on the edge of a cliff looking down and knowing I have to jump. Two years late.

"You're n–not supposed to be here."

"No. I'm not."

He opens his mouth to scream for help and I launch myself out of the TM, kicking him directly in the jaw. His head snaps to the side and he starts to drop, but I grab his body before he can fall and lower him gently down. He's still breathing, his chest rising and falling with the steady movement, but his mouth is sagging, his eyes closed tight. I only have a few minutes at best before he wakes up.

I drag his body under one of the large desks that run along the side of the wall and set him on the dusty ground. He is wearing spotless wingtip shoes, and I pull them off, followed by his white cotton socks. I tie them together to create a gag. There are wires under the desk connecting to the consuls above and I rip out two long pieces and use them to bind his hands, then feet together. As soon as someone finds him, they will know there was a breach in security, but there are fewer personnel in the Facility in 1945. I just have to pray no one was watching us from the two-way mirror on the other side of the room.

I wait for one minute, then two. No one comes. I glance at the now-silent TM. It is connected to a large computer system that sits on the desk above me. There are no digital screens against the back wall, no slick tiled floors. It is a simple room, a deceptively simple machine.

Maybe I should try and travel through the TM again, hoping I can reach 1943. But this machine is so new that the metal base still gleams, and the glass top that stretches to the ceiling is barely clouded. The TM wasn't always accurate before 1950—Faust and his team were still perfecting the machine, and the time travel serum I have in my body hadn't been invented yet.

I think of LJ's file, with plans for every scenario, pressed tight against my back. The most important thing is that I stop the Project. It's still possible in 1945, just more difficult.

It's too dangerous to stay in the Facility while I decide how to adjust the plan. And now that I'm in 1945 there are a few people I need to see again.

I slowly inch out from under the desk, pressing my body to the side of the wall as I move toward the exit. Thank God there are no surveillance cameras in the forties.

I open the door a crack. The hallway is empty, so I slide into it and run, half hunched over, my eyes, my ears, everything on alert. The walls and floors are as white as I remember—freshly painted, lit with the fluorescent bulbs that Tesla invented, too.

I turn a corner and hear voices coming from up ahead. There's nowhere to hide here, but the door to my right is unlocked. In 1989, it leads to a storage area, so I quickly slip inside.

The small, shadowy room overflows with towels and cleaning products. The smell of bleach is strong, and I wrinkle my nose as I turn back to face the door. My foot hits a discarded bucket and it slides across the floor. I lunge for it. I can't get caught down here. It's bad enough that blond scientist saw my face, and I can only pray that the kick to his head will disorient him enough to forget.

My palms are slick with sweat, but I wipe them on the fabric of my dress, forcing myself to relax. I am not the same girl I was when I first traveled through the TM. I know this Facility inside and out. I have studied it, walked these hallways as a recruit, and trained in the gyms on the lower levels. I know mixed martial arts and how to kill someone thirty ways without a weapon. I refuse to be scared of what's out in those hallways.

The footsteps are coming closer. I lean forward and press my ear to the door.

"I'll bring the samples to your office," a male voice says.

"What are the effects of the new formula?" I recognize the faint Eastern European accent. Dr. Faust.

"Inconclusive, but I think it will ultimately be rejected. It's not helping them travel any easier."

Formula. Traveling. I wonder if they're talking about the polypenamaether. Is Dr. Faust in the process of inventing the serum?

I move closer to the door. I can only see a sliver of the hallway, but I make out Faust, with his slightly heavy frame, his broad shoulders and thinning brown hair, newly laced with white strands, even though I last saw him only a year ago.

"We're running out of resources. We couldn't get that much of a sample after the boy was shot. There are no second chances," he snaps at his companion. "All you have to do is isolate the foreign agent in the blood. It's not that hard."

"Yes, Doctor."

After the boy was shot. Could he be talking about Wes?

A year ago, I watched Wes's blood drip to the floor of the TM chamber, so dark against the white tiles. From the beginning, Dr. Faust had been fascinated by Wes and the quick, efficient way he acted. He saw Wes as an example of what the Recruitment Initiative could become.

Was that day the birth of the time travel serum? Was it derived from the mixture already embedded in Wes's blood?

It would mean that no one ever really invented polypenamaether, but that it was simply brought to the past inadvertently, creating a continuous cycle of discovery. I tighten my grip on the doorknob, the cold metal biting into my skin. If it is true, then I'm glad Wes will never know. He wouldn't want to be responsible for aiding the Project in any way, let alone creating the basis for what makes traveling through the TM possible.

Then the two men are gone, and I ease the door open again, stepping out into the hallway. It does not take me long to reach the stairs near the exit, and I sprint up them. They are dark and dingy, with no lights embedded in the floors or ceiling.

I rip open the door at the top. There's a guard standing in front of the wide concrete doors that lead out into the woods of Camp Hero. He has his back to me, his hands wrapped around a rifle, and he is just starting to turn around.

I spring onto his back, locking my legs around his waist. He makes a grunting noise, and I grip his neck between my arms. His hair is an oily brown, pressed tight against my face. It smells unwashed, like musk and soot, and I struggle to take a breath. He drops his gun, but it makes no sound on the soft dirt floor. There are pieces of broken furniture scattered around the room, rotting wood and discarded nails and screws. The back wall is lined with metal doors. The one I came through is still ajar, and the thin light from the bottom of the stairs spills across the shadowed floor.

The man claws at my arms, his blunt fingernails digging into my skin. I wince as he draws blood, but I don't let go. He is wearing the black uniform that all guards in the Facility wear, though this one is in the boxy, high-waisted style of World War II uniforms. I tighten my hold. I'm not trying to kill him—it only takes five seconds to knock someone out. I soon feel the man's body go limp. As he falls, I drop my feet to the ground and then take his weight, staggering under his heavy build. I lay him down in the dirt, and then look up at the concrete doors. They are sealed shut, with only a tiny line down the middle that lets in a strip of sunlight.

I turn to the passed-out soldier and rifle through his pockets until I find what I am looking for. It is a rectangular piece of metal with random shapes cut out along the thin surface.

I feel along the right side of the wall until I find a tiny slit and quickly slide in the key. The doors part with a scrape, stone rubbing against stone, the whine of a rusted gear. I move to the center. As soon as there is a large enough opening, I step out and into Camp Hero.

The green army truck makes a rumbling noise as it drives down the packed-dirt road. I crouch in the back, half-hidden under an empty burlap sack.

I found the truck parked near the bunkers and mess hall, the white buildings disguised to look like civilian homes from the air. Now we are headed toward the heavily guarded entrance of the camp, not far from the Montauk Lighthouse.

"Just you today, Johnson?" one of the soldiers at the gate

calls out as soon as we approach.

"Yup," the driver answers.

The back of the truck is open, with rough canvas stretched over the rounded top. I pull the sack closer to my body. It smells like old grain, and I can only see an inch in front of me: the scarred metal of the truck bed, a corner of dusty road, a man's khaki pant leg as he walks past.

I think back to what the scientist said. It's the spring of 1945. Thanks to my endless history studies as a recruit, I know that Hitler killed himself five days ago, and American and Soviet troops have successfully taken Berlin. Japan is still fighting, but in only a few months America will drop the atom bombs that will finally end the war.

When I traveled to 1944, World War II seemed like it would never end. Mary's friends were signing up to fight; her brother, Dean, and her crush, Lucas, had already fought overseas. Food was rationed, and everyone was on edge, waiting for bad news, fearing for loved ones. But a year has passed now, and the war is almost over. I feel the change even at this gate. Before, a guard would have inspected the back thoroughly, but now he just waves the driver through. "Get us some more Spam, will ya? Mess is almost out."

"Sure thing."

The truck starts moving again, and the wind picks up, rippling the canvas overhead. I know we're on the long highway that stretches from Camp Hero to the downtown area of Montauk and I pull the sack away from my face to watch the low, scrubby trees pass by, light green with new leaves. The ocean is to my right, the waves breaking against the beach in rolls of white foam. Now and then we pass a small roadside stand selling fish or vegetables with hand-painted signs. As we get closer to town I see a few fishing shacks tucked into the dunes. Made from blue and gray weathered wood, they are sea tossed and crusted with salt, as if they sprang up from the ocean rather than made by men on land.

We reach the downtown, and it is exactly as I remember: a few low buildings, the general store with a sagging porch, one tall, brick, Tudor-style town hall.

The truck does not stop in the center of town; the driver must be headed to East Hampton, where the army picks up most of their supplies. I pull the sack off and crawl to the back end, waiting for the truck to start climbing the short hill that's not far from the school. As soon as we reach it the truck slows, and I feel the driver shift down and then down again, the engine whining, the wheels churning under us. Bracing one hand against the bumper, I throw my body toward the side of the road. I roll and roll, stopping when I'm lying on my back, gasping for air. The cut on my leg burns, and I sit up, pulling stray pieces of grass from my shoulders. There are no other cars on the small highway, and the truck keeps going, quickly disappearing from sight.

I circle the pond that sits near the middle of town. It is only steps from the road, and the water reflects the few houses and trees that run alongside it. The day is bright and cool, the spring air sharp.

Soon I leave the main road and turn onto a narrower, more private street. The trees are thicker here, and I walk in the shade, watching the shadows of the leaves make interlocking patterns in the dirt. It's not long before I see the house: two stories, white, a bright-red front door.

I climb up the steps and knock. My breath is short, and I bite my lip. It has been a year since I was last here. They might not even remember me.

"I'll get it, Daddy!" I hear shouted from inside. There is a clomping sound as feet quickly hit wooden steps, and then the door is flung wide-open.

Mary Bentley, my great-great-aunt, only eighteen years old in 1945, freezes, one hand at her chest, the other still wrapped around the doorknob. "Lydia?" she whispers.

"Mary." My voice breaks on the word. I take in her dark-red hair, a mirror of my own, her Bentley-green eyes, high cheekbones, and full mouth.

"Lydia!" This time she squeals it and flings herself at me. Her arms are tight around my neck, our cheeks pressed together. I hug her back. Beyond Mary's head I see her mother, Harriet Bentley, emerging from the kitchen holding a dish towel. Dr. Bentley must be in his study; I smell his pipe, sandalwood and spice.

For the first time in a year, I feel like I have finally come home.

CHAPTER 18

Mary crosses her legs, and the blue shirtwaist dress she's wearing falls across her knees. She is sitting on the cream-and-yellow stuffed couch in the den, and as she leans toward me the tea in her cup sloshes against the rim, threatening to spill over and onto her lap. "We didn't think we'd see you again. I had completely given up on you, but then—"

She's cut off by Mrs. Bentley, who comes into the room holding a tray of small cookies. "Real sugar and butter." She smiles at me. The lines around her eyes are deeper than I remember, and her dark-red hair has a touch of gray at the temples. "Now that the fighting in Europe has ended, we're getting some rations back."

"Thanks." I take one from the tray, realizing that I haven't eaten—or slept—since I was hiding in the dark in the back of the banana truck. I swallow the butter cookie whole and reach for another. The chair I'm sitting in is old and soft and I sink back against it, trying not to close my eyes.

"Oh, you're exhausted!" Mrs. Bentley sits in the chair adjacent to mine and looks at me with concern. "Your trip must have been grueling, Lydia. Why don't you go upstairs and take a nap?"

Mary waves her hand dismissively. A drop of tea flings out of her cup and lands on the coffee table. "She can't sleep here; it doesn't make any sense."

"Why not?" I sit up again. "Should I find somewhere else to stay? I don't want to burden you."

"Nonsense. Of course it's not that." Mrs. Bentley nudges the cookie tray toward me and I take another one. "But you'll be eager to get settled on your own, I'm sure. Where is your man, anyway? Why isn't he with you?"

I feel the heat rise in my face, my cheeks staining with color. "Well, that's—"

"Lydia!" Dr. Jacob Bentley is standing in the doorway. I get up from my seat as he approaches me with both hands held out. "It's a pleasure to see you again."

His fingers are warm and dry in mine and he squeezes once before letting go.

"Dr. Bentley." I smile and sit back down in my chair. "It's been so long."

He moves next to Mary on the couch, adjusting his

wire-rimmed glasses as he takes a seat. Like Mrs. Bentley, his dark hair has a bit more gray in it, stretching along the side of his head and down into his short beard. "You've returned, and the news is reporting that Hitler is dead. It's a good day."

"We're not sure it's true yet, though," Mrs. Bentley says. "There are rumors he might be faking it, since he knows our troops are closing in on him."

"Don't worry, it's true. Hitler's dead." The words are out of my mouth before I have time to process them.

Mary moves forward in her chair. "How do you know that?"

"I mean, I'm sure it's true. . . . I want to believe it's true."

Dr. Bentley nods. "You were in Europe, weren't you, Lydia? We heard you followed your fella overseas for a while. Do you have any adventures to tell us about?"

"Um, not quite," I hedge. "I'm more interested in your family. How have you all been?"

No one speaks. Even Mary is silent, her knuckles white against the delicate china of her teacup.

I press my lips together, realizing my mistake.

"I'm sorry," I say quietly. "I shouldn't have . . ."

"Oh, don't be sorry." Mary rests her cup back on the tray, then reaches over to take my hand. "It's just that Dean went missing last year, around the same time. We're all not . . . well, it's been a real hard time."

"I'm so sorry," I repeat. "Dean was . . . kind to me." I

glance down, remembering the last time I saw him at that hotel in 1989. He didn't recognize me then, and he wouldn't recognize his family now. The Project stole everything from him. But of course I can't tell the Bentleys that.

"He was always a good boy." Dr. Bentley clears his throat and reaches for a cookie. "It would be easier if we knew what happened to him. It's the wondering that makes it hard."

"It would be hard either way," Mrs. Bentley whispers.

Mary squeezes my hand and then lets go, reaching up to wipe at the corners of her eyes. "I'm being a real pill these days, Lydia. I just can't seem to stop crying." She forces herself to smile, her teeth white against her signature red lipstick. "I'll just go take a powder. When I get back we'll stop talking about all this unpleasantness."

Mrs. Bentley watches Mary closely as she leaves the room. Dr. Bentley sits back with a sigh. "Mary isn't taking it well."

"She and Dean didn't always get along," Mrs. Bentley adds, "but she secretly idolized him. She can't seem to move past it."

I think back to something my grandfather said, about how his aunt Mary was never the same after she lost her brother. It's why she eventually left town with her husband and almost never returned to Montauk. "Is Lucas helping at all?" I wonder.

The two exchange a glance. "Perhaps Mary should tell

you more about that." Dr. Bentley dusts the crumbs off his hands and stands up. "I need to get out to the hospital for a few hours. But I'm glad you're back, Lydia. Mary sure missed you. Losing both you and Dean at the same time . . ." He shakes his head. "Anyway, maybe you'll be able to reach her. We certainly haven't been able to."

"I'll try," I promise, though I know I don't have much time.

I'm glad to see the Bentleys, but I can't lose sight of what I need to do. I will no longer be able to infiltrate the Facility by trying to apply for an assistant position—the TM is already up and running, and I can't spare the few months it would take to get a job there. That means I'll need to do a hit-and-run mission, stealing into the Facility at night and destroying the TM and Tesla's notes without getting caught.

But everything is different now. If I don't have enough time to help Mary before the mission, I can do it afterward. I'll have the Bentleys in my life again.

Before, I thought I would be stuck in the past forever, with no one who remembered me. But now if I succeed in killing Faust and ending the Project, I will not be trapped here without a family. I will not be alone.

Mary appears in the doorway again as Dr. Bentley moves to leave the room. He touches her shoulder as he passes and she smiles up at him, though we can all see the dried tear marks on her cheeks.

"Lydia, get up!" She waves her hand at me. "There's someone you just *have* to see. You are going to flip your wig, I swear it. I'd tell you who it is, but I've decided that it's going to be a surprise, and there's nothing you can say to change my mind."

"Thank you for the tea," I say to Mrs. Bentley as I stand.

"We're so glad you returned." Her voice is soft and serious. "Our house is your house, you know that, Lydia."

"Come on!" Mary bounces over to me and grabs my arm. "I can't wait to see the look on your face."

I smile one last time at Mrs. Bentley before Mary pulls me from the room.

I follow behind Mary as we walk along the paved road that leads to the north part of town, where the navy set up their own base near Fort Pond Bay.

"Jinx is still working in the factory, and Mick's coming home in a month or two. Suze is over the moon. He wrote her every week, just like he promised; isn't that swell? Sometimes the letters would come in a big batch, twenty at a time, and Suze and I would read them for days. Billy wrote to me too, sometimes. But then . . . the letters stopped." She turns her face toward the rough pavement.

I picture the young man dancing with Mary on the sand, laughing as they spun in circles. "What happened?"

"He died overseas." She lifts her head and her eyes are wet again. "German sniper, we heard. It's just awful. His sister was the year below me in school and she hasn't spoken a word since they found out. Ma and I baked their family a cake—we used real sugar, even though supplies were low, but there was no other choice, obviously—and brought it by a few months ago, and their whole house was stuffed with food from neighbors. Isn't that nice? We could barely fit it in on the counter." Her voice drops. "Though half the women sitting in the parlor clucking like old hens were those fuddy-duddies from church who always whisper about Mr. McDonald, Billy's dad, being a philanderer. He *is* one, everyone knows it, but still."

She spins around and starts walking backward in her scuffed saddle shoes. It is chillier the closer we get to the ocean, and I rub my hands together, wishing my dress had longer sleeves.

A grayish-blue navy jeep passes and Mary waves. The soldiers honk their tinny-sounding horn at us, but don't stop.

"I've been talking your ear off, haven't I?" Mary asks once it has disappeared farther down the road. "It's just that Suze is so busy setting up house for Mick, and I've been so lonely lately."

"What's going on with Lucas?" I ask. "When I left it seemed like something might happen between you two."

She smiles quickly. "Lucas is keen on me. Who would have guessed it? He's been coming around on Sundays for dinner, and he takes me to the movies or dancing on

Fridays. You know I've been stuck on him for years, ever since De—" She takes a quick breath. "Lucas is getting discharged soon, and I know he's gonna ask me to marry him. He wants us to go live on his farm in Georgia with his sisters."

I look sideways at her. "Aren't you excited? You don't sound it."

Mary shrugs. "Georgia? It seems so far away. And how can I leave Montauk? Especially now."

I speed up a little until we're side by side. "You don't want to leave because of Dean."

She doesn't answer. I hesitate, glancing over at her profile. Her red hair is in short tight curls, her skin glowing pink in the afternoon sun. "Mary, I don't think Dean's coming back. Be happy with Lucas. If you want to go with him to Georgia, then you should."

She tilts her head at me, her mouth twisted to the side. "It's a nice thought, Lydia."

I start to speak but she cuts me off, her voice bright again. "Can you picture me as a farmer's wife? The thought of waking up at five just to milk cows." She gives an exaggerated shiver, her shoulders wiggling up and down. "I'd have to get rid of all my dresses. I'd probably never even do my hair again. I'd be too busy chasing after chickens."

I try not to laugh. "You're a nurse, aren't you? I think you can handle a few cows."

"Easy for you to say, when you're not the one shoveling

manure for a lifetime." She bumps into me on purpose, locks our hands together and swings our joined arms back and forth as though we're little kids.

This time I don't bother trying to hide my laughter as I pull away.

She laughs too, though the sound quickly dies away when she glances over at me. "I'm so glad you're back, Lydia. If only you had been here a year ago. It would have made things easier. But you just disappeared. I never even heard from you."

There is enough accusation in her voice for me to stop walking. I turn to face her. "I'm sorry I left so suddenly. I didn't mean to abandon you. I know I don't have a great explanation, but the truth is that I couldn't help it."

She folds my left hand in both of hers. "I know. You had a man to follow. I understand, I do. I just wish you'd been here."

"I missed you," I say. "This year . . . it hasn't been easy for me either."

"And here I've been blabbing away, not asking about you at all." She squeezes my hand. I reach out and touch her shoulder, my fingers brushing against the soft wool of her sweater.

She turns to look up the road. "If we weren't in a hurry, we'd sit right here in the dirt and I'd make you tell me everything. You'd have to spew your guts out. But you're back now, and we'll have plenty of time later. We'll talk for hours and hours and hours, don't worry."

I smile and follow her as she starts walking again. I'd bet anything we're going to Susie's house, a small cottage near the ocean, or maybe we're visiting Jinx, just home from her day at the factory.

We finally reach the top of the hill, and I see the wide bay spread out in front of us, deep blue and shining where the sun hits it. To the left is the naval base: small seaplanes are floating in the water, while men in blue-and-white uniforms stand in groups along the shore. Some are talking and smoking cigarettes, while others kick at the waves.

"It's nice to see, isn't it?" Mary asks. "Just a few months ago they were rushing around, training the new soldiers, or blasting torpedoes out into the water. The booms would shake the whole town! But now they're just goofing around. It makes me think the war truly is over, or close to it."

"It is. It'll be over by the end of the summer," I say.

"What are you, a fortune-teller?" She smiles. "From your mouth to God's ears, Lydia."

She steers me in the opposite direction from the navy camp, where several one-story houses sit next to larger wooden buildings advertising for bait and tackle and fresh fish. A group of older men are standing around a beat-up truck with high, rounded hubcaps. Mary waves as they watch us approach. "Hiya! Heard Mick's coming back. Suze is real excited."

A grizzled man leaning against the rusted-out bumper

nods. "Yup. Back on the sixteenth of June. 'Bout time, too, need him on the lines."

"Mr. Moriglioni, there are more important things than fish, you know!"

"None come to mind."

Mary laughs, and the men join her.

"Old man Moriglioni is a real gas." She clutches my arm, leading me down a dirt road that is quickly narrowing. It looks more like a bike path now, with long grass shooting up out of the middle. There aren't many houses around us, and the beach to the left is becoming rockier and steeper. Up ahead I see where the cliffs start forming, growing taller and taller until they eventually reach the lighthouse at the point.

"He's as crusty as stale bread, but he knows all kinds of dirty jokes that he's always telling Mick . . . who then tells us of course. It's hard to even keep a straight face around him. Oh, we're here!"

She pulls on my arm and we leave the road to follow a grassy, beaten-down path. It winds toward the beach, and stops at the door of a one-story shack made of battered blue and gray boards. The roof is slanted to the side with a bent black chimney sticking out of the top. There's a window in the front next to a wooden door, but I cannot see into the shadowy interior.

"Is this where Suze lives?" I ask.

Mary doesn't answer, just yanks me forward. I trip a

little as I try to keep up with her, and the simple leather shoes that Tag gave me slide in the high sea grass that surrounds the house. "Hang on a second," I say.

And then the front door opens, and I feel the world go still. Mary drops my arm and beams at me. Silhouetted in the doorway, the dark interior of the house at his back and the sunlight shining full on his face, is Wes.

CHAPTER 19

"*It's* you." I lift shaking hands to my face, press them against my mouth.

"Lydia." The hammer he's holding falls to the ground, bouncing off the wooden door frame. And then he is there, in front of me, and I am in his arms, pressed to his chest, his hands in my hair, his mouth to my forehead.

I rise onto my toes to get closer to him, burying my face in the crook of his neck. He smells like pine needles, like salt water. "You're here. How are you here?"

"I followed you," he whispers against my skin, and I start to cry, not just for him but for Tim, for my parents, for all the people I will never see again. I was resigned to leaving everyone behind in order to defeat the Project, but just seeing Wes's face makes me realize the magnitude of what I was giving up.

"I never thought I'd see you again." The tears are choking my throat. Wes runs his hand down my hair.

"It's okay. I'm here."

I twist my hands in the rough material of his shirt. He lifts his head to look at Mary, but I don't let go of him or turn around. I can't.

"I'll leave you alone now," Mary says. I hear the smile in her voice. "But don't get all wrapped up in your love nest, you two. You have to come to our house for dinner later. Daddy got some fireworks from the general store, and Lucas will be there, too. If you don't come I'll hunt you down, I swear it."

"We'll be there," Wes tells her.

"Six o'clock sharp." Her footsteps barely make a sound on the grass.

As soon as she's gone, Wes lifts me up. I move my arms to curl around his neck, my body against his, my feet swinging a foot from the ground.

He carries me into the house, setting me down on the floor in the middle of the one open room. I slide my hands from his neck to his chest. He leans back, fitting my face in the palms of his hands as he tilts my head up. For a minute we just look at each other. It is darker in here, the windows small and narrow, but I see that his skin is tan, his cheeks lined with dark stubble. His black hair has been recently cut, though it still falls down over his forehead. He is no longer so thin, and I can feel the muscles curving along his shoulders and back. "You look different," I whisper.

His black eyes move over my face, taking in the sharp bones that press against my pale skin. "It was only days ago, wasn't it? That you were in the woods?"

I nod, feeling his thumbs rub my cheeks. They are rougher than I remember, newly calloused and dry.

"God, Lydia."

He leans forward, and I know he means to kiss me. I start to close my eyes, remembering what it feels like to have his lips on mine, but then I stop. The last time we were together, he told me why he betrayed me to the Project. I've been so focused on my destiny and the decision to come back here that I haven't had time to process what that confession meant.

Wes feels me tense and pulls back. "What is it? Are you okay?"

"Yes. I'm—" Suddenly it feels like I have eight limbs, and they are all tangled around his. I carefully move out of his arms.

"Right." He looks thoughtful as he watches me take a step back, toward a wooden table that sits against the wall. "I was hoping . . ."

When I don't speak, he spins around, walking toward the kitchen that's on the other side of the house. "When was the last time you ate?"

I stare at his back. I know he wants everything to be easy between us, but I'm not sure what I want. "The Bentleys gave me some cookies," I say quietly.

He looks at me over his shoulder, his lips curved into a smile. "Let me feed you."

I sink down into one of the wooden chairs at the table as he moves around the tiny kitchen. It's just a long counter that's built into the wall with a small gas camping stove. There's no running water, I realize. No electricity, no plumbing.

I glance around the rest of the space. The walls, ceiling, and floor are all made of the same untreated, gray wood. There's a bed in the corner with a woolen blanket thrown over it, and the only other pieces of furniture are the small table and two chairs. "Is this your house?"

He nods and rummages around the counter until he finds a butter knife. There's a parcel in brown paper tucked up under his arm.

"How do you have a house? How long have you been here?"

"Six months." He walks back over to the table and drops the items he's carrying.

"Six months," I repeat, my voice flat. "You've been waiting here for six months."

"Yes."

"For me?"

"Yes."

Wes opens the brown paper and pulls out a loaf of dark bread. "Harriet made the bread and the jam. She keeps sending food over, worried my wife isn't here to take care of me."

I think of that moment in Mary's bedroom, when I told her I was eloping with Wes. "Your wife."

He sits down in the chair next to me, avoiding my eyes. "I told them we got married and you followed me overseas for a few months, and then went to Boston to study journalism."

"And now you have a house."

"It's not much, but it works."

I lean forward, resting my elbows on the table. The wood scratches at my skin. "What happened in the woods, Wes? How did you get here?"

He cuts off a chunk of bread and spreads pink jam on it, then holds it out to me. He doesn't answer until I bite into it. "I watched you get into that truck and the FBI swarmed. They thought I would be an easy capture, and they only had a couple of men on me. They didn't even use handcuffs, just those plastic ties. I still had the knife that . . ." He trails off.

"That Twenty-two used on me," I say slowly.

He nods without looking at me, and I know we're both thinking of being by the stream and him taking her side.

"I kept picturing your face, Lydia."

His words pull me back and our eyes meet. "I could still

see you lit up by the gunfire, so scared and pale. I don't know where the strength came from, but one minute I was standing there in handcuffs, waiting for an ambulance, and the next all the soldiers were on the ground bleeding."

It was me, not Twenty-two, who made him feel like that. Even though he lied about her, I know he is telling me the truth now.

"I stole a car, and used the grid to get to New York," he says. "I made it to the park just in time to see you leave with Tag. I followed you, saw the car disappear, and realized they had some kind of hideout. It took me a few hours to break into it, but I did."

"You were the one who shouted my name." The bread is dry in my mouth, and I force myself to swallow. Wes watches me carefully.

"It was a shock, seeing Tag and LJ again. They told me where they sent you, though they wouldn't say why. I demanded access to the TM. LJ didn't want to let me use it, but Tag made him, in the end. They said they'd send me to the exact time they sent you. But the TM must have screwed up. I was early and you weren't here yet."

I drop the bread back onto the table. "What do you mean you were early? I was late."

Wes narrows his eyes. "What date did they send you to?"

"May fourth, nineteen forty-three. I'm two years late."

His jaw becomes more pronounced as he clenches his

teeth together. "They told me they sent you to May fourth, nineteen forty-six."

"Why would they lie?"

He shrugs. It's not a gesture I've seen Wes make very often.

"Maybe he didn't want you to interfere with our plan," I say.

"What plan?"

I hesitate, pushing crumbs off the table with one finger. Wes reaches over and touches my hand. "I know there's a lot of mistrust between us," he says. "And I know that's my fault. But you *can* trust me. Believe that."

"I want to."

"Just try." He lets go of me and sits back in his chair. "I was able to fight back like that against the FBI because I love you. I followed you here because I love you. You're the only reason I'm still alive."

"Wes . . ."

"Trust me, Lydia."

I take a deep breath, and then I tell him what happened in New York. Meeting the future me, Colonel Walker, and the choice I made.

"She told me I was supposed to become Director Bentley. I would run the Project one day, change it. That was my destiny all along." The words are hard to say, and I stop, looking down at the table. I can't bear to tell him the rest— like what his fate would have been in the other time line.

"Lydia." He shakes his head. "I just . . . how is this possible?"

"I don't know. General Walker kept talking about my destiny, but I never dreamed it was something like that. I had no warning when she walked into the room."

"I didn't know about this." He leans forward, his hands clasped between us on the table. "I swear I didn't. I would have told you."

"I believe you."

And I do believe him. At that realization I take a slow, deep breath. Maybe I am starting to trust Wes again.

"I knew there was something, though." He pushes away from the table and walks across the room to the kitchen, then back again. He can cross the short distance in three strides, but the movement seems to comfort him. "General Walker told Twenty-two and me to keep you alive at all costs, and I knew it had to be about more than just the Sardosky mission. But I didn't know it was that big."

"It was strange, seeing an older version of myself. She was so different in the meeting with Colonel Walker, and then when we were alone . . ." I wrap my arms around my middle, remembering her eyes, so much like my own, but wounded in a way that was permanent, that stretched into every part of her.

"She was probably just trying to protect herself," Wes says. "I understand that better than most."

I think back to when I first met Wes: his blank, empty

expression, that frustrating recruit mask he rarely took off. He was always protecting himself, and I lived for those moments when he let his guard down and let me in. It was why his betrayal hit me so hard—I thought I was different, that I was the one person he would never pretend with. But was it unfair of me to have those expectations for someone conditioned not to feeling anything? Future me seemed blank too, but she showed me that we were still the same person on the inside. Did I ever really trust Wes before, if at the first sign of betrayal, I believed the worst in him?

"How did you end up with the resistance?" Wes asks.

I focus on him again. "The message. It was from LJ." I tell him the rest, about meeting Tag and Nikki again, and my ultimate decision.

"You're going to stop the Project?" Wes sits down again, his body falling into the chair heavily. It looks handmade and creaks under his weight. "Are you sure that's what you want?"

"Yes. I won't let them destroy anyone else."

"But you're already here, Lydia. We could run away." He leans forward. "They don't have the same resources in the nineteen forties. We can get away more easily."

"We can't run, Wes. Not anymore. I don't want to spend the rest of my life wondering when they'll find me. What they'll do to my family. This is the only way to give everyone a chance at a new life, one that's not tainted by the Project." I stand up, suddenly feeling that same urge to move, not to be confined to one chair, to one space.

Wes stands to face me, and I see the doubt in the downward curve of his eyebrows. "But you came late, Lydia. The Project has been going on for two years now. They already have a TM. It won't be as easy to stop them now."

I move across the room to the bed, then back to Wes. "The only one who knows how to create the TM is Faust, and he's not the type to share his secrets. I'll destroy the notes and the TM. He won't be able to rebuild."

"Lydia." He touches my arm as I pass, stopping my restless movement. "That only works if you get rid of Faust, too."

I don't meet his eyes, and he squeezes me once, gently. "Are you going to kill him? Are you prepared for that?"

"Yes." I face him fully. "Kill one person to save thousands, right? That's what the Project taught me."

"It's not as simple as that and you know it."

"I killed Sardosky, didn't I?" My voice comes out softer than I intended, and Wes sighs.

"That wasn't your fault. You didn't have a choice."

I shake off his arm. "Maybe I won't have to kill him," I say. "What if I treat him the same way he treated Dean? Send him far, far back in time through the TM. He'll end up in the prehistoric age."

"But the TM is unpredictable now. He could land somewhere in the future, like Dean did. And then he could start the Montauk Project over again."

"Without Tesla's notes?"

He runs his fingers through his hair, the short black strands tumbling around his head. "You have a plan, right?"

I point over my shoulder, feeling my cheeks get warm. "Yes. But I need your help."

Wes stands slowly and moves until he's behind me. He places his hand on my back, right where the folder is taped to my skin. "I was wondering what this was."

"I can't get it off by myself."

He doesn't say anything, but runs his hand along my back, feeling where the edges of the file start and end. His touch is too soft, too deliberate, and I swallow hard.

"I, uh. I can't get to it when you have the dress on," he says softly.

"Right. Okay." I reach up and start to unbutton. I get halfway to my chest when my fingers start shaking. "How about now?"

He carefully pulls the fabric away from my back and reaches down. I feel his fingers brush my skin and I close my eyes. We are both silent, and all I can hear is Wes's breathing. "I got it." He slowly peels the folder away from my skin. I wince as the tape comes undone.

Wes pulls the folder out and sets it on the table, sitting down again and keeping his eyes averted as I quickly button my dress back up.

There's an awkward silence as I sit down next to him. Finally he opens the folder, flipping through the pages. I watch as he skims one of the backup plans.

"Obviously, I need to make changes," I say. "I'm here too late, and some of LJ's ideas won't work. But it's possible, Wes. Imagine a world without the Project."

He lifts his head. "You really think you could do this?"

"I know I can. I have to."

He sets the folder down on the table and rests his fingers against it. "I've spent most of my life caught up in the Project. I know how powerful they are, but for the past six months I've been free from them. No one has come looking for me. I know you're valuable to them, but I still think we could get away from them, if we wanted to."

"It's only a matter of time before they'd hunt us down. This is the only way to guarantee our freedom."

"I don't know, Lydia." He stares down at the file. "This is a lot of information all at once. LJ never said a word about eliminating the Project when I found the resistance."

"Then why did you think I came here?"

"I thought you were running away."

"What?" I feel my chest get tight. "From you?"

"From everything." He stares down at the scarred wood of the table.

"But you still came."

"Even if you were trying to run away, I had to follow you. I needed to make things right between us."

"Wes." I lean forward until there's only a foot separating us. I want to close the gap, but something holds me back.

"I know I've been angry, but I would never run from you."
I pause. "I think that maybe we haven't been trusting each
other enough."

His head snaps up. "I trust you. I didn't blame you for
wanting to get away from me, from all of it."

"Then maybe you didn't trust that you'd be enough for
me."

"You *were* leaving me, Lydia." He speaks softly. "The
reasons may have been different, but you came here thinking you would never see me again."

He's right. I wanted to protect him, to keep him safe,
and I made that choice without him. Isn't that the same
thing he did to me?

"I'm not angry you came here," he says. "I've had a lot of
time to think about all this, a lot more than you have. I'm
not expecting anything." He looks out the window at the
fading sun. "It's almost time to go to the Bentleys. But . . ."
He hesitates, glancing across the room. I follow his eyes to
the small bed that is tucked into the corner.

"What is it?" I ask.

"Everyone thinks we're married. And they assume you're
coming back to live here. With me."

The bed looks smaller than a twin, and there's hardly
enough room for someone to lie down on the untreated
wood floor.

We'll be sleeping here. Together. Alone.

My mouth opens, but I can't say what I'm really thinking.

"There's not even a bathroom in here," I blurt out.

He laughs, and I stare at him. I've heard him laugh before, but not like that. Not easy and bright and free.

He stands up and reaches out, his hand skimming against mine. "Come on, the Bentleys will be waiting for us."

CHAPTER 20

"*Wes* seems happy." I follow Mary's gaze to where he and Dr. Bentley are talking together in the middle of the backyard. Wes is nodding at something Dr. Bentley is saying, his face soft in a way I've rarely seen. He catches me staring and lifts his chin in acknowledgment. I smile.

"He looks relaxed. He likes it here, I think."

"You know he's been working as a fisherman with Mick's father. He's the one who's renting him the house by the beach."

"I know. He wrote to tell me." But that's not true, of course. He filled me in on the way here, after he led me to the ancient truck that was parked behind his house.

"Where did you get this?" I asked him.

"I bought it." He held the passenger-side door open for

me. As we drove to the Bentleys, he told me he was working as a fisherman, and that he even had his own boat now. He described getting up at dawn, casting his nets into the churning ocean, or sometimes not getting up at all, but spending the day in bed reading novels and then taking long walks around Montauk.

"I've never had so many choices before," he said. "The Project decided where I would go, what I would do. I didn't remember what freedom felt like. And now I don't think I can ever go back."

"When I stop the Project, you won't have to."

He looked over at me. "If we ran away, I wouldn't have to either."

Now Mary dumps some chicken pie on a plate and hands it to me. "Go take that to your beau," she says. "Though I suppose I have to start calling him your husband now, huh?"

My husband. I am only eighteen. Wes is nineteen. We're too young to be married, but the word still makes me feel oddly warm.

"Thanks." I take the plate and a fork from her and walk over to Wes.

Dr. Bentley eyes the food as I approach. "Please tell me that's for me."

"I was instructed to bring it to my husband."

Wes tilts his head and our eyes meet. We both quickly look away, and I shove the plate in his direction. "Here."

Dr. Bentley winks at me, then excuses himself. "I'm famished, and I better eat while I can; I know Harriet will enlist me to get the fireworks ready soon. You'll help, won't you, Wes?"

"Sure, Jacob."

Wes takes the plate from my hands as Dr. Bentley walks over to join Mary at the table they've set up near the back of the house. "You call him Jacob?"

He nods, and eats a bite of the pie, chewing absently.

"This is so weird."

He raises his brows. We are standing alone in the wide, green lawn. It is just starting to get dark out, and fireflies spark in bursts of green light at the edge of the woods that circle the house. "What do you mean?"

"I was only here for about a week, a year ago. The Bentleys and I grew close, but you've been here for six whole months. You've created an entire life."

He lowers the plate and stares down at me. "It was because of you."

"What do you mean?"

"Wes!" The high-pitched shout is piercing, even from across the lawn. I turn to see a small boy running through the grass toward us. It's Peter, I realize when he gets closer. My grandfather as a little boy. "You're here." He leans over, panting from the run.

Wes drops one hand and ruffles Peter's neatly cut dark hair. "I said I would be, didn't I? Where's your mom?"

Peter points toward the house, but he has noticed me, and his head tilts back to examine my deep-red hair, my green eyes. "Do I know you?"

"I'm Lydia. I was here last year. Maybe you remember me?"

He shakes his head and looks at Wes's legs, suddenly shy.

Wes kneels down until he's at Peter's eye level. "Remember how I told you I was waiting for a pretty girl to come find me? That was Lydia."

"This lady's your wife?" He looks up at me and squints his eyes, the same color as mine. They are my grandfather's eyes, and I clench my fingers together to keep from reaching for him. "I remember you. You looked like Aunt Mary and played airplanes with me. But then you disappeared."

"I had things to do."

"My daddy disappeared too. Did you know him?"

I exchange a glance with Wes. "I did. I'm sorry."

"Do you know where he went? Did you disappear to the same place?"

I shake my head. Wes reaches over to touch him on the shoulder and Peter leans into him, an unconscious gesture he doesn't even seem aware of.

"I'm sure your father is happy though, wherever he is."

Peter gives me an assessing look. He must be eight now. He's grown a few inches since I last saw him, but he still barely comes up to my chest. He's only a child, but he's still my grandfather, and the last time I saw him he was trapped in a cold cell under Central Park.

This is why I need to stop the Project. So this little boy will never have to experience the same fate.

Wes sees my strained expression and straightens. He grabs both of Peter's shoulders and turns his body toward the house. "Why don't you go find your mother? I'm sure she'd like to say hi to Lydia too."

"All right. I'll be back soon, I promise. Don't go anywhere, okay?" Peter runs across the lawn again. From the back he looks like a miniature version of Wes, with his white shirt and dark pants.

Perhaps the reason my grandfather tried so hard to find out what happened to Dean was because he never had a father figure to step into that role. Could Wes already be starting to fill a void that was always there?

Peter's mother, Elizabeth, steps out of the door at the back of the house, and I almost gasp at the sight of her. She is like a walking ghost, pale and vacant, her eyes dead in a way that reminds me of the newly broken recruits.

"Oh, God. She's not handling it well."

"No." Wes's voice is grim. "Peter is mostly taking care of himself. He's over here all the time, with his grandparents and Mary, but it's not enough."

"That's why you've been spending so much time with him."

He nods. "I know what it's like to feel abandoned. And he's your grandfather, after all."

It is getting darker by the minute, and stars are starting to appear, small dots of light that mirror the fireflies blinking in the corners of the lawn. I reach over and touch Wes's arm. Already, the movement feels easier. "Thank you, for looking out for my family."

"You don't have to thank me for that." He smiles down at me. "I've never had a family before. For the first time in my life, I think I'm finally starting to understand what it means."

Lucas wraps his arms around me, his head close to mine. "It's swell to see you again, Lydia," he says in his honey-soaked southern drawl. "We've missed you."

I press my open palms to his back. "I missed you, too."

He pulls away, but keeps his hands on my shoulders as his gaze travels from my feet to my head. "As pretty as always, I see."

At that point, Wes has had enough, and he grabs my arm, moving me into his side and forcing Lucas to let go. "Wanna take your hands off my girl, Clarke?"

Lucas laughs, revealing his slightly crooked bottom teeth. "At ease, Private Smith," he says, using Wes's fake name from the last time we were here. "I was just sayin' hello."

"You can say it from a distance."

"You know my heart is elsewhere these days." He tips his head to the right, where Mary is bending down to talk to Peter. She smiles, and even in the dim light of the lawn I see her eyes soften as she straightens Peter's shirt collar.

"How's it going?" Wes asks quietly.

Lucas shrugs. "Mostly she seems like herself, but any time I bring up Georgia or Dean, she gets real quiet. Which is a strange thing to see, coming from Mary. I don't know what to say anymore. I feel like a fathead around her."

"She'll come around."

Lucas runs his hand over his buzzed blond hair. He is in his olive-colored army uniform, the starched khaki stretching across his broad chest when he raises his arm. "I'm getting discharged in a month. It's time for me to start making plans. I want her to be a part of that, but . . ." He looks over at me. "Think you could work your magic, Lydia?"

"I can try."

Mary stands up fully and turns to face the house. When she sees us standing there, her smile widens and she bounces across the lawn. Behind her, I watch Peter run to where his mother is sitting silently in a wooden folding chair. Mrs. Bentley is standing over her, holding a plate and trying to get her to eat. But Elizabeth just stares straight ahead, oblivious to even Peter, who grabs her sleeve when he gets close enough.

"Lucas!" Mary wraps her hand around his arm and tugs. "Why didn't you tell me you were here? I would have come said hello."

"I've been standin' right here for ten minutes. What do I need to do, grab a bullhorn?"

"Har har har." She looks over at me and Wes. "Is your fella this funny, Lyd?"

I smile. "He's not one for jokes."

"Don't I know it." Mary lets go of Lucas to poke Wes in the shoulder. "He's been moping around for months, waiting on you to get back from Boston. I think he cried himself to sleep every night."

Lucas laughs, but Wes just shakes his head. "You see what I've had to put up with while you were gone?"

"So how about it, Lydia, are you gonna settle down here now?" Lucas asks.

"I don't know what our plans are yet," I answer vaguely.

"Oh stay!" Mary hops up and down once. "The paper in East Hampton just fired one of their reporters. Ma was telling me about it earlier. You'd be perfect for it, Lydia! You can get a spiffy little car to drive around in; I'll help you pick it out and everything. It should be blue. No!" She points her finger at me. "Red. A convertible, and we can go get sundaes when it's warm and Pricilla Harold—her daddy owns the ice-cream shop and she thinks she's the cat's meow—will just *die* of jealousy. What do you think, Wes; shouldn't Lydia take the job? Make her take it. Don't let her go back to Boston, not yet."

Wes hesitates a second before he says, "That sounds good to me."

Lucas's blue eyes are bright as he stares down at her,

though his shoulders tense slightly. If Mary is so excited about Wes and me staying in Montauk, what happens when Lucas tries to take her back to Georgia?

If I succeed in destroying the TM, it means Wes and I will stay here forever. I would always miss my family in 2012, but I wouldn't be alone here. I'd have the Bentleys. I'd have Wes. I don't want to lose Mary again.

But that's assuming I succeed. I still have to figure out a way to sneak into the Facility, to get to the documents, to get rid of Faust, and to destroy the TM. I can feel the anxiety building and I rub my hands together. I shouldn't even be here right now. I should be planning and plotting, making sure I will not fail.

Wes must feel me tense; his hand settles on my lower back. "It's okay," he whispers into my hair, and I start to relax. I might not make it out of the Facility again alive. I can spare one night to spend time with the Bentleys, with Mary and my grandfather as a little boy.

"Oh, look, Peter found the sparklers." Mary points to the side of the lawn.

As soon as her face is turned away, Lucas raises his eyebrows at me and jerks his head toward her.

I look up at Wes. "Weren't you guys going to help Dr. Bentley set up the fireworks?"

"Right." Wes steps away from me and clasps Lucas on the shoulder. "Let's go do manly stuff, Sergeant."

"Get off me, Private." Lucas pushes his arm away, and they both laugh.

I watch them walk across the lawn, shoving each other back and forth. It's clear they've spent a lot of time together, and I remember how hostile they were when Lucas showed interest in me. But now they are friends. Wes, the boy who was so closed off, who pushed away even Tag, has made a friend.

"Boys are such goofs." Mary shakes her head, smiling after them. Her eyes linger on Lucas's back.

"He's worried about you." I move closer to her. "He thinks you might not want to marry him."

"That's not true." Her smile fades, and I almost regret bringing the subject up, wishing I could hold on to the giddy Mary from just a moment ago. "Lucas has been such a rock through this whole thing, but . . ."

I follow her gaze to Elizabeth, still sitting near the house in her stiff-backed chair. She hasn't moved at all, not even to speak, since she got here.

"Everything is so different now," Mary whispers. "Sometimes I think we'll never recover from this."

I reach over and touch her hand. "You will. It just takes time."

"Can I tell you a secret?"

"Of course."

"Lucas reminds me of Dean. That's why I panic about our future sometimes."

Wes and Lucas are in the center of the lawn, holding long, cardboard tubes of Roman candles and skyrockets while Dr. Bentley points at the ground. Lucas doesn't look anything like Dean—he is light where Dean is dark, from hair color to personality. But I see what she means. Both of them are loyal, always trying to do the right thing. They were best friends, and the only reason Mary even met Lucas was because Dean brought him around so often.

"But they're not the same person," I say. "And Dean wouldn't want you to put your life on hold because of him. He wasn't like that."

"I know he wasn't. That's what makes it harder. But how can I leave now? We've barely pieced ourselves back together."

My eyes wander over to Wes again. "There's something I've realized recently. You have to choose to be happy, and sometimes that means letting go of the past." I turn to face her. "If you want to go to Georgia, you should."

"That's the problem! I honestly *don't* want to go to Georgia! I want to stay here with you and Suze and my family. But I don't want to lose Lucas either." She buries her face in her hands, then spreads her fingers, peeking at me through the open spaces. "Do you think Lucas would stay here?"

"You won't know unless you ask him."

Before she can respond, Peter runs up carrying lit sparklers, smoke and light trailing in his wake. "Here!" he shouts, shoving them at us. Mary and I bend down and carefully take them from his outstretched hands. "Wave them in the air. You can make pictures."

Mary moves her sparkler back and forth, painting the night sky with glittering yellow and orange light. "How's this?"

"Perfect!" Peter hops up and down. "Now you, now you," he says to me, the shyness from earlier disappearing.

I wave my hand too, and the flames follow, sparks that die out so fast they are just fleeting bursts of color. I draw a heart in the air, watching as it slowly fades away.

Wes jogs back over to us, his long body framed by the lingering smoke. He is smiling, his hair flopping as he moves, and that's when I notice that I haven't seen him shake at all today. He has lost those razor sharp edges, lost that careful watchfulness, that feeling that he is both the hunter and the prey.

Just like the Bentleys, he is working on putting himself back together. Even though I pushed him away, even though the Project tried to break us both, he kept fighting. And now he is almost healed.

I'm the last piece, the only thing keeping him from being completely whole again.

When he is close enough, he circles and stands at my back. He laughs at something Peter says, but I can feel the way he resists coming any closer to me. I take a deep breath and then lean back, knowing he will be there to stop my fall.

He freezes when our bodies touch, and then his hands

slide around my middle. The sparkler fizzles out in my hand, but that is when Dr. Bentley lights the end of a Roman candle, holding it at an angle, the end pointed above the treetops. Sparks fly out. I hear Peter squeal. There is a low booming sound and the firework shoots out of the stick and up in the air, a ball of light that arches over the sky, suspended for a moment like any other star, falling just as the next one moves to take its place.

CHAPTER 21

Wes holds the door open for me and I step into the shack. A sliver of moonlight falls in through the window, but it is not enough to light the dark space and I bump against the kitchen counter when I take a step forward.

"Hang on," Wes says.

I hear him step in behind me, then watch the outline of his body as he moves around the room by instinct. He strikes a match, the sulfur hitting me even before he can light the few candles that rest on the table.

A faint glow spreads across the room, and I see his face now, half in shadow as he stands next to the bed.

It isn't late, but I'm exhausted, the past week finally catching up to me. Time has been changing so rapidly. First it is evening, then afternoon, in the blink of an eye, and I am disoriented from traveling through time.

I glance down at the bed, which suddenly looks even narrower than it did this afternoon. Wes and I last slept near each other on a bed of moss, a clearing four times this size. I am suddenly awkward, gripping the fabric of my skirt in my hands, avoiding his gaze to stare at the splintered wooden floor.

"Lydia."

At his serious tone, I turn to face him.

"We need to talk about this." He reaches around and pulls out the folder that he tucked up under the back of his shirt, refusing to leave it in his house where someone could find it. He sets it on the table. I sink down into a wooden chair and rest my hand on the thick paper.

"You won't run away with me, will you?" he asks.

I look up, willing him to understand. "There was a time I would have, but that was before I made the decision to end the Project. If we run, we'll always be running. And I don't think that's what you want either, Wes. I saw how you were today, with the Bentleys. You've found something you've always been looking for."

He watches me for a moment, then sighs and pulls out a chair, the wood scraping loudly against the floor. "Where do we start?"

I sit up straighter. "You'll help me?"

"You're right, Lydia." He rests his hands on the table near mine. "I don't want a life where I'm on the run forever, always wondering if they're right behind me. And I won't make you do this by yourself."

I reach out and touch his palm. It's just the slight pressure of my finger on his skin, but we both go still, staring down at our hands. "Thank you," I whisper. "I didn't want to do it alone."

Wes clears his throat and sits back, breaking the contact. "LJ was right that the easiest solution is to get rid of Faust and the documents."

I take his cue and carefully open the folder. "Which we can do by sending him back through time, and burning his files."

He nods. "But now we have the TM to deal with. We'll have to destroy that, too."

"One of LJ's suggestions is to blow it up, and I think that's the best idea. If there's even a trace of it left, then they might be able to rebuild it."

Wes looks up at me. "Bombs are messy, Lydia."

"But what else could work?"

He stares down at the pages, spreading them out until they fan across the table. After a minute he shakes his head. "You're right. A bomb is the only way."

"We could steal them from the Facility. They have a weapons room."

"Or we could make our own. All we'd need are gunpowder, potassium nitrate, and charcoal. I'd rather have our own weapons than rely on theirs."

I frown. "Could we even get those things in this era?"

"It's easier now than it would have been in yours. We'll have to go to East Hampton tomorrow, but it's possible."

I stand up from the table, almost afraid to say what I'm thinking. "If there's an explosion, we need to talk about the consequences. The aftermath. What about the soldiers and scientists who work in the Facility? They could die."

"The greater good?" He sounds like a recruit again, his voice blank, and I know we're both thinking of our training, hearing that phrase over and over to justify what the Project does.

"Is this one of those lines?" I curl my fingers around the back of the chair. "One of those lines, that, if we cross it, we become like them, and there's no going back?"

"That we're even asking that question means we're not like them."

"Still . . ."

"The explosion doesn't have to be large." He leans back in his chair. "We can't make more than a basic pipe bomb anyway, and it will be contained within the TM chamber. There might be injuries, but you have to remember that these soldiers are grown men. They know what Faust is doing with the kids. They're not totally innocent."

"But what *about* the kids? The recruits they've already started to train?" I picture the room of children, their vacant stares. "They didn't choose to be there."

Wes frowns. "We could try to get them out beforehand."

"We don't want to get caught, trying to move so many people before we can get rid of the TM. It's too much of a risk."

"We can't just leave the kids in there. You know what the Project will do to them."

I do know. If the Project were ever in serious risk, they would do anything to destroy all evidence of its existence— and that includes the people, recruits, children, and anyone else who might talk.

I lean forward against the back of the chair. Wes is right—we can't leave the kids vulnerable in there. "There has to be a way to draw attention to the Project, fast enough so the Project can't react, so that they can't sweep it under the rug anymore."

"What do you mean?"

I tilt my head in Wes's direction. "How much do the officers on the army base at Camp Hero know about the Montauk Project?"

"Not much, I don't think. Maybe some of the generals know right now, but probably not very many."

"*That's* our leverage. If we can draw enough people's attention to the Facility, then no one will be able to cover it up . . ."

". . . and other people will be there to rescue the children after the bomb goes off," Wes finishes my thought.

"But we need to figure out how to get people to notice, and not just the soldiers at Camp Hero."

Wes stands up from the table. "What are you thinking? How would we do that?"

I shake my head. "I don't know yet. I have to think about it. I'm just worried we don't have enough time."

"We're not doing anything tonight." He leans his side against the back of his chair so that we're facing each other. "Tomorrow we'll get the supplies to make the bombs, and we'll finalize our plan. But we won't be ready until tomorrow night at the earliest."

I lift my hand and bite at my right thumbnail. I've never been a nail-biter, but I've also never been this anxious before. "Maybe it makes more sense to go during the day," I say, thinking aloud. "To draw attention to ourselves."

"The bombs will draw attention either way, but we need to make sure it's the right attention." His eyes sweep up my body, taking in the way I'm slumped over the chair. "Let's talk about this tomorrow. You're exhausted."

I know I'm tired, but don't feel it right now, especially not when Wes looks at me closely, and then over at the tiny bed.

"I can sleep on the floor," he says softly.

"Wait." I stand up fully, turning to face him. "I need to say something."

"What is it, Lydia?"

I force myself to meet his eyes. "I'm sorry."

He raises his brows and takes a step forward, but I put my hand up to stop him. "I blamed you for everything that happened between us, and it wasn't right. I should have trusted you enough to know that you wouldn't betray me like that. I'm sorry that I doubted you for so long."

"I'm sorry I lied." He ignores my hand and steps closer until my palm is resting on his chest. I feel his heartbeat, steady and even. "About the mission, about Twenty-two. I thought that if I could shelter you from everything, it would show you I loved you. I didn't know how to have the kind of relationship I wanted us to have."

I look up at him. "But you do now. I watched you with Lucas and Mary. You have friends. You have a family."

He puts his hand over mine and I feel the heat of it spread through my fingers. "I went to the Bentleys in the first place because I knew that the minute you came back, you'd want to see them, and I wanted to be a part of your life as much as I could. Living here, waiting, taught me that I *can* be happy, that I have the capacity for happiness."

I lean into him. "Of course you do, Wes. You always did."

But he shakes his head. "I thought they stole that from me. The only time I ever felt like I might be happy was when I was with you, and you were asking me question after question, being unpredictable in a way that threw me off balance. When I . . ." His voice lowers. "When I kissed you, I felt like maybe, maybe it could be within my grasp, if I worked hard enough to get it. But even then, we had the Project at our backs, the constant fear of being torn away from each other. I was lying to you every day, and I knew I was getting sicker. There was no time for happiness."

"But now it's different," I whisper. "You look so healthy. You're not even shaking anymore."

"I feel stronger. I feel like I finally understand what time means, after they screwed with my head for so long. I needed to stop running, to just . . . stop for a while. I got that here. And now you're here. That's why I want to help you stop the Project. I want us to have a real life together."

Wes has finally become the person I saw glimpses of from the very beginning. All I've ever wanted was to see him like this, to see what he would be like without the Project's rigid control holding him back.

I move my hand away and he closes the gap between us. "I love you, Lydia," he says softly.

I circle my arms around him and stand on my toes, try-ing to get closer. "I love you too."

He leans forward and kisses me, just a brush of his lips against mine. "I won't let you go."

Our lips meet, for longer this time, but still slow. We break away only to lean in again, and I move my hands through the dark threads of his hair. He starts to walk me backward toward the bed and his fingers glide from my shoulders to my sides, to the front of my dress. I touch my tongue to his as he undoes a button, then another and another. My skin feels so fragile, like every brush of his hands will mark me, will leave an invisible bruise. He parts the fabric of my dress and I watch him pull back to look at me, hear the ragged breath he takes. I feel the mattress behind me, then beneath me. He moves his body over mine. My heart is beating so loudly that he places his hand on it, whispers, "Don't be afraid."

"I'm not," I answer. "Not anymore." And I reach up to pull his weight down onto me.

We lie side by side beneath the blanket, only an inch of space between us. The candles have burned down low on the table. One flickers and then goes out, making it harder to see Wes's face. But I don't need the light to trace my finger over the dip below his cheekbones, the curve of his brow.

"I want to give you something," he says. He lets go of my hand and stretches his arm over his head, reaching for a shelf that I didn't notice before, tucked between the wall and the bed. He pulls out a small tin, the kind that holds mints or chewing tobacco. "Here."

I take it from him and pry open the lid. Inside is his gold pocket watch, delicate leaves etched onto the surface.

I touch the smooth curve of it. "Are you sure you want me to have it again?"

He traces the edge too, his finger so much larger than mine, almost covering the locket entirely. "I've always wanted you to have it. I'm sorry I ever had to take it back."

He pulls it up out of the tin and leans over to clasp it

around my neck, his fingers lingering in my hair.

I start to move in closer to him, but I'm distracted as another candle sputters out, and the room grows darker. It must be midnight by now, or even later. The moon is hovering somewhere over the small cabin, no longer visible through the smudged glass.

"You haven't slept in days, have you?" he asks.

I shake my head against the pillow.

"Sleep, Lydia." He closes the tin and puts it back on the shelf. My eyes are half shut, the metal of the watch cool against my chest. In that heavy place right before sleep, I feel his lips against my forehead, his hand settling, warm and solid, over mine.

CHAPTER 22

The choppy waves beat against the sides of the boat as Wes pulls in his fishing net. I sit on a small wooden bench, watching the muscles in his back flex, his arms strain. With a grunt he yanks it over the edge and it drops to the bottom of the boat in a rush of salt water and green, twisting seaweed.

Fish are flopping back and forth inside the net, their tails caught in the coarse rope, iridescent scales reflecting the hazy morning sunlight. Wes is already kneeling, his dark pants wet at the knees, his shirt rolled up over his forearms. He sifts through the net, detangling the fins and ignoring their constant, churning movement. "You can help me throw back the ones that are too small."

I am only a foot away from him on the bench, but I

still crouch down, feeling the water soak into the cotton of my dress. Wes has opened the net and he hands me a fish, firmly caught in his grasp. I take it, unprepared for how slimy it is, how slippery, and it slides from my fingers back down to the floor. I laugh, chasing it with my hands across the wood as it tries to flop its way to freedom.

"There." I finally catch it, tilting it up over the side of the boat and sending it back into the blue waves. "Be free."

I look up, pushing my hair out of my eyes with my forearm. Wes is smiling at me, so widely that I see the dimple in his cheek. He leans over the fish and presses his mouth to mine.

It is a firm kiss, over in a second. "You're here," he says.

"You're here," I repeat.

I'm not naive enough to think it will last, this easy feeling. In a few hours we will go to East Hampton to buy supplies for the bombs, and later tonight, we will finalize our plan. I want to be in the Facility, destroying the Project, by tomorrow night at the latest. It doesn't give us much time, and whenever I close my eyes I smell the bleach and battery acid from those endless white hallways.

I try not to think about it as I help Wes sort through the rest of the fish. The feed store where we'll buy the potassium nitrate for the bombs isn't open until noon, and Wes insisted he take me out on his boat first. I think he is worried this is the only chance we'll have, that he wants to show me the life he's built in case we fail tomorrow.

Wes puts the fish he'll sell to Mr. Moriglioni in a deep metal bucket. I stare at their unseeing eyes, and I think of Tim and Wes catching the fish together in that small stream. Already it feels like so long ago, a different lifetime.

We are headed back to shore when I see a figure jumping up and down on the sand, her skirt flying up, her arms waving over her head. "That'll be Mary." Wes jerks his chin toward the beach. He is rowing the boat through the rough waves with quick, efficient movements. "She asked me when you were coming back every single day. Kept trying to get me to take her to Boston to visit you. I'm glad you showed up. I don't think I could have lied to her for much longer."

"That's why you're glad I showed up?" I ask.

He just grins at me, and I stare at his teeth, so white against his tan cheeks, his hair windswept and damp. Behind him I see that Mary is not alone on the shore— Lucas is leaning back against his jeep, and Peter is running along the water, kicking his legs into the surf and bending down to examine rocks and seashells.

I have no idea if we will succeed in stopping the Project. But on this boat, next to Wes, the waves rocking us from side to side, I feel something finally click into place. The Project spent months creating the jagged edges inside of me, chiseling and chiseling away at them until I was only broken pieces. It was just in the last week that I have started to put them back together. It began with Tim, who would not let me turn away from him, who knew that the only way we would survive was if we leaned on each other. But it was forgiving Wes that has made those edges soft again, and I feel like a piece of sea glass, battered on the shore, letting the steady rhythm of the water turn me smooth.

"What's with that look on your face?" Wes does not stop rowing, his arms laced with muscle, his breath even despite the weight he's pulling.

"Nothing." I smile at him through the spray from the crashing waves that sends mist up over my hair, my bare arms. "I'm just happy."

On the beach, Mary has spread out a picnic blanket. We reach the shore and Lucas wades into the cold springtime water, grabs the thick rope that Wes uses to tether the boat, and pulls us in. Wes hops out and holds his arms up, lifting me onto the dry sand.

Peter is standing on the beach, trying to reach the rope to help Lucas and Wes pull the boat in.

"Whoa." I grab his shoulders and bring him back a few feet. "The waves are strong today. Let them do it."

He twists away from me. "I'm not a little kid, you know. I can help."

I look down into his face. His cheeks are nothing like my grandfather's. He's still a little boy, his face round and soft where my grandfather's was angular. But the direct, stubborn way Peter speaks is startlingly familiar.

The grandfather I remember might be gone, but, in a

way, he's still here. I'll have a different role in his life—caretaker instead of charge—but he'll always be someone I love. And now I'll be able to watch him grow up, instead of knowing he would probably pass away during my lifetime.

I lean down close to Peter.

"I know you can," I say softly. "But Wes will tell you when he needs help."

"I help Wes a lot. Sometimes he takes me fishing."

"I just helped him too."

"And she wasn't very good at it. Not nearly as good of a helper as you are, Peter." Wes walks toward us in the sand, wiping his hand across his face. The boat is now several feet up the shore, well out of the high-tide line. "She kept dropping the fish back in the water."

"Hey." I put my hands on my hips. "I was a great helper."

"You're a girl," Peter says. "Girls don't know how to fish."

"That is so sexist. Girls can do anything boys can do."

He cocks his dark head at me and scowls. "What's sexist mean?"

I open my mouth, then shut it. Wes starts laughing. "Oh shut up," I mumble, pushing his stomach as I walk past. He clutches his middle and gives an exaggerated groan, which makes Peter start to laugh.

I shake my head, sitting down next to Mary on the blanket.

"Lydia." She waves her hand in the air. "You reek of fish."

"Wes made me throw back the little ones. My hands are all gooey." I hold them in her direction and she shrieks.

The boys join us, and Wes lies down on his side, tucking my back against his front, his arm around my waist. Lucas sits near Mary, resting his hand behind her. She scoots back a little so his forearm is pressed to her side. Despite Lucas's fears, they look comfortable with each other.

"I have hard-boiled eggs," Mary says. "Ma packed breakfast for us, and there's eggs and apples and root beer and brown bread and butter, I think, maybe a little and—"

"Mary!" I interrupt. "We got it, there's food."

I feel Wes's body shake behind me as he laughs and I lean into him.

"I'm just trying to tell you what there is." She huffs.

"I'm starving." Wes pushes up until he's sitting beside me, keeping his left arm wrapped around my waist. "What's in there, Clarke?"

"Well, there's eggs and apples and root beer and brown bread and butter . . ."

We all laugh, even Mary. I watch the way she looks up at Lucas from under her lashes, and I know that even though she is still mourning Dean, she is going to be okay.

Peter runs over to eat with us, squeezing in between Lucas and Wes, and they both rumple his hair. I give him a plate with chicken and he thanks me, smiling.

While he eats he lays his treasures on the blanket: rocks smooth and pale from the waves beating against them, a white seashell, curved and hollow. Lucas shifts through them, pointing to a dark rock with lighter-colored stripes. "I like this one best."

"Me too," Peter says, though I know he would have agreed regardless. Lucas is a lot like Tim, I realize, and it's not just their build—both a little stocky with light eyes and broad shoulders. Lucas is just as easygoing, just as comfortable in his kindness.

"I'm still hungry." Lucas reaches for the basket, but Mary holds out an apple.

"Here."

"Feed it to me?" He bends his head close to her, opening his mouth wide.

"You have arms, don't you?" She tosses the fruit at his face and he catches it right before it connects with his nose.

"Oh, I have arms." He throws the apple to the side and lunges at Mary.

"Get away!" she shrieks as they topple over into the sand. "Ahh! Lydia! Save me!"

I do not move from the blanket. "Peter, go rescue your aunt."

Peter jumps to his feet and hurls his tiny body onto Lucas's back. "Get off her." He giggles.

"You're like a monkey!" Lucas shouts, sitting up with the smaller boy clinging to his neck.

Mary sits up too, patting at her hair and glaring at Lucas.

"It took me two hours to set these curls, and now look at them. You're a menace, Clarke."

"And you're beautiful, even covered in sand." He leans forward and pecks her on the cheek, Peter still hanging off his shoulders.

"Oh stop." Mary waves her hand in the air, her face tinted pink.

Lucas pries Peter away, setting the boy to the side. "Eat more food," he commands.

"Don't wanna." Peter jumps up and runs to the water's edge to look for shells.

I watch him lean his face close to the sand, and then my gaze wanders over to Wes's shack, to his rundown truck, to the dunes above us.

My body goes solid.

"What is it?" Wes whispers into my ear, too quiet for Lucas or Mary to hear.

"On the dunes. Something reflected the sun. I think someone's watching us."

Wes scans the ridge above us. "There's nothing there."

"I'm sure I saw it."

"It could have just been a shell, or a piece of glass."

"What if it's a recruit? What if they sent someone to find us?" I breathe the words.

"There's no way. Don't worry."

"What are you two whispering about?" Mary asks.

"Nothing." I force myself to relax, and Wes squeezes

my side. He's right. It was probably nothing. Trying to shake the uneasy feeling, I hold up a raspberry and his lips close around my fingers. Our eyes meet and I remember how it felt last night when those same lips grazed my neck, when he whispered in my ear. I glance away, clearing my throat.

Mary is watching from across the blanket and she rolls her eyes. "You do not get to take up all of Lydia's time." She points her finger at Wes. "I haven't seen her in almost a year and we have so much to catch up on, and we need to—well, no offense, Lydia, but we need to fix that hair of yours. It is so old-fashioned; I mean, honestly."

Wes chokes on the raspberry and I hand him a root beer. When he has taken a long sip he grins at Mary. "I promise I won't occupy her all the time."

But Mary and I will only have time together if Wes and I succeed tomorrow. If we are caught in the Facility, it's all over. We have one shot at destroying the TM, and we can only hope we don't destroy ourselves in the process. Wes feels my shoulders tense and he moves even closer, resting his chin on the top of my head.

Mary smiles, missing the stiff way I'm holding my body, and I do my best to smile back. I will not be afraid on our last day together, not when we are on this deserted beach, the sun high and bright overhead, and people I love sitting right in front of me. They are gifts, moments like these, and I have learned not to waste them.

When we are driving back from East Hampton, the supplies for the bombs in the truck bed behind us, I turn to face Wes. "I think I have an idea," I say.

He glances at me, his hands loose on the steering wheel. "What is it?"

"In order to save those kids, we need to draw attention to the Facility, right? We need civilians there. It's the only way to make sure the scientists and officers who are involved can't cover up what's happening."

"How will we get people out there?" He sounds thoughtful. "It's pretty far in the woods, and not many civilians go near the army camp."

The windows are partially down, and air whips through the small space. I move closer to Wes. So he can hear me better, I tell myself, ignoring the half grin he gives me.

"Dr. Bentley goes to Camp Hero every day to work in the hospital." I almost have to shout over the wind. "You *know* he wouldn't be involved in any kind of cover-up, and if he brought the other doctors with him to the Facility, there'd be too many people for the Project to keep quiet."

"But how are we going to get him out there? And when?"

"Tomorrow morning. At first light."

We are both silent for a minute. It is only hours from now, but it will give us more than enough time to make the bombs and map out how we'll get in and out of the Facility. I've been having fun, reconnecting with Wes and the

Bentleys, but I can't forget why I'm here. Destroying the Project has to come first. It's the only way any of us will have a future together.

"We need to go when it's light," I say, and Wes nods. We're getting closer to Montauk, to his home, but also to the Facility. I watch the low trees and dunes fly past the window.

"I think we should write Dr. Bentley a letter." I lean back against the seat, my head tipped toward Wes. "We can leave it in his study tonight when we go for dinner. That way we won't have to answer any questions in person. I'll tell him to be at the camp at a certain time, that something is happening in the western woods that will require medical aid. He'll go; he trusts us."

Wes reaches down to change gears and the old truck jolts, rocking my body forward. Instead of putting his hand back on the wheel, he rests it on my thigh. "You'll need a better story than that."

"I'll think of something. But this is the best solution I could come up with for now."

He squeezes my leg, and I imagine that the layer of my dress isn't there, that he's touching my bare skin. "It's a good idea, Lydia. I trust Bentley. He'll make sure those kids are safe."

Later that evening, as the sun is setting a deep red behind us, Wes and I walk back toward his small shack. "I love

Mrs. Bentley," I say, "and maybe we can blame it on the war, but I cannot eat any more of that horrible cake."

"It's bad, isn't it?"

"Cakes should not be made without sugar and butter. It's a crime."

Wes laughs, his hand curled tight around mine. I move closer to him, wanting to be in the moment, but I cannot shake this nagging feeling I've had since we came back from East Hampton.

"Wes? Do you feel like someone is watching us?"

He stops walking, his body still as he listens. "I can't hear anything but the water," he says after a moment.

"I'm not saying it's something you can hear, I just have this feeling. Like there's someone staring at my back. I've had it all night. And then this morning on the dunes—"

"Do you think you're being overly suspicious?" His voice is soft. "You spent the last week in the woods being hunted. It's normal that you'd still feel that way."

"I guess so." He starts moving forward again and I let him pull me along, our hands still clasped together.

He might be right—maybe I am overreacting, still remembering how it felt to sleep with my heart in my throat, wondering if every sound, every breeze was a sign that the Secret Service had found us. But Wes has also spent the last six months alone, never looking over his shoulder. Am I paranoid or has he lost his instincts?

"Don't worry." He squeezes my hand, turning to look

at me in the fading light. "Tomorrow morning this will all be over."

It's not exactly reassuring, but I try and smile at him. I must have been mistaken; there are not many places for a person to hide out here, with the ocean to our left and the dunes to our right.

Inside his tiny house he pulls out the bags of supplies we bought in East Hampton and we sit side by side at the table. We are silent as we separate out the ingredients, using small lead pipes to contain the explosions.

"The fuses can't be too long," Wes says when we are almost finished mixing the materials. "Otherwise a guard might be able to stop them before they explode."

"But how are we going to get out in time?" I lift up one of the small fuses he's already cut. "This would only give us thirty seconds."

He takes it from my hand, fitting it into the end of the pipe. "We have no choice. We'll have to steal timers from inside the Facility. We can wire and rig the bombs in the TM room after we send Faust through time, and set the countdown for two minutes. Even if they find the bombs, a guard wouldn't be able to stop one in time. Deactivating a timer isn't as simple as cutting a fuse."

"Will we have time for that? It won't be easy to sneak around, especially if we have Faust with us and we're trying to keep him quiet."

"We'll have to make it." He sounds distracted, and I

stare down at his bent head as he concentrates on installing the fuse. "We need to make sure the TM explodes, but I'm also planning on living a long life with you, Lydia. That means we need to make it out alive."

I smile. "Only you can be romantic while assembling a deadly weapon."

"I try." He looks up and grins, the dimple cutting deep into his cheek.

Earlier, I left a note for Dr. Bentley on the desk in his study. I wrote that I had heard some soldiers in town talking about testing bombs near the southwest bunker of Camp Hero at dawn, and how they're sure it won't be safe. I asked him to check it out with the other volunteer doctors and nurses from the hospital, because I thought some men would end up injured. I know he's the type of doctor who will go, even if my information wasn't certain.

As soon as Wes and I have assembled three bombs, we lay out the contents of LJ's file. Most of the documents are things we already know—a layout of Camp Hero, a brief description of how to get into the entrances. But one paper is a detailed map of the Facility, and another is a write-up on Faust, including details about his schedule. He lives in the Facility, eats and sleeps there, and almost never leaves. It will make him easy to find, and we use the map to pinpoint the exact location of his office, and the entrances we'll use to get in and out.

When it is close to midnight, Wes stands up from the

table. "Come here." He lifts his shirt over his head and I stare at his bare chest.

I move toward him because I cannot help it, we are magnetic, and his fingers tangle in the loose strands of my hair. He kisses me, then pulls back. "I love the freckle you have right here." With his opposite hand he touches my face, just below my eye.

I run my fingers over his shoulders. He has twin bullet holes, one on each arm, and I trace the raised white flesh on his right shoulder. The one on the left side is newer, still an angry pink. "It's strange to see this healed. For me, it happened three days ago."

He twists, pulling me down beneath him on the bed. "Wes . . ."

"What?" His voice is muffled against my collarbone.

"We have to concentrate."

"On what?" His hand cups my cheek, his mouth moving lower.

"The plan."

He lifts up until he's staring me in the face. "We've been over the plan a hundred times. We've made the bombs. We put the letter on Jacob's desk. All that's left is to execute it, and we can't do that for hours."

"Aren't you scared?" I ask.

He twists his finger around a lock of my hair. "A little. But we've been in the Facility before, and this time there are fewer soldiers and no cameras. We'll be fine."

But I can't relax. Everything is riding on tomorrow.

"We're trained for this," Wes says. But then he sees the way I bite my lip and he sighs. "Lydia, don't worry. We're ready. And you're here, in my bed, and I don't want to think about what could go wrong tomorrow." He moves his hand from my hair to my cheek, running the backs of his fingers down to my chin. "Let's think about something else, okay?"

I nod, knowing I need to trust him, to believe that we will succeed. He leans over and kisses me, and then I stop thinking about anything at all.

We get dressed in the early morning, when the sky is just starting to lighten and the moon is low on the horizon. I put on Wes's old recruit uniform, washed and tucked away in a drawer. It is too big on me, but I roll up the sleeves and the pant legs. Wes is dressed in black too, in a tight T-shirt and rugged work pants.

When we leave the shack, the fog from the ocean hits us, damp and thick, making it hard to see where we're walking. Wes takes my hand and we stumble over to his truck, our shoes slipping on the wet grass.

Maybe it is the mist, maybe we are both still wrapped up in what it felt like to lie in each other's arms all night, but neither of us senses her presence until it is too late. Wes reaches for the handle of the passenger's-side door when he freezes, slowly turning to face the beach. I turn with him,

CHAPTER 23

She steps down off the sand, the high sea grass winding around her legs. Neither Wes nor I moves as she approaches. "You need to come with me," she says, the sound of the crashing waves nearly drowning out her words. "General Walker sent me to bring you back."

"You're alive," I whisper. "I thought . . ."

"That I was dead? Is that why you left me?" Neither of us answers. "I eventually broke out of a federal prison, and made it to Montauk on my own."

Wes steps away from the door of the truck so that his body is partially in front of mine. "How did you find us?"

She turns the gun until it's pointed at him. "One of the scientists here logged that he saw a girl who had a similar appearance to Seventeen exit the TM. The general said that if I found her, Eleven would be there, too." Her mouth twists slightly.

"We tried to go back for you," I say. "There were too many bullets. We couldn't reach you."

She keeps the gun on Wes, ignoring me. The wind from the ocean whips through her sleek, dark ponytail, sending pieces of hair fanning out over her shoulder. "I've been instructed to use force, if necessary. He doesn't need you both, just Seventeen. Eleven is expendable."

I jerk forward, but Wes puts his arm out to stop me. "I'm not going." I spit out the words.

She steps closer, her eyes on Wes's arm, curled protectively across my body. "I'll shoot him if you don't."

Wes is silent, his muscles tight, his gaze trained on Twenty-two. Her hand trembles. It is just a moment, just a second, but we both see it.

"I have to complete this mission," she states. "I have to do whatever it takes to bring Seventeen back to General Walker."

"I know why they want me. But I won't do it." I am shouting at her now, and still the words are lost, muted by the constant wind.

"Seventeen is valuable to the Project." Her eyes flash, though otherwise she keeps her face carefully empty. It is like she is a thin sheet of ice—tranquil on the surface, water

raging underneath. "Eleven is too old. He has been traveling too long."

"He saved you." I push against Wes's arm, and he lowers
it slowly. "He saved your life and you fell in love with him.
I watched how you looked at him in the woods. Do you
think I didn't see it? You can't shoot him, any more than I
could."

"And I watched you!" Her voice finally cracks, the
gun swinging toward me. I stop moving, and Wes's body
becomes even more solid beside mine. "I watched you flirt
with Thirty-one. I watched Eleven staring at you anyway,
trying to protect you. I even watched you an hour ago,
sleeping in the same bed together. I'll be *happy* to deliver
you back to Walker."

"What will happen then?" I demand. "You'll keep
going through the TM until your body falls apart, until
you're killed, like Tim? Is that what you want?"

"What else is there? You don't know. Not like we know."
Her eyes dart toward Wes, then back to me. "You weren't
tortured. You didn't have to . . ."

"You're right, I wasn't tortured. But Wes was, and he's
not choosing to remain loyal to the Project. He's choosing
to get out."

"There is no way out!" She screams the words. "They're
everything, they're everywhere!"

"There is a way—" I start to speak but she cuts me off.

"You've brainwashed him," she says harshly. "You've made him doubt the Project. It's your fault they want him dead."

I rear back and Wes touches my elbow. Twenty-two glares at me, so hard I can feel the heat of it.

"It's not Lydia's fault," Wes says. "She hasn't done anything other than help me change, and help me realize that they don't have the right to control us."

"Lydia," Twenty-two spits out. "Her name. You all knew it. Why? How?"

"Because I told him."

Wes's grip on my arm tightens. He looks down at me briefly before he turns back to face Twenty-two. She is watching him with a desperation I didn't know she was capable of. "Because for the first time in years, I cared about someone else's name." Wes's voice is steady. "For the first time in years someone asked me what mine was. She helped me remember."

"Wes?" She half chokes on the name.

I clench my hands into fists, not liking the way she says it, as though it belongs to her.

"And you could remember too," Wes says, "if we stop the Project now."

The gun drops half an inch. "What are you talking about?"

Wes lets go of my arm and steps forward. Twenty-two

swings her gaze to his, her eyes widening, her mouth parting as he draws near.

"There's a way to erase everything that happened," he says. "There's a way for us to go back to the beginning."

"What do you mean?" she whispers. I cannot hear her over the wind and the waves, but I watch her mouth the words. I take a step closer, but as soon as I move she lifts the gun again, her eyes narrowing on mine.

"Okay, okay." I hold my arms up like a criminal. "I'll stay here. I'm not moving."

Wes raises his hand, moving it downward in a soothing motion. It works to distract her, and Twenty-two stares at him. "Don't you want to make it all go away?" he asks. "Don't you want to stop being a recruit?"

Her recruit mask cracks and breaks apart, and I can suddenly see the longing in her eyes. "Yes. It's all I want."

"What was your name?"

She swallows. "I don't remember."

"Think. What's your name?"

She opens her mouth and a low sound escapes.

"What?" He leans forward. "Say it louder."

"Althea. My name is Althea."

"Greek," I say, and her eyes swing to me. She is blinking rapidly.

"My mother was Greek. She . . . died. I had no family. They found me." She raises one of her hands and presses it to her forehead. I can see it shaking, even through the fog that surrounds her.

"Althea." Wes says her name. "We can send you back to your own time. What year were you taken from?"

"Two thousand and four."

"You can go back there. We'll send you back, and you'll rejoin the time line. We'll destroy the TM and then no one will be hunting you. You'll be free. You won't forget the Project, but you can have your life back again. Create a new life. A family, maybe."

"A family," she repeats, as though it is both sacred and forbidden, a word that must be whispered instead of shouted.

"Give me the gun." Wes holds his hand out. "Help us."

"I . . ." She looks at him, down at the gun, over at me. "I don't know how."

"Just let go."

She stares at him blankly.

"I understand that it's hard," Wes tries again. "The Project has been making choices for us for too long. But this is *your* choice. They can't do it for you, not this time."

I watch her wrestling with the decision, her brown eyes darkening, her small, compact body braced against the haze that rolls in off the ocean. It is not the choice that is hard, it is the making of it, the act of remembering freedom. She closes her eyes, her jaw tightens, and then she slowly drops her arm. Wes takes the last few steps to reach her and forces the gun from her limp hand. She doesn't fight him, her body swaying toward his.

He turns to face me. "Let's go."

I nod and open the door of the truck.

"We should use the bunker in Sector Three-J," Twenty-two—Althea—interrupts me.

She sits between us on the bench seat of Wes's truck, listening to me fill her in on our plan, her back straight, her eyes on the windshield. The old, nearly broken-down vehicle lurches along the road, whining over hills and vibrating under us.

"It makes more sense to use Four-B. It's closer to the entrance, and less commonly used by the Facility," I explain.

"That's because it's more exposed. The army base patrols that area. Three-J is the better option."

"The base patrols it in the evenings. It's morning now. This is the quietest time for the camp, but the Facility will be all over the J entrance. We're using Four-B."

"But it isn't—"

"Lydia's right," Wes says. "We need to focus more on the Facility than the army base."

"Fine." Althea crosses her arms over her chest. "Keep going."

I try not to sigh.

Before we reach Camp Hero, Wes pulls the truck off the main road, following a small beach path and parking behind a sand dune. "We're on foot now," he says as he turns off the engine and opens his door.

Wes swings the canvas knapsack containing our bombs onto his back, and we walk through the woods until we reach the edge of the camp. There is no fence around the perimeter in 1945, but civilians rarely come out here; HIDDEN LAND MINE signs are posted in the woods to keep out enemies, and soldiers routinely patrol through the trees. The lack of a fence allows us to approach from the west side of the woods, and we keep low and quiet, ducking beneath branches and avoiding the dry patches of leaves underfoot.

The sky is now a light blue, with rays of sunlight just starting to break at the edge of the trees. Dr. Bentley will be here soon, waiting to see what my letter meant by explosions in the woods.

The Four-B entrance is in the southwest area of the park, and we reach it quickly. We only hide once, when the patrol passes along the road in front of us. Instead of the larger groups of alert soldiers I saw in 1944, this one has only a few men, smoking cigarettes and talking loudly as their guns swing against their backs. They pass by, never once looking into the woods where we're crouching, still and silent.

The concrete bunker is in a small, empty clearing, hidden in the woods off one of the main roads. It is embedded in a man-made hill, two wings fanning out on either side of it. In my time, the concrete would appear sealed shut, but in 1945, there is a large metal door on the front, a padlock with a thick chain coiled around the handles.

We all move toward it quickly, though I'm the first to reach the lock. Althea makes a noise and steps forward, but Wes stops her. I pull a bobby pin from my hair, fit it into the small opening, and quickly twist until I hear the tumblers give, one by one. The lock pops free. I yank it off and Wes helps me untangle the heavy chains around it.

We pull open the metal doors that are set into the cement. The dusty room inside is being used as a storage unit for the army base; wooden crates are stacked against a side wall and a quadruple fifty-caliber machine gun is perched in the middle. It looks like a small tank, with wheels and a space at the top for the driver to sit.

"The door's in the back," Wes whispers.

We skirt the gun and move to the far wall. Althea and I both take out our metal keys at the same time, and this time I gesture her forward.

The light is weak in here, with only the blue gray of morning spilling in through the open door. Twenty-two runs her fingers along a section of the wall until she finds the tiny slit and slides in the key. As soon as she pulls it out again, a door opens in the concrete, the lines of it so smooth that no one would ever suspect it was there.

Wes pries it open with his fingers, and we go in, walking slowly down the long, dark flight of stairs in front of us. Twenty-two is first, I'm in the middle, and Wes follows.

As we descend, the musty smell from the bunker above

us slowly disappears, overwhelmed by bleach and acid. I suck in my breath. There is a dim overhead light at the bottom of the stairs, just enough to make the small landing visible. We crowd together in front of a scarred metal door that looks like it hasn't been opened in months. There is another slit by the side of it and Althea jams in her key again. A red light flashes above the door. I grab the handle and push it open to reveal a clean, white hallway ahead of us. It is so much easier to break into the Facility in the 1940s, before there were rooms that scanned your body, and DNA testing.

The three of us slip inside. Wes, still holding the gun, is on point. I follow behind him, hugging tight to the walls. We move slowly, peering around corners before we turn them, crouching in door frames when we hear footsteps up ahead. But this part of the Facility is quiet. The soldiers bunk in the opposite wing, and the TM chamber is in the very heart of the Facility. The scientists have their offices here, not far from the labs and the dormitories where they keep the newly kidnapped children.

We round a corner and I immediately recognize the hallway where Faust's office is: the white walls, the bright lights overhead, the three metal doors.

"That's it," I whisper to Althea. "The door in the middle is Faust's office."

She nods. The corridor is empty, and she strides across

it. Wes and I follow, pausing when she stops in front of the door.

"The gun." She holds out her hand.

Wes doesn't move, the weapon tight in his grip. It has a silencer, which means she brought it from the future. At the look in her eyes, I lean forward, ready to react if she tries something. Is she about to turn on us, now that we're trapped down here?

She impatiently juts her hand forward. "If he's in there, someone will have to detain him. You two know what you're looking for. I don't. I'll handle Faust while you find the documents."

Wes glances at me. I think of Althea's face earlier, when Wes told her she could go back to her own time, and I nod. He slips the gun into her hand.

She twists the doorknob and pushes. We enter the room. Dr. Faust is sitting behind a wide desk, a journal open in front of him. He looks up, startled. "What—"

But he doesn't have the chance to finish before Twenty-two raises the gun and shoots him in the chest.

CHAPTER 24

Blood blossoms across his white shirt like a rose fully opening for the first time. It would almost be beautiful, if I couldn't see his pale face, his mouth open in horror, the way he claws at the edge of his desk.

"What the hell are you thinking?" I snap at Althea. Wes quickly shuts the office door.

I run forward, pushing Faust back in his chair, and press my hands to the wound, a little below his shoulder. It has missed his heart, but he could still bleed out.

Wes pries the gun from Althea's hands. She stands in the middle of the room, watching me impassively. "He needed to die, didn't he? I knew neither of you would do it. I had to."

"Not here." Wes's voice is harsh. "Not like this. We can't

have a dead body on our hands. What if someone finds it? What are we going to do with him?"

She lifts one shoulder. "Dump him in a supply closet. Who cares?"

The doctor groans, sweat forming on his forehead. I can almost smell his fear, sour and sickly sweet.

"He's not dead yet," I snap. "Stop talking about him like he's dead."

"Give me the gun and I'll finish him." Althea holds out her hand and Wes scowls at her.

The blood is seeping through my fingers. I feel it, warm and thick. A red drop falls onto the white tile floor. All of a sudden I am crouched in the leaves and the pine needles, the gunfire drowning out Tim's wet, strained breathing.

"Wes . . ." I whisper. "I can't do this."

He quickly comes over, holding a large handkerchief in his hands. He nudges me out of the way and presses it onto Faust's bleeding chest. I step back on shaking legs. There's blood all over my fingers, and I wipe them on my shirt. Wes holds the gun out to me with his free hand and I take it from him and tuck it into the waistband of my pants.

I spin to face Althea. "We were going to send him through the TM. It's a better punishment for him."

She crosses her arms over her chest. "He should be dead. He's the one who started all this. Without him, none of us would have ended up here." Her fingers are digging into her arms, so hard they are turning white with the pressure.

Soon she will break through the skin. "We have to kill him. He stole our lives. It's only fair."

She is starting to snap. Being in this room, seeing the man who created the Montauk Project is breaking her. "We need the timers," I say quickly. "They should have them in their weapons room; there's no Assimilation Center here yet. It's in the East Wing, Level Three—"

"I know where it is." Her arms drop and she squares her shoulders. "I'll get what I can and meet you in the TM chamber in fifteen minutes."

"Fine. Just go."

She quickly leaves the room, perhaps grateful to have a task to get her out of this office, even if it does come from me. I have a moment of panic, wondering if we can trust her, but then I turn back to Wes. She shot Faust because he's connected to the Project; her only priority is to make it out of here.

"How is he?" I ask.

"Alive." Wes keeps the handkerchief pressed to the wound. The blood is slowing. "He'll make it; it's mostly a flesh wound. But we can't leave him here."

"I know. We'll take him to the TM chamber. It's what we were planning anyway."

Dr. Faust is breathing heavily, slumped back in his chair, and he turns his glazed eyes to Wes. "It's you," he whispers. "You were here before."

Wes doesn't answer him. "Lydia, the journals."

"Right." I turn to the file cabinet, ripping open the bottom drawers. They are filled with files on dead soldiers, information on the subjects they've sent through time—but nothing about the TM or Tesla. I try the top two drawers, but they're sealed with the kind of combination locks that look like they belong on an industrial safe. "What is it?" I ask the doctor. "What's the code?"

"Not . . . telling you," he croaks out.

Wes leans onto his chest, pressing into the bullet wound. The doctor groans again. "I can't. . . . I won't."

"The more you fight us, the worse it will get," Wes says.

The doctor stares up at him and suddenly smiles, his teeth still clenched against the pain. "You're magnificent," he breathes.

Wes flinches, moving his head back.

I glower at Faust. "If he's so magnificent, then tell him the codes."

Wes presses down again, not hard, but enough to show we're serious. The doctor gasps. "Seven, ten, one, eight, five, six." He spits the numbers out.

"Tesla's birthday," I mumble. "I should have known."

I spin the dial quickly, and the first drawer opens. Inside are personal documents—a birth certificate from Austria, a passport, proof of US citizenship. I open the lock on the second drawer. The first thing I see is a folder with NIKOLA TESLA on the front in bold letters. I pull it out and leaf through the handwritten sheets of paper. Most are covered in equations; a few have pictures of machines with detailed instructions. I stop at one that resembles the TM. Tesla's Machine. It is circular, stretching up and narrowing into a tube that only stops at the top of the paper, implying that it goes on and on. I shove it back into the folder, and tuck the whole thing under my arm. There is only a thick notebook left in the drawer and I open it. It is in different handwriting—it must be Faust's—and is filled with more detailed notes on the TM, various formulas and possible renderings.

I turn, holding both the folder and notebook in my hands.

"You can't take those!" Faust yells though his voice is weak, his face lined with deep wrinkles. "There's nothing else like that in the world. If you destroy it, you destroy me. You destroy everything Tesla and I have built."

"From what I've read about Tesla, I don't think he'd approve of what you've been doing with his ideas," I say.

The doctor's mouth falls open. It is the worst insult I could have given him.

Wes looks up at a clock on the wall. "If we want to meet Althea in the TM chamber, we need to go now."

"Should we hide his blood?" I glance around the room and see a lab coat resting on one of the chairs in front of the desk.

I grab it as Wes lifts the doctor up. He's a short man, but heavy, with thick arms and a rounded stomach. We shove him into the new lab coat, keeping the thick handkerchief pressed against the wound in case it starts to bleed again. It makes him look like he has a slight growth on his shoulder, but all we need to do is get him to the TM chamber without anyone noticing.

Dr. Faust groans and leans heavily on Wes, who winces under his weight. I pull out the gun and point it at him. "Stop being so dramatic. You can walk. You weren't shot in the leg."

As soon as he sees the weapon, he stands up straighter.

I hand the notebook and the folder over to Wes. He takes them, then reaches down and grabs the open journal off Faust's desk, a few drops of blood already drying on the pages. "We can't leave this here either. Who knows what's in it."

I press the gun into Faust's side and lead him to the door. "You're going to be really quiet, or I'm going to shoot you. And I won't miss like Althea did."

"What are you doing with me?" The fear is back in his voice.

"We're going to send you into the past." I push him forward. "Just like you tried to do with Dean Bentley."

"Tried? He didn't end up there?"

I don't answer.

"And you, how did you make it out?" He looks over at Wes. "Your blood was on the floor of the chamber."

"Stop asking questions," Wes growls. "If you're quiet, we won't kill you. It's that simple."

The doctor presses his pale, thin lips together. I hide the gun in the folds of his lab coat, prod him in the back, and we slowly walk out of the room.

We turn another corner, and I hold my breath, only letting it out when I see that the hallway in front of us is empty. I keep my head down, the butt of the gun jammed into the doctor's side. He winces with each step he takes. Wes is behind us, ready to act if Faust tries anything.

"You won't get away with this," the doctor whispers.

"That's such a cliché," I respond softly. "Now be quiet."

We reach the end of the corridor. We are so close to the TM chamber, only a few feet away. If we can just make it around this corner—

"Doctor!" The shout comes from behind us. I slowly turn, guiding Faust's body.

A younger scientist with white-blond hair is running down the hall. He reaches us and bends over, breathing heavily. "I've been looking for you," he gasps. "But you weren't in your office. I have the results of the new serum. We were up all night testing it, and it seems to be working."

"Incredible," Faust breathes. "Did the subject make it through alive?" He jerks forward, and I dig the gun into his back in a silent warning.

"We're still waiting, but so far his body has not rejected it. We'll test it on the TM if the results are positive."

Wes shifts so he's standing in front of us, blocking Faust

as much as he can without looking suspicious.

This is taking too long. I push the gun into Dr. Faust's back and he hisses under his breath.

The scientist narrows his blue eyes. "Are you all right?" He looks from Wes to me, taking in our black uniforms, our grim expressions. "Who are these people?"

I tense. If Faust says the wrong thing then I'll have to kill both him and this scientist. This is not the same as handing Sardosky a drink. This is blood and bullets and staring into their eyes as they die. But there's too much at stake not to pull the trigger.

"They are new subjects," Faust answers. "I am bringing them to the TM."

The blond scientist's expression turns assessing, and he appraises us like we're cattle. "Are you sending them through now? Should I come help?"

"There is no time for that now. The serum is more important."

"Of course. I'll bring you an update as soon as I can." He turns to leave.

My muscles finally loosen. Wes takes a deep breath and lets it out slowly.

"Dr. Roberts!" Faust yells suddenly, stopping the younger scientist in his tracks.

"What are you doing?" I whisper urgently.

His voice changes, deepens, his accent thicker as he says, "There's a sliver in my foot."

The blond man's eyes widen, then he turns and takes off down the hallway, disappearing from sight.

"Shit, it was a code." Wes moves to run after him, then looks back, clearly not wanting to leave me alone with Faust.

"Let him go," I say quickly. "We don't have much time. We can barricade the door and fight our way out after we set the timers."

He looks doubtful, but turns with me and grabs Faust's arm. We don't bother to be subtle as we sprint with him down the hallway. When we reach the door of the TM chamber, Wes shoves it open, pushing Faust through first. He stumbles and falls to his knees on the floor.

Althea crawls out from under one of the desks. "Where have you been?"

"We've been made." Wes runs toward her. "Help me block the door."

Althea jams a chair under the knob, while Wes sweeps pencils, paper, and a telegraph machine off one of the desks. They each grab an end, drag it to the door, and shove it up against the chair.

I point the gun at Faust, still lying on his side, one hand pressed to the bullet wound in his chest. "What happened to keeping quiet?"

He lifts his uninjured shoulder. "What was the risk? You're going to kill me anyway."

"We're not going to kill you, just send you back in time."

"Isn't it the same thing?"

Althea steps away from the door and looks at Wes. "The timers are on the table. Send me back now. I already set the date." She points at the large, boxy computer consul sitting on one of the desks. "You just need to push the button."

She starts walking to the TM, but stops and turns back to Wes. She steps close, hesitates, then puts her hand on his arm. Wes doesn't move at all, his face unreadable, and she pulls away slowly. "I guess . . . well, good-bye."

"Good luck."

She nods and approaches the TM, the door sliding back for her when she gets close enough. She steps in and spins around to face us. Her brown eyes seem larger, the color in her cheeks high. "They won't be able to control me any-more, will they?"

Wes walks over to the consul and clicks something on the keyboard. The door to the TM closes, cutting off the look of careful hope on Althea's face. The machine starts to shudder and quack. The room fills with throbbing light and the familiar buzzing. I shield my face when it gets too bright, when the TM seems to explode outward, the glass on top swirling with smoke and color, Althea's body disap-pearing into time.

I can't say that we liked each other, but I hope she finds what she wants—a life without the Project.

Wes is still at the keyboard, typing rapidly. "What date for Faust?"

"I don't care. Maybe sometime in the Middle Ages."

I hear the doctor's sharp intake of breath.

Wes pushes another button. "Maybe we'll get lucky, and he'll get the plague."

I glance at Wes over my shoulder. And then I see his face change, his eyes getting wider, his mouth opening. I hear a scraping noise from behind me and turn to look, but something hits me in the stomach, the impact throwing me to the ground. Faust is standing over me, panting. The gun falls from my hands, slides across the floor, and he lunges for it. I launch to my feet, but it's too late. Dr. Faust is holding the gun, and he's pointing it at me.

"I made a mistake, last time, trying to send you both through time." His voice is still weak, but it is angry too, lashing out at us.

I back up, inching closer to Wes.

"Don't move!" Faust screams.

I freeze.

"I should have killed you. Shot you, like you shot me. I won't make the same mistake again." He looks over at Wes. "You'll be first. I need more of your blood. We're so close to making the serum. If we just have a bit more, we'll succeed, I know we will."

Something hard slams against the door, and all three of us jump, the gun wavering in Faust's hand. The table and chair start to shake as the metal is hit over and over.

"See? They're coming already. You have no hope."

Wes moves forward so slowly that at first I don't even

notice. If we can just stall Faust for another minute . . .

"There's always hope," I say quickly, and Faust's attention swings back to me.

"You think so?" He smiles, a teeth-clenching grin where it looks more like he's in pain. "How about now?" He points the gun at Wes and pulls the trigger.

"No!" I shout, or maybe breathe, or maybe think the word. One minute I am standing near the door and the next I am in front of Wes, pushing his body out of the way.

Wes gasps as he falls to the side and slams into the corner of the desk, his head whipping back to stare at me in horror. I hear the bullet leave the chamber of the gun, I watch it cross the room in slow motion, and I feel it when it rips into me, tearing through skin and muscle, leaving only blood and burning in its wake.

CHAPTER 25

"*Lydia!*"

Wes's voice. Screaming.

I fall to my knees, clutching my elbow. "I'm fine, I'm fine," I whisper. "Stop him."

Wes takes half a second to see the neat hole in the flesh of my lower arm, spilling blood across the white floor. But it's not enough to kill me and we both know that.

He flies across the room, before Dr. Faust figures out that the weapon is automatic. He raises it in Wes's face at the last second, but Wes spin-kicks him in the chin. I hear the bone crunch, watch the doctor's face twist. By the time Wes lands on his feet, Faust's mouth forms a distorted O that he cannot reshape. He tries to speak, but only moans, incapable of moving his jaw. Wes kicks the gun across the floor, grabs the doctor's arm, and drags him over to the TM, throwing his body into the base of it as soon as the door opens.

I crawl across the cold floor on my knees and grab the gun, holding my other arm tight against my body. The bleeding is slow, but the pain is so strong that I'm pretty sure the bone broke when the bullet hit it.

"You've earned yourself the prehistoric age," Wes says to the doctor.

Through it all, the banging never stops, as if the guards outside are using a battering ram to try and push their way through the metal door of the chamber. The table and chair are holding for now, though there is a large dent forming in the middle of the door.

I stand up, holding the gun high and pointed at Faust. Wes turns his back on the TM and keeps his eyes on me as he walks to the consul and pushes a button hard. Faust scrambles to his feet, ready to throw himself out of the machine. I step forward. When he sees the gun he cowers against the metal wall, whimpering as the door closes in his broken face.

Wes and I both ignore the rumbling and the lights and the smoke as the doctor is torn into fragments, hurtled through the wormhole. He has sent so many other people to this fate—lost in time, no thought to where they would end up or how it would destroy their lives. Now he is the one displaced, and hopefully he will die in some forgotten era, if the TM doesn't kill him first.

Wes strides over to me and carefully grabs my shoulders. "Are you okay? Tell me you're okay." He has to shout over the banging from outside, over the constant buzzing of the machine.

"I think my arm might be broken, but I'll live." I glance at the door. "We don't have much time. We need to rig the bombs now."

He nods, but doesn't let go, his gaze roaming over my face. "Don't ever do that again."

"Save your life?" I try to smile. "Shouldn't you be a little more grateful?"

"I'm grateful. Believe me." He leans down and presses his mouth to mine. His lips are hard and the kiss is more harsh than pleasant, as though he is trying to convince us both that we're still alive. He pulls back, then leans in again, and this time it is softer, a graze, a promise, his hands cradling my face, his nose brushing against mine. I wrap my good arm around his bicep and tilt my head up, and we kiss as the TM dims, then flashes, the light so powerful it would blind us both if we let it.

As soon as the TM quiets, Wes rips off part of his shirt and wraps it around my arm as a makeshift bandage and sling. I feel my vision blur when he touches the bullet hole and shake my head to focus it.

Together, we yank open Wes's knapsack and pull out the

bombs. I lay them on the table as Wes gets the timers, and together we start to fit them into the pipes.

The pounding on the door echoes the pounding in my chest, and the fingers of my good hand slip around the delicate wires.

"I'm done," Wes says.

"I can't . . . my hand."

"Let me." While he finishes, I grab the two bombs that are ready and set them on the floor on either side of the TM. Each bomb has a small timer attached to it manually, with a long wire connected to a master timer that sits on the desk.

Wes grabs a screwdriver from the bag and fiddles with the back of the larger timer. I take Tesla's notes and Faust's journal and place them on the floor, right next to one of the bombs. The small blasts will be enough to cave in this room and demolish the TM, though the outer wings—where most of the officers, scientists, and kidnapped children are—should remain unharmed.

"Done," Wes says again. He sits back from the desk and wipes his forehead.

"Wait." I put my hand out, still crouched down next to a bomb. "Do you hear that?"

He turns to look at me. "I don't hear anything."

"Exactly."

"The banging stopped."

I glance over at the door. The dent in the middle is more pronounced, a concave point, but the guards weren't able to break through.

"They must be trying to find another way in." I straighten from my crouch, my bad arm suspended against my chest. The bleeding has stopped, but the pain hasn't, and I fight the urge to throw up as I move toward the door.

Wes stands, placing the final bomb on the floor in front of the TM. "We'll only have two minutes to get out of here before the bombs start to go off."

A loud cracking noise cuts through the room, and I twist my head to see a small spiderweb of lines appear in the middle of the blackened two-way mirror.

Wes quickly turns to me. "I think it's time to unblock the door."

I push the table out of the way, but then I hear another crashing noise. The fracture in the mirror is getting bigger, spreading across the thick, bulletproof glass.

Wes concentrates on the main timer, and I stare at his back as he sets it for two minutes from now. "Ready?" I ask.

He nods and pushes a button. Nothing happens. He pushes it again. The analog clock on the front should start counting down, the small hand sliding slowly backward. But it isn't working.

"What's wrong?"

"Nothing," Wes answers, but I can tell he's lying. "The

clock is jammed, but it'll be fine. I'll reconnect the wire." Another crash. The spiderweb of cracks now covers the entire mirror. "You should go, Lydia. I'll be right behind you."

I don't turn away from Wes. "Do it now. Reconnect the wire now."

"Lydia . . ." He smiles at me over his shoulder, but he can't quite hide the panic in his eyes. "It'll be fine."

"Just do it now!" I shout.

He turns back to the timer. I see a drop of sweat slide down the side of his bent neck. His arms move quickly. Another crash, and a tiny piece of glass falls from the mirror, hitting the floor with a pinging noise.

"They're coming, Wes," I whisper.

"I know. I know. I almost have it. Go. Get outside."

"Not without you."

Thirty more seconds pass. He throws the timer down in frustration. "It's not working. The master timer's broken. We'll have to set the other timers. It'll take a little longer."

"We tore out that function when we connected them to the main timer, remember?" I can't keep the horror out of my voice.

He stares down at the useless clock in front of him. "Then the only way is to light the fuses manually."

"Wes." More glass falls to the floor, sparkling against the white tiles. "That won't give us any time to get out of here. We won't be able to leave before the bombs go off."

He turns to face me, his expression grim. "I'll have thirty seconds. I could get out."

"Why are you saying *I*? What happened to *we*?" My voice is shaking, my hands, my body, everything is shaking. I step toward him.

"Go, Lydia. If I don't—" He stops, swallows. "You still have your family here. This is your only chance."

"I can't leave you. It's not enough time. You'd die." My voice is as jagged as the broken glass, and suddenly I am on that field again, watching the blood fall from his shoulder and thigh, abandoning him when he needed me most.

"Go!" He shouts the word, his hands balled into fists at his sides. "Let me set the bombs. Let me know you're safe."

Another crash. Glass trickles down. The hole is getting larger, and I can hear the guards now, yelling in the opposite room.

"I'll set the bombs. You leave." I don't know how he hears me over the falling glass, but he does, and then he's right in front of me, his hands clasped around my upper arms.

"We'll both leave. We'll abandon the mission. We can find another way."

"No. We can't." My voice is hard, unyielding. "You know we won't get another chance to stop the Project. We have to do it now." I reach up to cover his hand with mine. "We'll both stay. Thirty seconds, right? We can make it, I know we can."

His eyes scan my face and he opens his mouth to respond, but then a louder crash echoes through the room, and we turn our heads to watch a large chunk of the mirror fall, splintering into pieces when it hits the floor. The guards can't get through, but they see us now, and one raises a gun.

"Okay," he says.

"Okay." I try to smile at him. Thirty seconds is a suicide mission and we both know it. But I would rather die here with Wes than know that I'd left him here to die alone.

"You pull the chair away from the door," he says quickly. "There's a lighter in my bag. I'll set the fuses and then we run."

"Got it." I take my hand away from his so he won't feel me shaking.

Wes steps away to light the fuses and I pull the last piece of furniture away and put my hand on the doorknob. Bullets fly into the room, but the angle is bad and can't reach us. I hear the shots ricocheting off the TM, see the tile floor cracking and breaking.

"Now," Wes says from behind me.

I rip the door open. The hallway is empty, the guards all in the room with the two-way mirror. But they see me open the door and I hear shouting as they order some men into the hallway after us.

"Hurry!" I yell at Wes. I step into the empty corridor and turn back to make sure he's following me.

He is standing in front of the doorway. Behind him, I

see that the fuses haven't been lit yet, the bombs lying quietly in front of the TM.

"What—?"

"I love you," he says, his eyes wet and locked on mine.

"No," I whisper as I realize what's happening—and then he shuts the door in my face.

"Wes!" I throw my body at the door, but it will not budge. "No! Wes!" I pound on the warped metal. My arm throbs and the wound starts to bleed again. I slump forward.

"She's there!" a man's voice shouts from down the hallway. I keep my hands pressed to the door.

"Please," I whisper into the metal, tasting copper and salt. "Don't do this. Wes. Open the door."

The guards are running toward me. I hear their footsteps getting louder. But then the first blast erupts in the TM chamber, flinging me away from the door. I hit the opposite wall and sink onto my knees. My ears are ringing, a sharp noise that will not fade. "Wes." I crawl forward, but the second blast blows the door off, and I see into the room beyond: fire and ash and debris. The TM is destroyed, a hollow burning chunk of metal, and the ceiling melts down around it, the flames so hot they make my face burn. There is no way Tesla's papers survived in this room. There's no way anything could have survived. "Wes!" I scream his name.

The guards who were after me sprint past, but one slows, grabs my arm, and pulls me to my feet. I fight against him, trying to run back into the room, but he tugs me forward. "The ceiling!" he shouts. I look up. The tiles in the hallway are starting to crumble, the dust floating down to coat our hair. "We have to get outside!"

He pulls me to the end of the hallway. I wonder why he's helping me now, when moments ago he thought I was the enemy. I push his arm off, trying to get back to the chamber, to Wes. But then the third and final blast goes off, and I watch the hallway fill with flames.

"There's nothing left!" the guard yells, and he yanks me forward. I stumble after him. He's right. There's nothing left.

Outside is chaos: soldiers and shouting and trucks and smoke. I see Dr. Bentley in the crowd and he runs for me. "Lydia." He wraps his hands around my shoulders. I know he is jarring my elbow, but I can't feel the pain anymore, not with my heart broken open and bleeding like this. "What are you doing here? Are you okay? What happened to your arm?"

"Wes. Wes. Wes." His name is a mantra. "He was inside. He's—he was—the fire—I think he's—" I fall to the ground near the door of the bunker the guard just dragged me out of. It was the same one I traveled through the very first time I wandered into the Facility.

Dr. Bentley crouches down next to me, his face lined and tired. "Are you saying Wes was in there? The whole ground caved in. I think there was some kind of underground explosion. The army base is trying to rescue people now. If Wes is still alive, we'll find him."

But they won't find Wes. I was in front of the exit. The only other way out was through the two-way mirror, filled with guards who wanted to kill him.

Wes is gone. After everything we went through, it's over. Just like that.

"Lydia?" Dr. Bentley shakes my arm. "You look like you're going into shock." All I want is to curl up in a ball like my grandfather did in his cell, rocking back and forth and trying to forget what just happened. But I can't. I won't let Wes's sacrifice be for nothing. We came here to stop the Project, and it's not over yet.

"The children." I lift my face, tear-stained and covered in soot, to look up at Dr. Bentley. "We have to get the children out."

"What are you talking about, Lydia?" he asks. "Let me fix your arm."

"The navy. Call the navy and ask for help. Not the army. I don't know how much they know. We have to get people in there before they cover everything up."

"Lydia—"

"Just do it!" I scream. A few more soldiers in black tumble out of the bunker. One is clutching his shoulder, another has blood dripping from his forehead. They melt into the crowd, ignoring the doctors who hover around them.

Dr. Bentley releases my arm and stands up again, his face creased with worry. "Please, Lydia, let me look at your arm, and then I'll do what you want."

"No." I force myself to stand too. My legs feel like water, but I have to do this for Wes. There will be time to fall apart later. "If I stop now I won't start again. My arm can wait. We have to save the children."

I go with Dr. Bentley while he radios the naval base. The blue jeeps arrive in ten minutes, bringing dozens of soldiers. A fire truck emerges from the trees, cutting a path through the dense woods. Men climb down off it, dressed in thick suits, carrying a large hose. They disappear into the smoke.

Dr. Bentley and the other doctors organize a makeshift hospital near the edge of the woods, and I help them set up cots and lay out sterile bandages, though most of the Project's guards and soldiers dissolve into the crowd instead of visit. A few scientists sit on the ground nearby, coughing and pressing their hands to their foreheads. I see Dr. Bentley eyeing my arm, my face, the low, defeated set of my shoulders, with concern. But I ignore him. Wes is gone, and I do not have the time to stop and think about it. I don't *want* to think. I want to keep going, to never stop, to never acknowledge what happened in that room filled with flames, the TM as gnarled and broken as Wes's body must be.

The sky has turned hazy from the smoke that seeps out of the ground in black waves. The Facility is large, and these explosions have only wiped out the TM chamber. There are still so many corridors down there, crawling with scientists and soldiers.

Some of the soldiers from the navy follow the firemen down into the smoking bunker. But they need to find the children, and I'm the only one who knows how to get there. I approach a group of soldiers and say, "I know another way in. We have to hurry."

One of the soldiers looks at me skeptically. "You're just a girl. And you're hurt."

"I said, I know another way in. There are children in there, and they need our help. Follow me." My voice is stern enough, cutting enough that a few of them exchange glances. An officer steps forward, his expression dark.

"Show us where," he says.

I lead them to one of the nearby bunkers. It is deeper in the woods, more hidden in the trees, but the concrete doors are wide-open. When we get closer, I see that the secret door in the back is open too, left askew as soldiers and scientists fought to escape the blasts.

"It's down there." I point into the darkness. "Follow the corridor, then take a right, a left, a right—"

The officer holds up his hands. "You said you were going to show us, and that there's not much time. We'll follow you. Lead the way."

I hesitate at the top of the stairs. Wes died down there, and now I have to go in again, smelling smoke on top of the bleach and the battery acid. But I can't give up now, not when the children are still inside.

I lead the navy men down the dark staircase, ignoring their gasps as they see the white corridors for the first time. It is darker than normal down here, the black smoke thick, but I do not falter, keeping my head low as I bring them directly to where the children are kept. A few guards from the Facility run past, ignoring us as they speed toward the exits.

The firemen have already found the room, thankfully, and they are carrying the children out one by one. A tall man passes me, and the girl in his arms blinks as our eyes meet. Her head is shaved, her arms are limp, but her mouth is curved up the smallest bit, making me think she's not completely lost.

Wes was like her once, though no one ever came to save him. I shove the thought away. Being in the Facility is like being inside his tomb.

The navy men are silent and grim as they wade into the group of children. They each carefully pick up a child. Only about ten remain in this large room, and already more firemen are coming back for them. These small recruits are like dolls, expressionless as they are lifted into different arms.

I lead the soldiers out again, knowing that I do not have the strength to carry one of the kids. I barely have the strength to carry myself, but I will keep going until this is over.

Outside I take a long, slow breath. The soldiers and kids around me are coughing in the fresh air. We were being suffocated by smoke in there, but I didn't even notice.

I follow the soldiers back to the nearby bunker where everyone else is gathered. The crowd is thicker, and I see a few women scattered here and there. Some are nurses, some are women who live near Camp Hero. It means word of what happened today is spreading, making a cover-up almost impossible.

We have exposed the Montauk Project and saved the recruits. I am no longer beholden to the Project, not because they've stolen my grandfather, and not because of the destiny that the future Lydia laid out for me. I'm free.

The cost of that freedom was Wes. He sacrificed himself so that I could have the life I wanted. But he was always supposed to be a part of my future, and I do not yet know how to believe that he is gone.

The smoke is still trickling out of the bunker, though it's thinner now and more gray than black. Another fireman emerges, a child in his arms. I wonder if they are finding the labs, or any proof that this underground Facility was run by the government.

I can't stay still for much longer or I will start to think about what happened to Wes. I turn toward where Dr. Bentley is tending to the children, but something makes me stop.

A soldier comes out of the smoking door of the bunker,

his dark hair plastered to his forehead, his skin covered in black dust. He is bleeding from his cheek, from his shoulder, but I watch the way he moves, even graceful when he stumbles on the wet grass.

"Oh God," I whisper, and then I am running, pushing soldiers and doctors out of the way.

"Wes." I scream, I whimper, and I throw myself at him, my body slamming hard against his. He takes a step back, his arms folding around my waist.

I feel my legs give out, but he pulls me up against him. He is an anchor, holding me in place.

"I hate you." I say the words into the skin of his neck, tasting ashes and Wes. "I hate you so much."

"I know." His voice is like sandpaper.

"I thought you were dead. I thought I'd never see you again."

"I'm sorry." He winces as I squeeze him tighter, and I know I should loosen my hold, but I can't.

"I love you," I whisper. "I love you so much."

He lays his hand on my hair, heavy and strong. "I know."

The Project is destroyed and he is alive. The nightmare we've lived is over. We're together now. Nothing else matters as he pulls me closer to him in the sunlight.

EPILOGUE

Mary slumps down onto the bed, her white dress falling around her like deflated meringue. "I just can't believe Suze isn't here. How could Mick choose *today* to come back from the war? It was supposed to be next week!"

I pick up the veil she flung onto the floor only a minute ago. "I don't think he had much of a choice."

"Oh, applesauce. Stop being so cheerful, Lydia. My life is ruined." She throws herself back against the pink bedspread.

I laugh. "Your life is not ruined, but your hair might be if you don't sit up."

She pops up again, smoothing the soft curls that frame her face. Suddenly her back goes straight and she smiles. "Why don't *you* be my bridesmaid? I thought about asking you in the first place, but Suze has been my oldest friend for forever and it just didn't seem fair to her, what with you getting back into town only a month ago. And Suze seems a little jealous of you since we both have red hair and everyone says we're like sisters, but this is perfect! Wes is already Lucas's groomsman and the four of us will be a little wedding party up there at the altar. What do you say?" She clasps her hands together as though she's praying. "Say yes, please, please, please."

"Yes!" I say. "Of course I'll do it."

"You're the best, Lyd, the absolute best. And you look like such a Grable today, no one will even notice me."

"Now you're just lying."

She smirks and hops up from the bed. Her dress is a long, fitted flow of white satin, with princess sleeves and a sweetheart neckline.

"Sit down." I point at the chair in front of her vanity. "I'll put your veil on."

She does, smiling at me, her lips red against her powdered face. I arrange the crown of white flowers in her hair, the lace veil spilling out the back and over her pale shoulders. "There. You're all set."

Our eyes meet in the mirror. "Remember how I did your hair when you first came to stay with us?" she asks. "You wouldn't sit still and you had the strangest long bangs. It's so much prettier now."

I touch the curls that rest against my shoulders. One

afternoon a few weeks ago, Mary insisted that I let her cut it, saying that she refused to look at it anymore.

"And I'm so *glad* you let me take you into town to buy your dress. That blue is divine against your skin."

I smile. She would like this dress—she picked it out, insisting that the column of blue silk with the fitted bodice would be perfect for her wedding. I stare at myself in the mirror over her head. I'm starting to lose the defined muscles from the constant training, and the hard angles of my face are softening. I look like myself again. Like Lydia, instead of Seventeen.

Mary reaches her hand up and clutches mine where it rests against her shoulder. "Do you think I'm doing the right thing? Even though I don't want to go to Georgia?"

I bend down until our faces are close together, looking back at us in the mirror. We really do resemble sisters, with the same green eyes, the high cheekbones, and full lips. "You are absolutely doing the right thing. Lucas even told Wes that he's happy to leave the farm to his brother-in-law. He says he has no interest in smelling like cows for the rest of his life. Besides, he loves you and you love him."

She squeezes my hand. "I want us to be like you and Wes. You make me believe that I can forget . . . that I can just be with Lucas without any other darkness."

"There's always a little darkness," I tell her. "But Dean would want you to be happy anyway."

At the mention of Dean, her eyes fill with tears and she

looks away. "Oh, I'm being so silly." She grabs a handkerchief off the vanity and blots at her face. "It hasn't even started and I'm already crying."

"Cry all you want. We can always redo your makeup."

She gets up from her seat and turns to face me. "That's why I like you, Lydia. You're unbelievably practical."

I laugh. "Not really."

"You are! You've only been here a month and you already got Wes to put in indoor plumbing."

"That's because I refused to live in a place without running water. He was just scared I would leave him."

She picks up her bouquet of wildflowers from the bed and links our arms together. My left arm is still in a cast, though Dr. Bentley says I won't have to keep it on for much longer.

He didn't ask me why I was there in the woods until a few days later, after the rescued children were adopted or placed in orphanages. I told him that Wes and I went out to the camp to see if the bomb testing was real, then saw that the bunker door was open, and realized there was some kind of secret facility underground. While we were exploring, the bombs went off. I'm not sure he believed me, but he let it go. By then the papers were reporting that several civilians had built an underground hideout and were kidnapping children for nefarious purposes. According to the papers, the police never found any evidence that the facility was connected to the government, and I know the labs were all destroyed before they reached them. No one was even arrested; police claimed that the culprits must have disappeared in the confusion and the smoke. Only the children and three dead bodies remained—unidentified soldiers who were too close to the explosion.

"I can't believe you're already thinking of moving away, even though you just got here," Mary pouts at me. "Lucas wanted to talk to Wes about starting a fishing business."

We leave her childhood bedroom and walk down the stairs of her parents' house. "Don't panic," I tell her. "We don't know what our plans are yet. I just always thought I would get a degree, and Wes has been thinking about it lately too. We can always come back."

"But you're already working at the paper! And you said you liked it!"

"I do like it." I pull her skirt out of the way before she trips on it. "But I still want an education."

"Just so you can lord your degrees over the rest of us humble folks."

"You're a nurse! Not exactly humble."

She rolls her eyes. "Oh, let's not argue. I'm about to get married." We reach the front door and she stops me, her fingers digging into my arm. "How do I look?" Her voice shakes as she asks. I step back and examine her, from her rosy pink cheeks to her new satin shoes.

"You look perfect. Lucas is going to freak out, trust me."

She laughs. "Lydia, you do say the oddest things."

"I'm here; I'm here." Dr. Bentley walks down the hall toward us, still knotting the tie at his neck.

"Daddy, we're going to miss the ceremony if you don't hurry up."

I disentangle my arm from Mary's, and open the front door. "I'll see you out there, okay?"

She gives me an anxious look. "If I faint, swear you'll catch me."

I reach over and squeeze her hand one last time. "You won't faint. I promise."

"We should have just eloped, like you and Wes."

I smile, then give her a tiny wave.

The sun is high, shining bright and hot on the crowded backyard. I start to walk down the aisle. There are only a few seats set up in the grass, and most of the guests are standing to the sides, facing the priest. A few turn to look at me as I pass. I see Wes and Lucas up ahead, talking quietly.

Someone grabs my arm and I look down. Peter is smiling up at me. "Hi," I whisper.

"Hiya." Peter's mother is sitting next to him, still drawn and ghostly. But between Mary, Lucas, Wes, and me, we've been able to keep Peter occupied, and he seems to be doing better—asking fewer questions about his father, and making more friends around the neighborhood.

I miss my grandfather and my parents every day, but having Peter here is making it a little easier. I haven't completely lost my grandfather. He's still a part of my life, and

I've become like an older sister to him in the past few weeks.

"When's Mary coming?" Peter asks me. "I'm hot, and I want to eat cake."

"Soon. But I have to get up there or Mary's going to yell at me."

His green eyes get wide. "Mary doesn't yell."

"No, you're right, but she might talk me to death."

He giggles and sits back in his chair.

"After the ceremony's over, go ask your grandmother for cake," I tell him. "I bet she'll sneak you some before anyone else."

"You better hurry," Peter says, sounding a lot older than eight. "Uncle Wes is staring at you."

I look up. Wes *is* staring at me, smiling slightly, his hands in the pockets of his dark suit. I smile back, and continue walking down the aisle toward him.

I take my place on the left side of the aisle just as a hush falls over the crowd. Mary and her father appear across the lawn. She is beaming, and I hear Lucas take in a quick breath.

There have been times when I catch myself in a mirror and am startled by my own reflection—the tight curls, the smart dresses, the large hats. It feels as though I am playacting, as though I will wake up at any moment and still be in the Facility, or at home in my bedroom in Montauk. But then there are times where I am wholly in the moment, and it feels more like reality than 2012 ever did.

Wes catches my eye and smiles again, and I know this is one of those times, surrounded by family, in a sun-drenched backyard in August, knowing that the Montauk Project is gone forever, where I can almost forget that I ever had a life before this.

Hours later, after I have eaten cake and danced with Lucas and Dr. Bentley, after the sun has gone down, shedding red and pink rays across the makeshift wooden dance floor, Wes finds me at a table in the corner, my heels kicked off and my legs propped up on a chair. "Tired?" he asks, leaning over me.

I tilt my head back to smile at him. His tie is hanging loose against his white shirt, and his newly cut hair is just starting to fight back against the grease he used to slick it into place.

"My feet are killing me," I tell him. "I hate new shoes."

He picks up my legs, sits down in the chair, and starts to massage my insoles, digging his thumbs into the arches. "Oh God," I groan, leaning back against my own chair. "Have I ever told you that I love you?"

He gives me his half smile. "Once or twice."

We are silent for a while, watching the last few couples spin in lazy circles around the dance floor. Most of the band has gone home and just a trumpeter is left. He is drawing out the notes, mournful and slow.

Wes drops my foot into his lap. "Are you ready to go

home? Mary and Lucas left an hour ago."

I nod. We stand, I slip my shoes back on, and we walk out to his truck. In the dark driveway, he holds the passenger's-side door open for me and helps me in, his hand skimming along the side of my thigh.

When we reach the small shack, he grabs my hand as soon as I get out of the truck and pulls me down toward the beach. The moon is almost full and it reflects off the water, the circle of light a halo on the black surface. Wes sinks onto the wet sand and tries to pull me down next to him.

"No way. I'm not wrecking this dress; it cost half my paycheck."

His voice dips as he says, "So just take it off."

"Don't get too excited." I raise my eyebrows. "The girdle I'm wearing covers more than a bathing suit."

"Fine." He reaches up and guides me down until I'm sitting on his lap. "Happy now?"

I nod, leaning back against him.

"Don't go to work tomorrow." I feel his lips against my neck. "Come out on the boat with me. I want to know you're close by."

"I have to go to work. We need the money."

His arms close around mine. "It was easier back then, in a way."

I know what he means. Being a Montauk Project recruit was mindless. Food, clothes, all the basics were provided. We never had to make any choices. Our futures were laid out in front of us. But I defied that destiny, and now Wes and I are two orphans trying to survive on our own. I never thought I would be talking about bills at eighteen.

"But this is still better."

He squeezes me. "Still better."

The ocean is calm, the waves softly pushing against the shore. "Regrets?" Wes whispers into my hair.

I tip my head back against his shoulder and stare up at the waxing moon. It is a question he asks me once a week, sometimes daily, and I know he is worried that I miss my family and my original life in 2012.

"I won't ever regret what we did. We had to end the Project, for us and for the other recruits. I'm just happy we both made it out alive."

He rests his chin against my forehead. "I'm sorry I scared you."

"You should be. That was the worst hour of my life."

Before the first bomb went off, Wes used those thirty seconds to rush at the soldiers in the observation room. By then the mirror was almost completely broken, and he dove through, hiding behind the wall when the explosion hit. Most of them blindly copied his actions, and only one soldier died when he didn't duck down quickly enough. Wes managed to get out of the observation room and into the hallway before the other bombs went off, but amid the chaos and the smoke and the confusion, it took him almost an hour to make his way back out of the Facility.

A few weeks ago, I convinced my boss at the newspaper to send me to Camp Hero to try to get more answers for a bigger story on what happened out in the woods that day. I interviewed the major general who oversees the army base. He gave me the same stock answers that he gave the other reporters. *We're shocked and saddened by how sick these men were. Camp Hero is in no way affiliated with the events of that day.* But his right eye twitched whenever he lied, and I knew he was aware of what was happening down in that Facility.

But I tried to put his words behind me. Even if the men leading Camp Hero knew about the Montauk Project, it doesn't change what happened: without Tesla's notes, without a time machine or Dr. Faust, the Montauk Project is gone forever. Wes and I succeeded.

Wes's hands are resting against my stomach. I pick one up and hold it in my lap, playing with his long fingers, the flat, broad shape of his nail beds. "I can't pretend that I don't think about my parents a lot, or wish I could see them again. And I love Mary, but I miss Hannah's sarcasm and how cynical she could be."

Wes sits up a little, his body curving around mine.

"I always had this vision for how my life would play out," I tell him. "I'd graduate from high school, go to Northwestern to study journalism, then start writing for a local newspaper and work my way up the ladder."

"Some of that could still happen."

"I know. But I think I've learned that you can't make

grand plans and expect everything to work out the way you want it to. Maybe that was the problem with the Project all along. They wanted to control every piece of history, but it kept getting away from them."

"Isn't it hard, not knowing what will happen to your parents, or to Tim? Not knowing if they even exist?"

I nod against his shoulder. I hope a new version of Tim is with his mom and sister, never knowing what could have become of his life. That the future version of me is free somewhere, with no Project left to perform for. I like to think there could be another Lydia, at home with her parents, hanging out with Hannah and loving her grandfather more than anything. And maybe there's even another Tag and Wes, out on the streets of New York, hustling to try to get by. But without a TM, I'll never know what happened to any of them. The Montauk Project is gone, and Wes and I are the survivors, living in a world neither of us was born into.

"I know we did the right thing," I say. "This world is better without the Project in it."

"We did."

He says the words like he means them, though we both know they are only meant to reassure us both. Because we can't know the future. No one can. Not anymore.

Suddenly Wes stands up, shifting his arms until he's cradling me against his chest. I shriek when he bounces me, then shriek harder as he starts walking into the waves.

"Wes, no! Put me down!"

He smiles. "If I drop you now, you're going to get soaked." He loosens his arms. "Is that really what you want?"

"No, no." I grip his neck tight with one hand, the other still in its cast pressed to my chest.

He turns in a circle, the waves breaking against his legs, the stars spinning overhead.

I laugh and close my eyes. "Don't drop me."

"I won't." He stops moving and stares down at me. The moon makes the angle of his nose stronger, his eyes darker. I reach up and rumple his hair until it looks like it does when he just comes back from his fishing boat: touched with salt and falling over his forehead.

He dips his head and I rise up to meet him.

That future Lydia tried to convince me my destiny was to be in charge of the Montauk Project, to turn it into a force of good. I destroyed them instead. There will always be consequences to that decision, but Wes was right when he said that we make our own choices. And I choose this—the boy I love holding me suspended above the dark water and trusting that he won't let go.

ACKNOWLEDGMENTS

I have been blessed with the most amazing editors, Sarah Barley and Tara Weikum. Thank you for pushing me in ways I didn't know were possible. Working with you has made me a better writer and I'm so proud of the books we created together. Sarah, your notes have been spot on, and I always trust your judgment. I already miss passing manuscripts off to you on the streets of New York, chatting and holding up foot traffic!

Without Full Fathom Five, I never would have had the opportunity to write this series and share Lydia's story with the world. Thanks especially to James Frey for trusting me from the start, to Jessica Almon for the constant support, both editorial and personal, and to Matt Hudson and Bennett Madison.

Everyone at HarperTeen rocks, and special thanks to my amazing publicists over the years. I seriously won the cover lottery with this series. Thanks so much to Alison Klapthor and Alison Donalty for creating it. Also thanks to the Epic-Reads gals, Aubry Parks-Fried and Margot Wood—you are awesome and crazy in the best possible way.

So much research has gone into these books, and I especially want to thank those people who let me pick their brains about certain eras and places. Thanks again to my grandmother, Virginia Gurdak, my expert on the 1940s. You've given me so much, and all I did was name a character after you. And thanks to Beth Barraclough, for teaching me all about NYC in the 1980s and 90s.

Montauk, New York, is a truly special place, and not just because it might house a government conspiracy. Thanks to the Montauk librarians and the Camp Hero park rangers who helped answer pressing questions about what their town looked like over the years.

Jeramey Kraatz, you are my rock. I would not have made it through the last few years without you. Christina Rumpf, you know me better than anyone and somehow still like me. Thanks for late night phone calls, fancy dinners, writing parties, and generally being the best friend a girl could ask for. Jessica Hindman, Asher Ellis, Mike Murphy, Starre Vartan, Michelle Legro, and Jordan Foster, you've been such huge sources of support throughout this process in different ways. Thanks for everything.

To all the people I've stolen names from, especially Nikita Schwalb and Jesse Levy: thanks for the inspiration!

I have a big, loud, awesome extended family, and their support has meant more than they'll ever know. Thanks for making up the bulk of my book sales, guys.

My sisters, Mary and Emma Carter—thank you for your honesty, your belief, and making me laugh more than anyone else can. You're my sisters but also my friends, and I'm thankful for you everyday.

To my mom, Terry Gurdak-Carter, and my dad, Phil Carter. I could not have written a word without the two of you. You've supported me from day one and made this life possible in every way. I love you both so much.

I've met so many amazing bloggers and fellow writers through this process, and I want to acknowledge everyone who has helped and encouraged me over the past few years. And, most important, I want to thank my readers. Without you none of this would be possible. Thank you for your emails, your tweets, and your tireless enthusiasm. You make everything worth it.

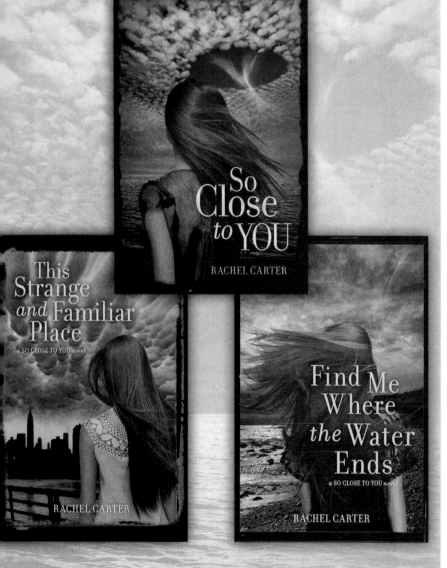